W9-BEP-745

EVE OF
DARK
HORIZONS

PART ONE OF THE DRACONIAN SERIES

MARVIN PROCTOR JR.

ARCHWAY
PUBLISHING

Mark Lewis, Richard Godfrey, Karl Schlig, Anna Michaud, Mark Dela Vega. For the people touched my heart dearly through this adventure, Allen M. Doug, and Peter Afiator; who seems to know me better than I know myself at times. And special thanks to my awesome creative friend Arthur Duval, you are a godsend. Thank you dearly, one and all, and may this be a long and joyous journey.

PROLOGUE

T he third sequence initiated. Unstable subject matter. Subject's secondary genetic sequence is resisting the connection of the primary target gene, M771 sequence, from coding. Resistance is imminent. Code red. Syntax error. Incompatible test subject XJ5-221-CH10!" announces the advanced self-automated (AI) computer mainframe for the top-secret laboratory that's deep underground in Washington, DC. It was named MARC (for multi-tasking artificial response computer), a creation of the genius mind of the late Dr. Johnathan Daniels.

Meanwhile, Eric James, the observation tech on duty and a veteran of his position for twenty plus years, continues to monitor the enclosed human sedation pods that house three youth test subjects who are monitored for their mental and physical vitals. In the calm but artificial monotone voice of a man, MARC declares, "Test subject XJ5-221-CH10 is proven incompatible … and is registered as a fail, Mr. James." James looks over the results and relays the findings to his superior, who is dressed in a knee-length shiny silver lab coat. The man has an ICB (identification clearance badge) with his name, Dr. Brandon Kline, and his station as the supervisor of special operations. Approaching him hastily, "Dr. Kline, subjects XJ5-221-ML16 and XJ5-221-SC17 are green for go. However, subject XJ5-221-CH10 will not comply as needed."

Reading over to the displays, Dr. Kline gives the information a quick once-over while comparing the results from his own personal handheld tablet device. "Mr. James subjects SC17 and ML16 can be transferred to the DH sector. Use Laboratory Alpha Charlie Tango to prep the DH16z1 inoculations."

A slightly graying technician, Eric James is gaining a moral consciousness about the tasks he is required to perform. He turns slightly to see the supervisor and says, "D-Dr. Kline, are you certain that this is really advisable, given the results of the last ten candidates. We sent them all through to the DH sector processing only to prove fatal. Each one of them."

"Are you questioning this protocol by wishing to overstep your station, Mr. James? You do remember signing the EDCCA (employee declaration of company compliance addendum), do you not?"

"Why yes, of course, Doctor." Mr. James swallows deep, looking uncertainly at the man he has worked long and hard for many years a little differently. It's as if the life force behind his eyes has suddenly dimmed. "But for all intents and purposes, the newest candidates are mere children, sir. The boys are slightly older than the girl. The eldest boy is seventeen, and the other boy is sixteen. However, the orphan girl you acquired is only ten years old, sir. She is the same age as your little granddaughter, Erica. You are aware of this?"

He feels some conviction in his resolve to find a reason behind the extreme measures the organization is taking. "What is the next step? The DH Program? What is its intended purpose? Why do we need to have such young candidates?"

Dr. Kline is not at all pleased by the line of questioning from his long-standing subordinate. Removing his fashionable protective lab spectacles, he gazes directly into Eric's pale green eyes. "Look! You have worked under my direction for the past twenty-five years. There is one thing you should always know and never fail to comprehend." He presses his spectacles squarely into Eric's chest. "Mr. James, you … not now, not ever, question the likes of me or the protocols of your assigned task! Always be mindful. You were hand-selected by me for this job, and reassignments are frowned upon. Just do what you were assigned to do and concentrate specifically on that task! Nonetheless, I will make this very clear."

Dr. Kline breaks down each word for clarity. "You are a great standing loyalist, and you express your wonders in the sciences. These candidates, albeit young, sweet, and innocent in their mere appearance, are by far anything of the sort! They are not random youth just yanked off the streets. Each subject we have collected has shown themselves to be an extremely dangerous and a high risk to themselves and to the society as a whole—that is, if they are left to roam around freely in society."

Eric makes a confused expression as the doctor explains to him the severity of the situation. "They need this testing. No questions asked, Eric. There need to be some preventive control measures taken to slow or stop the strange anomaly known as the M771 DNA gene strand before it becomes a worldwide epidemic. These frail-looking candidates are acutely aware of the potential dangers they may bring to themselves and their loved ones. For most of them, this may be their only means to possibly have a normal human existence."

Kline gestures with his hand, speaking candidly and calmly, "Stop your damn inquiry, Eric, and prep the two male subjects for the DH lab. Once you're done with that, get your ass back over here and begin resequencing the female child. Understood?"

Not wanting to engage in any further debates, Eric briskly returns to his duties.

child who burns with the fire of hell itself." (He directs his attention to the chamber where the female subject lies in stasis.)

Dr. Kline says. "Hold up! You think she is that child?"

"You said yourself that the kinetic discharge was off the charts for a kinetic, didn't you? And her power had an element within it. Then she could very well be … the one! She needs to fully awaken to her abilities and unleash what is required."

Dr. Kline continues, "The issue of candidates is starting to raise concerns, Mr. Black. This operation is not exactly sanctioned. We had to go to some extremes to acquire the latest candidates for your mission." Kline gestures to the three profiles on the monitors. "Like Mr. Shihan Gamo-Chin, better known by his alter ego, Ryuu-no-kage, the Dragon of Shadows."

Mr. Black snickers after he hears the translation of Shihan's Japanese name.

Dr. Kline continues, "He's from the elusive and secret society the Shinto Thunder Clan. We lucked out with this young man when our eyes caught him practicing his unique mystical craft at the empty Haiden Hall at Kamigamo Shrine in Kyoto, Japan. We believe he is a direct lineage of the once thought extinct and the first dynasty of the Gamo family."

"Interesting." Mr. Black nods his head. "He shall do … well."

Dr. Kline continues, "The other young man, Michael Landings, is a mix of half Cajun and Créole. He's a native of New Orleans. He is known for working his dark mystical arts at a young age, and he's a fearsome sleuth hunter of the supernatural variety.

"He has a reputation for seeking out the Versipellis, the werewolves of the south, specters, banshees, and even thought to have hunted and destroyed a five-hundred-year-old Vampryus. He is believed to relate to a highly sought-after group called the Dark Magicians. The adults are referred to as dark mages. It's an allegedly old mystical occult formed back in the old countries, involving mysticism and conjuring."

"Hmm. I like this one a lot. Maybe he can find the elusive Black Wolf? That's our precaution in case the stones of Ancestria aren't recovered?"

"The surprising twist about Michael's people is the mere fact that the reincarnation of a so-called high priest or priestess has yet to make itself known to the clan. He or she is to replace the one they call Bone Keeper, who ironically vanished some eighty years ago without a trace. Either way, the prophets of the Créole people say the new leader will be their savior or their doom, depending on his or her chosen path of life at the tender age of twenty-one."

Mr. Black nods contently, and Dr. Kline follows his statement with a wicked chuckle. "Hmm, sounds familiar. That reminds me of the pesky ancients and their damn rituals!" Mr. Black says, rubbing his chin as if in deep thought

"Who?" sharply inquires Dr. Kline. Mr. Black doesn't appear a day older than thirty, with his tailor-made black, pinstriped suit, and black aviator glasses.

"Oh, nothing. It is something of another time and place. Nothing relative to this era. That's something long gone eons ago, Doctor."

With a raised brow, Dr. Kline continues, "Oh ... I see. Well, to day their order is only referred to as the Mages. Nevertheless, both young men have passed the preliminary sequences with significant success and are now prepared for the final phase."

Mr. Black examines them through the thick glass wall, observing Eric manning the equipment. "Are there any concerns among your crew here? Anyone who may jeopardize the security protocols?"

Without hesitation, the doctor says, "No, I should think not!"

Kline's responds rather abruptly as if the question insulted his judgment.

With a sinister grin on his face, Mr. Black compliments him instead. "This is good news. I didn't want to be the one to terminate anyone's blood-binding contract prematurely. Understandable, am I not right?"

"There will be no need for that, Mr. Black, I assure you! My people are loyal to the tasks. They're quite aware of their duties."

"Let's just hope they remain that way, Dr. Kline. If not, I will gladly show them what Dark Horizons is all about!"

Dr. Kline's milky white complexion suddenly becomes even pastier after Mr. Black's threat.

"What is the problem with the specimen Cheryl? Why isn't she progressing?" Mr. Black inquires after seeing the girl in the third chamber pod.

"Oh, um … yes, Cheryl Hunters, we found her locally. Not much information on her—except she was in foster care and ran away. We just recently acquired her after a report of a pyro-psionic attack in the Eastern Street Market causing severe chaos and injuries earlier this week. She claims she was looting many of the unsuspecting vendors of their perishable goods. After capturing her, we had to wipe her memories twice. She kept crying out for some person named Liam, I believe. After we did a sweep of the grounds, there was no sign of a Liam. We could only assume it was a boyfriend or someone because she wouldn't give us any information on the identity of the male, and according to NSA, Cheryl Hunters doesn't exist. She has no family or relatives. It's just an alias. We administered a second dose, which calmed her immensely, but it may have completely suppressed all of her prior memory before her capture."

"Hmm, that may not be a bad thing, really. In this way, we can plant new memories, best suits our needs and interests!" Mr. Black points out manically, with a grimacing smirk.

"At the moment she's setting us back a little bit. Unlike the others, we initially thought it was because she had prematurely activated her M771 gene before the age of fifteen. But upon further inspection, we found a rarely unique anomaly within her. She hasn't activated the gene we originally thought. She seems to have an unknown marker in her DNA strand. We can't rightly isolate yet. It is tethering within her complex strand, short-circuiting the dormant M771 gene from fully engaging the telekinetic fields she can self-manifest."

"Okay, this is definitely a new development. So, the spike she unleashed wasn't her true psionic blast, correct?" Mr. Black whispers to himself while looking at the girl in the chamber. *This one may be the missing link after all! Her and the cursed, Black Wolf. I won't even need the damn crystals*, he thinks. "Interesting. A double gene strand, you say? Oh, how I wonder." *Is it possible? A soul gene ... surviving the purge after all?*

"We believe this marker is preventively protecting her from our sequencing attempts with some sort of immunity and thus not allowing the assimilation of her M771 gene."

"That absurd minuscule human child thinks she can divert my master's grand plan? She is so gravely mistaken, dear doctor. I most definitely want to see what this child is capable of." Mr. Black snarls as he reaches into his suit's inner pocket and removes a small vial with a black substance inside. "Give this to the child. She will be compliant for sure, and she will activate the M771. It will also significantly suppress whatever else is inside of her." Mr. Black carefully hands over the small vial to the nervous Dr. Kline as if exchanging unstable plutonium.

"What is this?" Dr. Kline questions.

Mr. Black merely grins.

"Is this blood? Why is it black?" Dr. Kline tries to examine the unmarked vial with curious concern.

"Consider it a one-of-a-kind gift to your species from the source of all sources, my dearest lord, and master."

Dr. Kline looks to the vial and turns back to Mr. Black.

"Source? Source of what? What in God's name, Mr. Black? Is this biological or synthetic? Is it compatible with—"

"Dr. Kline, you have something that no one on this forgotten, backwater planet can get their hands on. That vial will do the job that nothing else will. Guaranteed! You will find the subject much more cooperative, and it is a 100 percent compatible." While explaining to Dr. Kline the rarity of this sample, he slowly removes his shades, revealing his saturated black eyes with no visible white area. The doctor instinctively steps back. This is something that he has never encountered in his fifty-two years of science and medicine.

"What the bloody hell!" Dr. Kline exclaims, his voice trembling a bit. "What are you?" Nervous, he swallows hard. Mr. Black slowly walks toward the now paralyzed doctor.

"In simple terms young doctor, I am *the planet's coming future*! This wretched world has slept for far too long. As they say, it is time … to reawaken the sleeping giant and bring a new order to this mundane existence. We are repositioning the missing pawn, your planet, back on the current game board of the universe. There will be a great change in the days to come, and it all starts here with you and me." Mr. Black once again conceals his fierce eyes behind his tinted glasses. Still smiling, he nods just before turning toward the shadows of the room, but he stops short when Dr. Kline calls out to him.

"Mr. Black! Y-you, speak of change. What is it exactly? What are we doing or trying to accomplish here with these subjects?"

Feeling no need to turn around, his voice fills the room with reverence and echo. "Right now, we are planting the seeds to bring about a harvest of this planet's greatest acolytes. These children will serve and die for my master's return and bear witness to the most significant power this universe will ever be privileged to serve. The light of this world shall be enlightened by the darkness that is to come."

"Are we talking the book of Revelation here?"

"You could only wish it was that peachy. You may even pray for an apocalypse when the time has come." Like the preacher standing before his flock with hands in the air, Mr. Black revels in his own words. "What's coming is nothing short of majestic divinity! Prepare yourself for the inevitable Dr. Kline, for the Dark Horizons be within our grasp, o' faithful partner!" Never using the existing doors, Mr. Black sends scowling laughter as he vaporizes into the shadows, which sends a chill down Dr. Kline's spine.

Stumbling over to the workstation where Mr. Black was sitting, Dr. Kline spots something on the table that wasn't there before. It's a small business card. He picks the card up to inspect it and see a graven image of a black dragon. Its claws are gripping a double-edged sword, and there's an inscription at the bottom that reads, "My Lord and forever Master, Dark Heart."

CHAPTER 1

Six years later in the semirural township of Upper Marlboro, Maryland, the autumn harvesting season is in full bloom. And Franklin High School, barring the Dueling Dragons mascots, is buzzing with activity. It is late September. Some of the houses in the cul-de-sac are already exhibiting the festive Halloween spirit, including happy pumpkins stacks, black and orange lights, and fake webbing in the trees and bushes.

Mary Mathews and her husband, Gregory Mathew—parents of Kyra, Kyle, and Rissa Mathews—are preparing for the morning, and they are also disciplining their seventeen-year-old daughter and scholar, Kyra.

Mrs. Mathews places a gentle hand on top of her husband's broad shoulder as she sits down next to him. Sitting across from her parents, Kyra patiently awaits a punishment, while her siblings prepare for school, like normal. Today is a total first for Kyra as she sits and counts the seconds on the wall clock. Ironically, this is often the usual position her wisecracking twin brother, Kyle, would be in. For the first time, Kyra notices just how enormous her father's rugged hand is, nestled underneath her mother's silky, delicate one.

feet, popping her gum, and texting on her phone. "Seriously, K, I forgot how long it takes for the stinky cheese mobile to get here."

Kyra smirks while rolling her eyes. "Chill. It still has a few minutes. Besides, it wasn't that long ago, Julie. Three months actually!"

Julie replies after a loud pop from the gum, "Yeah, yeah, yeah ... whatever."

Meanwhile, as if in a daze, Kyra stares blankly at the house across the street. Out front, here are straw-filled mummies reaching out from around their mailbox and the sides of their house. Kyra's long, silky, chestnut brown hair flows smoothly in the cold morning breeze.

Julie realizes that Kyra isn't paying any attention to her rants about the bus. "Hello! Hello? Talking to you!" she continues until her friend responds.

Snapping out of her daze, Kyra looks to Julie and says, "Oh, my bad. I was in la-la land or something. Did you say something?"

"Not much, really. I just wish the bus would get a move on already."

"I hear that. I need to turn in my AP chemistry report before homeroom."

"Oh, snap! You are freakin' right!" Kyra looks to Julie with disbelief.

"C'mon, you're telling me you didn't finish and still went to that party last night?"

"Hah ... gotcha, Mom! You know I don't handle my biz like that. I am a girl with a moral compass and a wicked-ass chemistry software program. I don't slave like some people."

Kyra blows it off, "Ah, yeah! Whatever, Julie. I choose to be more—"

Julie cuts in hard, "Reliably *boring*!"

Meanwhile, back at Kyra's home, the phone rings several times before Mr. Mathews answers. He hears an older male's voice. "This is Mr. Mathews. How may I help you?"

"Umm, yes … sorry to disturb you at this early hour, Mr. Mathews. I am Kyra's AP chemistry teacher. Simply calling to thank Kyra for helping my wife yesterday evening. She returned to the school and retrieved the project notes she left behind from earlier in the day. I … just want to say … you have a uniquely gifted and compassionate daughter there, Mr. Mathews."

Confused by the caller, Mr. Mathews grunts with blinded agreeance.

"Please … let her know. I would tell her myself, but I won't be back at the school for a short spell. She doesn't have to rush her project in today. I already acknowledge her skill set and tenacity for earnest, thoughtful work. I know she wasn't able to put the time into it that she really could have last night."

Trying to wrap his head around the conversation, Mr. Mathews says, "I'm sorry, Mr. …"

"Oh, pardon me, Mr. Mathews! I am Professor Kim G. Ward. A teacher at Franklin High."

"Okay, Mr. Ward. I'm a little lost in this conversation. Forgive me. But you said my daughter was at the school and helped you and your wife last night and not at Wilmer's Park?"

The professor laughs. "Ha-ha. Honestly, Mr. Mathews? We are talking about the same, Kyra Mathews? The super achiever of the world, right? Her … at a party? The night before a project's deadline? Believe me! If I know your daughter well enough, you would have to grab her kicking and screaming to miss an assignment."

"Okay, I see your point, Professor. But what was it she helped you and your wife with?"

"My wife came to the school and started feeling light-headed. I kept telling her it was the shift in the weather and that when we get home, she should take an Allegra and rest."

Mr. Mathews expressed concern. "Is she okay?"

"That's just the thing! My wife and I thought there was nothing

CHAPTER 2

Well, if the automation is counter-free, only reset it as needed. In this paper, I have given a very constructive proof of Eilenberg's theorem." Kyra, finishes up her oral presentation to the class of half-interested teenagers, except Timothy Daniels, Kyra's lab partner, who is wide-eyed and full of excitement.

The teacher gestures to Kyra. "A well-thought-out presentation, Ms. Mathews! Class, you're doing splendidly with the premise of Krohn-Rhodes cascading theorem. We will start a new subject theorem tomorrow. Oh, Mr. Daniels, can you pick up your packet on the table. It was superbly written."

The teacher directs Kyra to have a seat while he sees to the door, announcing to the class as he stands behind the metal desk, "Just start closing down your workstations people and glance over your notes for tomorrow."

Kyra passes Timothy as she is returning to her seat, and he walks to the front of the class to pick up his work packet. When Kyra settles into her seat, she can't help but notice Timothy's secret journal of his innermost thoughts is laying there open. She sees writing within it appearing to be more of a poem.

> *Jason, oh, Jason, what can I say? Your fiery red hair and dazzling green eyes. How it is you send me, watching your one-man races outside my window? I cry a little bit each day, to just feel your face. Your biceps so firm, your athletically perfect body, like your chest and legs. Even your butt is perfection, too. I can only imagine such beauty, in my dreams, be it days or nights. Jason so fast, Jason so true, Jason your too beautiful to be true. I know my spirit wants me to tell you how much I lov—*

She doesn't know what to think, but her curiosity draws deep. She doesn't even know if Timothy has a friend within or outside of the school. He is such a loner to everyone. Unaware, Timothy closes the book, not realizing Kyra has already glimpsed at it.

Timothy gently taps Kyra's hand while the teacher addresses the people at the door, and with a soft whisper, he says, "Way to go. I knew you would be good. But you are really brilliant in your delivery." Kyra is taken by surprise that Timothy is making physical contact with her, which he has never been done before.

"Timothy, please. You're the smartest kid in this school, and you know it." He gives an awkward grin like an android trying to mimic a human reaction. Timothy lacks emotional responses with others around him. *Maybe it's Asperger's*, she thinks.

Two boys sitting in the last row behind them boldly taunt Timothy. They primarily do this because Timothy doesn't defend himself. He just ignores them.

"Yeah, yeah, we know you chicks are the super nerds in this

class, especially curly Sue Timmy right beside you. Don't get me wrong, Kyra, you are by far the hottest brain in the entire school."

His buddy Ben chimes in, "Hot damn, Jake!"

The boys fist-bump each other and return to the mean insults. "Hey, Ben, don't you think the little sister Timmy is looking especially sweet today?" He chuckles.

His partner gives him a hive five. "Kablam! Jake, bro, that's a good one. Yo, Timmy, lovin' those elastic drawstring cotton shorts. Tell me! Is romper room next mod, Yo?"

Jake wheezes while laughing so hard. "Fuckin' straight, Ben. You got it. Those are some cute-ass hip huggers. Those fresh, silky smooth legs are banging. Oh, yours are too, Kyra."

Ben blurts out, "Legs are fine. But seriously, did you not see that juicy rump when he swooshes his plump little ass up to the front of the class? Dude, baby got back."

The boys start to make a big scene with their mocking laughter.

"It's funny. We shared gym-time with the Dude, and yet we never saw him enter or exit the locker room during class."

Jakes laughs hard with eyes popped wide.

Ben follow suit in laughter.

"Do you think he uses the girl's locker room by chance?" Jake's statement makes Timothy very uncomfortable. Others in the classroom start to snicker.

Ben yells out, "Yeah, you may be on to something, Bro! Get this. I listened to some things about our boy Timmy. That's hilarious, man."

"Oh, really? Spill the beans, dude. What gives?" Jake's face is almost red from laughing.

"I heard Tim-o-thy is something of an enema man!" Ben announces louder than he should have, and the class roars with real laughter. Jake shakes his head, acknowledging how oblivious his buddy is that he used the wrong word at the worst time. Laughter billows out of control, and Ben is clueless about the reason.

Jake helps his poor buddy out with an elbow to the ribs. "Dude, I think you meant … enigma!"

Ben turns flush with embarrassment. "Oops, my bad, bro. You're right!"

"Anyway, why is Tim-o-thy such an enigma, bro?"

"You remember the mandatory physical we all had to take because everyone was afraid of an outbreak? Over in the track and field building? It turned out to be a false call anyway." Jake nods his head, remembering the event. "Dude, I remember the doc saying he had a boy Timothy's age who was completely prepubescent."

"Oh, freakin' sugar snaps, bro. Are you saying what I think you're saying, dude?"

"Bro! He is completely hairless like one of those … freaky lab rats, you know?" Ben cracks up.

"Bald? Are we talking, baby ass cheeks bald?" Jake questions for clarity.

"It's like … the freaking puberty train completely detoured when heading to the Timothy Daniels station, bro." Jake's words bring the class to a horrific roar—all except Timothy and Kyra.

The substitute teacher tries to calm everyone down while trying to talk with the people outside the classroom door.

Kyra notices Timothy's mortified expression. Unable to take any more lip service from the boys behind her, Kyra swiftly turns about and gives both a wicked glare. "Why don't you two jock straps for brains slip on a greasy banana and split?"

Jake places his hand over his heart, portraying the wounded victim, before laughing out, "Hey, I'm sorry beautiful. (looking directly at Kyra) I didn't mean to offend you. I resent that statement. (He clutches the bulge of his crotch.) You should get to know my brain personally. Right, sexy lips?" Ben is bent over with laughter, resting his head on Jake's shoulder. Jake continues, "You're welcome to chat with it. Just be careful. What comes out of its tiny mouth is always a bit messy."

Grinding her teeth, Kyra is disgusted, and she turns away from his sight, squinting her eyes. Under her breath, just audible enough for Timothy to hear, she says, "What a sick jackass!" Her voice burns with hatred.

"I should know, yeah? My brain gets swollen and needs some release from time to time. Your girlfriend Timothy is free to witness how big my brain is if he promises to control his queer ways. Hell, I'll be a sport and let him play a game of hairy balls."

Timothy clenches his fists tight. His breath becomes labored, and his stomach knots to the core. His rage burns at his sour mouth and dry throat. Even though Jake and Ben are track runners and bigger than him, Timothy lashes out with a verbal firestorm. "What a fucking Neanderthal! You twice-bent prick face, turd pond! Your intellectual is so bleak that it can only be measured by the length of your pathetic excuse for a freaking prick, which is not measurable, for it's too damn minuscule to register, even for a microorganism. Either way!"

The roar of laughter in the classroom brings the teacher scream-ing back into the class. When the laughter subsides, Kyra makes Timothy turn around, seeing the look of fierce anger on his face. He's almost in tears.

Jake tugs on his own manhood for Timothy's personal obser-vation. Ben cheers as Jake express himself in a whispered tone for Timothy ears only, "Look! Hairless twat! I will show you exactly what my IQ measures up to, freak show! Keep it up! I dare you!"

Not to let the overtly sexual gestures bother him, Timothy shies away. Kyra senses Timothy's inner torment as her blood boils over.

Kyra gives Jake a cold hard stare, "Jake, if I had to choose be-tween a thug like you or a charming, brilliant, adorable sophomore, you would lose every time. Get a life. Timothy is a real man with vision and planning. Your future is nestled tightly in the grip of your own hand … right now! Which isn't saying much. From where I am sitting, it's looking a bit bleak."

Ben starts laughing at Kyra's spunky retort, which makes Jake frustration explode. Kyra quickly redirects her attention to Ben, "Oh, and you, Mr. Giggles! …are no better. What is it like being Jake's little lap puppy. Woof, woof! Do you lap-up everything he drops to the ground for you?"

"Hey!" Ben shoots, slamming his fist hard on the desk, catching the attention of the substitute teacher, who points him down, to chill it.

"I'm no fuckin' Homo, like the freak-boy, Timothy! We heard about your secret spy fetish on the new kid Jason last week." Ben's voice cracks as he reveals Timothy's most hidden secret.

Kyra stands, brushing hard against the metal chair and locking eyes with Jake. "Why don't you two miserable excuses for unused condoms do everyone a huge favor?"

Jake lifts a brow with a snarky grin on his face.

"Find your own repressed sexual desires and play with each other. I hear little boys who always rag on other boys are secretly longing for something themselves. You know the adage. Only attack what you fear being labeled." Her voice resonates into their very souls. Her frightening tone of authority sends a shock wave through Jake and Ben's macho exteriors, shattering them.

The class erupts into utter chaos once more and gives no signs of stopping. The laughter leaves the guys speechless while chuckles resonate.

The substitute teacher rushes into the chaos and hushes the room for the last time. When the teacher gestured for someone to enter, everyone looks to the front of the room.

"I want everyone to meet the newest addition to our AP

chemistry class … outside of me, of course. She is a transfer student from Michigan. This is her sophomore year." A beautiful girl with shoulder-length blonde hair that has blue and lime crinkly curls enters the room. She's wearing a pleated skirt with the school colors that accent her hair. Her eyes glisten a bright green, and her lips shine with a glossy peach.

The teacher directs her to everyone, even though she has an unenthused expression plastered on her face. "Everyone! This is, Ms. Cheryl Hunters. Treat her nice, guys. I am, Mr. Wagner, the substitute teacher for, Mr. Wade, who is out indefinitely because of family concerns."

Cheryl does a panoramic view of the room and the students. The boys in the class appear fixated directly on how well she fills out the uniform. The girls all make a note of her sharp and fresh fashion sense. Mr. Wagner directs her to find a seat anywhere in the class. She locates an empty chair adjacent to Kyra and Timothy's station. With all eyes squarely fixed on her, she slowly makes her way to the seat.

Passing in front of Kyra and Timothy, she stops briefly, eyeing the two of them, and then she continues. Kyra receives a very odd feeling of distress, which makes the hairs on the back of her neck stand erect. Her stomach twists into a giant knot. She doesn't know what to make of it. Nevertheless, she makes a point to not dwell on the sick feeling but to focus on the rest of her reading. The sensation slowly subsides, but it leaves her wondering. It could have been the unneeded stress of dealing with Jake and Ben. The remainder of the day runs smoothly, or at least she believes so.

The school day finally runs its course, and Kyra is ready to leave for the evening after explaining to her after-school clicks that she can't stay. She finds herself dreading the idea of catching the miserable school bus. Her twin brother, Kyle, sees her and doesn't even make a gesture that he will take her home in his little souped-up

Nissan. Her senior status has now been reduced to freshmen status in the blink of an eye.

Walking through the crowded halls and saying her goodbyes to friends, she sees Jake and Ben talking with Eric and Carlos, a couple football jocks, about something intense. The boys appear to be in their usual buddy-buddy laughter routine. Ben glimpses over and catches Kyra within in his sights. He taps Jake and gestures in her direction. Jake hastily makes his way through the crowd of scattering students and staff to confront Kyra directly.

Kyra braces herself for the worst. His voice is wild and pitchy. "So, warrior princess, defender of the weak and pathetic, you think that little dance in class earlier was something special today?" Kyra says nothing but looks at her watch instead, not wanting to provoke a scene in the middle of the busy hallway.

"So sorry to hold you up, my lady! I just want you to clearly know that this is far from over, interloper. Your little pansy friend thinks that getting in my face and insulting my manhood was cool? Ha! A fatal flaw on his part. I am laughing so hard. Just let his sorry ass know that it's game on!" He smiles as he walks away. "Let him know that the hunt is on! And how does it feel to not be the only cute girl in class now? Damn, that Cheryl is hot!"

Though deeply upsetting, she only sees his words as a hollow threat at best. It's common knowledge to her that any athlete who wants to remain an athlete and keep their eligibility status won't dare threaten someone in an open environment, especially with all the, no bullying laws and rules posted all around the school. She proceeds to make her way down the last corridor toward the main exits.

Kyra is quickly blindsided by a group of rowdy cheerleaders who push their way through her. Trying to avoid a full-on collision, she dodges the last girl and unexpectedly slams into something thick, firm, and robust. The impact knocks her back onto the floor, and she flings her belongings all over the hallway.

The captain of the cheerleaders briefly looks back and chuckles, pointing out the commotion to the other copycats, Though Kyra is somewhat cute, they don't allow girls like Kyra into the squad. "What a klutz!" she taunts as she turns around to go on her merry way.

Her pride all over the floor, Kyra springs to her knees and gathers her belongings before they are all trampled on. The final bells begin ringing then. Time is clearly not on her side. She remembers that the third signal alarm is to let everyone know that the buses are now departing.

In her haste, she's completely unaware of the hand that is graciously reaching out to her.

A healthy adolescent male clears his throat. Her hazel eyes pan upward, and she sees the firm, lightly tanned, well-manicured hand. The boy is sporting thigh-hugging black denim. She catches the visible bulge of his manly nature and the bottom of a letterman's jacket. The jacket is unbuttoned. She doesn't look at the boy's face, but she steadies herself and gathers her items off the floor. A familiar voice speaks down to her, giving her instant goosebumps when he starts questioning her name.

"Umm, Kyra? Kyra Mathews, right? Do you need some help?" The base of in his voice indicates he is closer to manhood than boyhood. Kyra snaps her head back, her long locks flowing freely to one side. She flutters her eyelashes with astonishing disbelief.

Kyra's knees become gelatinous like Jell-O when she sees the young man she's been infatuated with for as long as she can remember. The man of her dreams, the knight she has imagined riding in on a mighty white steed, sweeping her off her feet and dashing with her into the amber sunset, happily ever after.

Here he is in his full Technicolor glory. Caught in a daze, Kyra soaks in his essence—the scent of his day-old musk and withered body spray. Nothing was overlooked, not his bright baby blue sparkly eyes or his short, feather, sandy blond hair with the fading sides.

Scott Tanner is the most revered young man in Franklin High. He's the varsity's star quarterback. He's charming, and he's a sex symbol to all his adoring female fans … and even some questionable male ones.

His road to glory is a fascinating tale of courage and will. Scott is a legend among the geeks and underclassman as well. He gives them hope and vindication that anything is possible if your heart is strong enough to endure. He was so talented he went varsity his sophomore year. Coach Johnson admired his talents when he tried out for JV basketball his freshmen year. The coach approached him afterward and asked if he wanted to try out for varsity football instead because of his physical prowess.

So, he did. Surprisingly, he made the varsity team and became the first sophomore in the history of the school to become starting quarterback.

This is the first time Kyra can gaze upon his perfection without the onslaught of needy groupies and fellow players orbiting him.

"Kyra. That is your name, right?" he inquires. Finally, she realizes that she should at least say something and stop drooling.

"Ah, I-I am sorry. No, I mean, Kyra? Yes, that is my name. I think. Oh, crap! Uh, hmm, not you, of course. I meant I am Kyra." Kyra is spewing out words in a jumbled mess. "I am sorry for smashing into you like that." She finally manages to calm herself.

The boy chuckles rather innocently. "No need to fret. I'm fine."

"I know you are—"

He's a bit shocked, but he finds humor in it. "Don't worry. It would take a lot more than a beautiful girl to damage this body. I mean … I am—"

He reaches out his hand, but she interrupts him, "Scott … Scott Tanner. Yes, I know exactly who you are!"

Scott smiles and blushes a little.

"The school's legendary varsity athlete and varsity starting QB three-years running. I mean … who wouldn't know who *you* are?"

A little deflated and yet flattered at the same time, Scott remarks with a little sarcasm, "Wow, I am beginning to think maybe that's not such a great thing."

Kyra smiles. "I didn't really mean to say it like that, of course."

Kyra feels that she's put her foot in her mouth, twisting her hair in her fidgety fingers.

"Nice to meet you, Ms. Kyra Mathews." Scott takes her hand and holds it firmly. He almost doesn't want to let it go.

Oh, my God! Is this really happening, today? Am I dreaming this right, now? Kyra's mind blisters with all the what-ifs. Scott stares warmly inviting, into her eyes.

CHAPTER 3

K yra feels overwhelmed, staring straight into the face of a living, breathing Adonis above her. Scott isn't like the rest of the guys in school.

Mature for his age and a classic kind of cool, Scott isn't perfect by far, but so amazingly close. Kyra is lost in thought, *He likes to horseplay with his buds, and make wisecracks on other athletes when passing in the halls. He's a bad boy sometimes, breaking bad when he needs to. Nonetheless, his mannerisms with girls and lowerclassmen are top notch. Unlike some of the guys, with notoriety around the school of being crass, bullies, or just acting like jerks. Scott, on the other hand, takes great pride in his appearance. He's very college-like. He is a big guy of six foot two and roughly a Buck-forty-five-pounds of sculpted, lean testosterone muscle. He narrows at the hips and broadens at the shoulders. His tight shirts show off his noticeable pecs and biceps. For a boy, his sun-kissed, peachy skin is a delectable delight to see. It also shows that he is an outdoors kind of guy. The only thing that seems to give a hint to his age is his rather boyish face and the wide-eyed puppy-dog stares he gives to people with is gorgeous blue eyes.*

Kyra is used to seeing Scott around the school daily, but he's usually surrounded by a flock of jocks and a lurid array of elite cheerleaders. This only makes him appear unattainable. Not that she's in the market for a boyfriend. Even she can't believe that fairy tale.

Nevertheless, she's unaware that the buses have started their departure. But she quickly snaps out of her reverie and confronts the stark reality around her. She must go!

"Uh-um, I thought you drove to school? Were you trying to catch that bus or something?"

"Huh!" She shakes her head as if something small has just flown past her face, "What … what's that?"

Scott points to the main entrance, which is about forty feet away, and with a little snicker, he says, "The buses … are leaving!"

"Oh, Crap!" she exclaims abruptly. She snatches the two remaining pages from a bewildered Scott's hand and catapults herself toward the lobby doors. She bobs and weaves in and out of people's paths with the greatest of ease like a well-seasoned running back.

Scott is amazed by her athletic ability and swift movements. "Damn! That girl moves like an Emmitt Smith. I need to put a jersey on her and bench, Wahler!"

Dashing toward the exit, she quickly surmises her bus has already left, and she feels defeated this day yet again. "Today is the worst … day … ever!" Scott along with everyone present hears her outburst.

The only positive out of the day was meeting her dream-hero Scott Tanner, face-to-face. The fact that he knew her name is even more mind-boggling. *'Hmm, why is that?'* She questions, *'It's not like I ever met him personally or had any classes with the guy. We surely don't swing in the same network of friends. So … what gives?'*

She's quickly startled by a familiar soothing voice, approaching from behind her left ear. "Don't worry Kyra. You need a ride?"

Kyra stands erect like a statue, hoping to turn invisible instead of turning to face the beautiful boy of her dreams. Goosebumps trickle down her back, and she feels the sensation of his warm breath caressing the nape of her neck.

She wants so badly to scream out to the hillsides, but she maintains her composure. "Oh? That's sweet of you. But I couldn't impose on you, Scott. You are too busy with after school thingies. You shouldn't be bothered yourself with a simpleton like me."

"I am not really sure what you mean by imposing. And I am quite certain you are anything but a simpleton, Kyra. It's not a problem to take you home. You are only a couple neighborhoods down from me."

That's another piece of vital information that takes her by surprise. Scott even knows where she lives. That's either exciting or scary. She still must weigh the balances. In her mind, she is on the floor with unequivocal joy, flailing around like a fish out of water.

Kyra tries to clear her throat before looking at him directly. "You know what?" She looks as though she has an epiphany. "You are right. I remember now. You lived on Red Pansy Drive in the Flower Village neighborhood, don't you?" Her dreamy stud cringes before her with embarrassment.

"Jeez! Shhhh! Seriously?" Flustered, his face turns red. "Don't remind me, especially not so freaking loud!" Scott smirks, which only shows the young boy that hides inside the rugged exterior, a look that reminds her of her self-assured brother, Kyle. "I am still trying to forget that—thank you very much. The guys in the locker room would never let me live that one down if they ever found out. I never forgave my father for moving us there instead of one circle over, and it would have been Gladiator Grove, which thankfully happened after middle school."

"Silly boy, you are aware that Gladiator is a flower name too, right? Like gladiolas?"

window in the afternoons? It is becoming quite a daily routine. They usually don't start the outside events for another twenty minutes or so, and I just saw Scott Tanner sprint down the hall."

Timothy is one of the rarest cases of underclassmen in the after-school program. In fact, he is the only underclassmen in the program for two years running. He essentially doesn't require any technical assistance in the labs at this point, but Jamerson is there only as a safety precaution. Jamerson helps the students with their independent projects as needed, covering the span of the sciences and botanical arts.

The school code of ethics and safety protocols must always be upheld. Timothy doesn't respond, and Mr. Jamerson's curiosity grows. He decides to investigate on his own and inspects the view by a nearby window.

Mr. Jamerson then sees the object of Timothy's fixation. Out of shock, Mr. Jamerson makes a double-take when he sees a young sprinter coasting the lap track. He shifts his view between the young runner and Timothy several times. Mr. Jamerson always figured Timothy was a little different than the others, but he thought it was rooted in his lack of social and emotional connection with the students his age. This appears to be somewhat more complex than he had originally thought.

Is Timothy interested in the running or the boy? It's very hard to tell at this point, Mr. Jamerson thinks before breaking the ice. "That kid is quite a sprinter. Do you know him, Timothy?" Jamerson asks.

Timothy is oddly shaken by the sudden presence of Mr. Jamerson, and he responds with slight hesitance, "Ah … who?"

Mr. Jamerson points to the boy jogging on the track, the one with the high-cut shiny red shorts and the loose-fitted T-shirt. Timothy looks out the window once more as if to confirm the presence of this person. "Oh, you mean him?" he points out the window.

Mr. Jamerson nods.

"Oh-no! N-not really! Not personally." Timothy shakes his head nervously. "I just know a little about him. He is a new student this year. I know that for sure." He places a finger under his chin as if contemplating a question, he already knows the answer to. "His name is ... um, Jason Brodie. He is a sophomore like me. He seems to enjoy doing sprints a lot. He's out every evening before the others come out to the fields. He is hitting record speeds when no one is there to see him. He can easily take out our fastest sprinter by a minute and fifteen seconds. The amazing thing is ... he manages to always get done before anyone in the athletic department can come out to witness his greatness. It's as if he doesn't want anyone to know he is so brilliantly fast with those strong legs of his. Many times, I never actually see him leave. It's like he just vanishes into thin air or something, which I know is impossible."

Mr. Jamerson finds himself admiring the young sprinter, especially since he was once a runner in his youth for his university. "Hmm, he's a powerful athlete. He must be in the three and a half to the four-minute-mile club. Yeah?"

Timothy feeling the need to correct him, "Actually, he seems a little off today! It's like something is weighing on his mind." Nevertheless, Timothy doesn't mention how saddened he was in witnessing the boy, berating himself, just minutes before Jamerson's intrusion. It is noticed by Jamerson, how the young male on the track has such a strong hold on Timothy.

Timothy continues in his robot mode of speech, "I have clocked his fastest mile in two-minutes, forty-two- seconds and point six-milliseconds. I can only estimate his run today is bearing three-minutes, ten-seconds and point forty-two-milliseconds."

Mr. Jamerson hits Timothy with an exceedingly fascinated scowl, "Are you serious? You actually clocked him with only your mind?" Timothy confirms with a bow of his head. He had never once thought about it. His mental calculations were always second

CHAPTER 5

The football team along with the practice squad are playing and training hard on the field, while Kyra observes very intently from the bleachers. Several of the cheerleaders, and the captain of the squad, Tiffany Bowman, who scrutinizes with some of the girls, over a routine that needed to be learned.

Tiffany fits the stereotypical role of a self-absorbed, egotistical cheerleader perfectly. Everyone knows how pleasing to the eye she is—her bubbly perkiness, blue eyes, and the glorious luster of her artificially treated blonde hair, which is her ultimate joy. Tiffany is shadowed by an overzealous BFF, a mediocre brunette lackey with ample bosoms, which make up for the lack of natural beauty, and intellect. Trish Faucet is the girl who doesn't mind being belittled by her self-appointed leader Tiffany.

Kyra is locked on Scott like a heat-seeking missile. This is her first time seeing him in such a charming setting. His hip-hugging, sweaty practice shorts and thin mesh jersey allows her to see the man and not the little boy. The tight dimples from his perfectly sculpted buttocks have her undivided attention. She admires his movements as he shifts from one cheek to the other. Scott is aware of her undivided interest in his every move. Each time he passes her location, he gives a little wink of approval. He loves seeing her bashfully try to look away.

After the long and hard practice in the afternoon's scorching heat, Scott jogs over to Kyra, who is standing nervously at the foot of the tall bleachers. Kyra is very distracted by Scott's visible male organ bouncing freely about in his sweaty white practice shorts.

Scott explains how they'll leave after he takes a quick shower. As he is talking to her, he notices Kyra's attention isn't directed to his eyes but further south of his belly button. Being so comfortable around the fellas, it didn't dawn on him how exposed he was to Kyra's unexpected viewable delight.

While practicing, it's a commonplace for the players to get a glimpse of another players junk, from time to time. The thin white practice shorts are very transparent when wet with sweat, and often the guys omit to wear their under-spanks. Resorting to the term freeballing. The guys never worry about what's visible available— until now, in Kyra's presence. His shorts leaves no mystery to his complete full frontal packaging.

Not wanting to be so exposed in front of the girl he loves, Scott rips off his saturated jersey, revealing his glistening biceps, broad chest, and bulging pecs. His dark crimson nipples are peeked with arousal, while His well-defined six-pack is dripping with droplets of glistening sweat.

Of course, this proves to be an excellent distraction to Kyra's line of sight, as he wraps soiled jersey around his slimed waist, covering his visible man bulge. Kyra ogles at his sparkling hairless torso.

Tiffany and Trish are just about to walk into the main building from the soccer field, where the girls practice their evening cheer routines. Trish spots Kyra and Scott flirting with each other in the distance. Without his jersey on, Scott gives them the perfect view of the small indent of his lower back, which leads to his plump peachy amble rump, peering through his shorts.

"Who the hell is that?" Tiffany exclaims, to Trish, seeing Kyra with Scott.

Trish peeks over at Tiffany's point of interest. "I've never seen her out here before. She isn't one of the second-string cheerleaders either. And she's not a baller, for damn sure!" Tiffany doesn't say a word as Trish continues to ramble on. "I don't know, Tiff. She is kinda cute in an off-Broadway sort of way, of course. I mean, look at that outfit, kind of yesterday's bag. You know what I'm saying? I mean! ...like, seriously? those shoes?" She annoyingly smacks her gum as she talks.

"Enough Trish!" Unable to take any more, Tiffany says, "I don't know who she is or who she may think she is. Scott Tanner is off limits. The bitch needs to recognize. This is common law, a known high school factoid. Quarterbacks and cheerleader captains are stated featured items, rule primo-uno!" She sneers with rolled eyes, "Even if she were the queen of the freaking Nile itself, little Miss Disney Channel Princess needs to learn, one doesn't mess with fuckin' destined shit, without a slap-back!"

Giving her buddy support, Trish adds, "Yeah, you tell her Tiffany. (She looks dumbfounded for a second) ...Um, Tiff? Is she like ... a real queen or something? With the whole palace and shit?" Tiffany can only look at her friend with absolute disdain for her naivety, and she simply shakes her head slowly and walks off.

Scott casually jogs from the bleachers to the main building, and his butt cheeks bounce the whole way. The sight makes Kyra blush ever harder as she steps from the bleachers.

While in deeply entranced in a fairy-tale-like daze, completely clueless about her surroundings, Kyra slams hard against a very solid frame, like Déjà vu all over again. Looking upward, she sees a glistening teen boy with scruffy ginger hair, a soft pale complexion, and green puppy-dog eyes with a smell of fresh soap and a hint of masculine muskiness. A bit startled by his undeniable adorableness, she graciously apologizes, "Oh, forgive me. I am deeply sorry. I was obviously not paying attention to where I was stepping."

"Oy' I say! Too busy eyeing the lad's perfectly shaped peachy rump?"

Kyra is in complete shock. She can't find the words.

The brassy boy continues, "I'd say for a big musty bloke, the lad has that cute pretty-boy face thingy happening there! If that's what you'd be really fancying, Oy'?"

He's surprisingly playful, which causes Kyra to blush. She questions his rather uncharacteristic descriptiveness of another boy so openly and with ease.

"See! You nae deny it?" He smirks. "Beautiful lassies like yourself … always running ugly blokes like me over so you can fawn all over them pretty faced Lads like Oy', Scotty Tanner." Kyra tries to shake her head in defense, "Not true!" She exclaimed, while subconsciously telling herself, *Well, not intentionally, I think.*

"But worry you not, wee lass. You sparkly thing sprinkled from heavens pure magic fount, I am built rugged and tough like a truck, Aye? A gentle bump from such a pretty wee flower could never hurt my bum." He turns his body slightly to let her see his healthy tush. "You see, It's a nice bum, Aye?" He even jiggles it slightly so that she can see it bounce. He chuckles, "… if I say so myself, I think it is." While he is talking, he starts to laugh most delightfully, warming Kyra's heart completely.

The ginger-haired boy was anything but ugly. He's a slightly slimmer, younger version of Scott. Unlike Scott, his thighs are more defined, as his lower shins are shapelier. The guy could either be a runner or a speed skater. His eyes are disarmingly gentle and warm. His demeanor is cockily cute and infectious. Kyra's completely stupefied by the fact she has never seen him around the school before.

He explains boastfully how he was probably moving too fast for her to see him. With a cheeky smile, Kyra states, "Hmm, maybe I should just give you a speeding ticket then, mister!" Kyra couldn't help but analyze the kid's use of words and subtle accents. "You're Scottish, aren't you?"

"What makes you think this?"

She softly giggles. "I don't know. The hair, your amazing green eyes, and your cute Gaelic accent."

"Noe, what ye be meaning … Gaelic accent? I have no accent. Ye be talking shenanigans. I am speaking clear, concise English, Aye? I am an … all-American-born and bred, bloke!"

Covering her mouth, as if in shame, Kyra apologizes, "Oh wow, please excuse my ignorance! So, so sorry! I meant no disrespect, honestly. I just think it is rather adorable."

The boy chuckles deep and hard. "Chill ye sweet wee nickers, Lassie. I was just playing with you. Besides, I am nae cute! Unlike your dream-boy Scott, Mac-Scotty pants, in there. (Pointing to the building he had departed to.) I'm just a scraggly rank bloke, out for a run, Oy'?"

Kyra blushes and nods her head, although she wants to tell him how wrong he is pandering himself as ugly because he is amazingly gorgeous.

He continues, "My folks were from the homelands of Scotland, in the northern highlands. However, this ugly-balach (boy) was born here in the good old US of A." Kyra smiles. Jason is helpless to her smile and laughs along with her.

Hearing the gentleness in his tone makes her cheeks flush. His charm is very alluring. His outer shell is rugged and tough, but his inner gentleness shows his warmth.

"Very rude of me! I am, Kyra Mathews." She cheerfully announces with a giggle and a wave of her hand.

The boy attempts to curtsy, which is oddly awkward. This is
an act which is more familiarized with the female set, rather than
males. Yet, it's cute to see him try, albeit badly.

"The pale young bloke before you, be none other than Jason
Brodie, me lady."

Kyra can't help but burst out into laughter, from his theatrics.

Jason was surely a true gentleman in another life.

Kyra ravels in the gentle innocence of Jason, as he huffs out
a quick breath and starts, "Please, excuse my vulgar smell, sweet
Kyra. I know I am still a bit rank. I couldn't thoroughly shower because of the brutes from Scott's pack. I needed to talk to a teacher
about a spying little bloke, up in the science labs."

"Oh, Mr. Jamerson, maybe?"

"Wow. You know the man, Aye?"

"Well, let's say, I am fairly familiar with the science labs in
general." Kyra doesn't want to divulge so much, too quickly, "You
know of Mr. Jamerson?" she counters the question.

Jason shakes his head. "Not really. Just met him not long ago.
He seems cool, for an older bloke, I guess. Had to talk with him
about a spying little curly head kid in the labs. He's rather persistent
in checking me out. It's getting a bit creepy, Aye! I don't want
poofter perv's spying on me, you know?"

"Really?"

"Yeah, If I am not mistaken, he was surely checking out my ass
earlier! Kinda caught the little perv red-handed, gazing out his lofty
window. Really freaked me out a bit. That's all."

His accounting of the incident triggers a memory for Kyra.
*Could this be the same Jason in young Timothy's secret trove of
thoughts and dreams?*

Kyra vaguely smiles. "Honestly Jason, you have nothing to

worry about." Kyra wants to avoid mentioning her acquaintance with Timothy. Even though she would love to tell him, how sweet Timothy really is, and he should have no fear of him. Regardless, Kyra changes the direction of the conversation, "You don't smell completely dreadful at all. B-e-l-i-e-v-e me! I've smelled musky rankness before and you my friend, are clearly not. Some of the opponents in last year's martial arts tournament would blow you over with their funky body odor, while never laying a hand on you."

Jason's eyes nearly pop clear out of his orbital sockets. "Tournaments? Whoa! You're like a Femme fatale, Lassie?"

She shakes her head firmly, "No, not hardly. I mostly do exhibitions. My father won't allow me to go full-point contact."

"Hmm, not wanting to offend such a cute thing as yourself, I am happy you don't. Much too pretty of a thing for bruises and such." Raising a brow, she wants to lay into him for his sexist remark. *Women are not just looks and makeup!* Her mental voice screams, all the while her face adorns a pleasing smile.

Looking passed his comment, Kyra extends her hand in a friendly gesture to Jason. Knowing she must cut the conversation short, for she must go and ready herself for Scott. Jason sees the gesture, and returns it in kind, reaching out to hers.

As their hands come into contact, a wild jolt of static electricity forces them to yank their hands apart. This is unlike any shock either of them has ever experienced.

They snicker and dismissed it as a freakish experience and attempted once more. Jason likes the smoothness of her hand, while she feels the strength in his full grip. Once more she can't help but feel a tenderness in the way he anchors that force.

Unbeknownst to either of them, a pair of ancient eyes studies them from far off, completely void of detection. 'First contact,' whispers the mysterious stranger's voice.

Ironically, an indescribable sensation comes over Kyra and

Jason simultaneously. A strong surge of energy hits Kyra's lower limbs and courses down to her feet. For him, however, it feels more like a zapping sensation. Legs feeling liquidly unstable.

The sensation passes as quickly as it came. Kyra feels vitalized with incredible energy. Breaking her eyes toward Jason, she senses the zest within him seems to have diminished. His eyes lack their full luster, appearing more wounded puppy like. Jason unnerved by the weak sensation in his legs, realizes he has accidentally wet in his shorts.

Feeling the urgent need to vacate, Jason cracks a half-witty grin, says a warm goodbye and departs. As he walks away, a droplet of urine slowly drizzled down his inner thigh, bring a whole new sensation of humiliation to his masculine nature, while praying Kyra isn't aware of it.

Still overwhelmingly baffled by the incident, Kyra watches Jason walk away. Yet, she can't help but ponder on the boy, as an enigma.

The similarities between Jason and Scott appear uncanny to her. Kyra continuing her comparisons. Both boy's exhibit strong athletic traits and great cocky personalities. Physically, Jason is every bit a jock; bold and strong. Ironically, she sensed a tender sweetness deep within. He is unique in this sense, actually feeling similar to what she feels in Timothy, to be precise. *What does this mean?* She ponders, while finally understanding a bit of Timothy's dark obsession with the guy. Jason is a true charmer.

A few minutes before Kyra and Jason's bumped encountering, Mr. Jamerson alerts the time to Timothy for late dismissal. This affords Timothy plenty of time to pack his materials and shut down the lab for the afternoon. Never fond of the idea of leaving before a task is fully exhausted or completed, Timothy's tact for punctuality is seconded to none, especially when involving his personal driver of two years, Ms. Susan Kemp. Ms. Kemp brings him to school daily. Timothy adores her amazing cuteness especially in the buttoned downed uniform assigned her, as he thinks her boyfriend has got to be one of the luckiest guys on earth. A twenty-something, smart, ambitious woman who appears to love her job, Susan never treats him like a bratty, spoiled rich kid, unlike some of the current housing staff.

CHAPTER 6

Timothy is yearning for a major growth spurt any day now. His stocky five-foot-seven stature isn't cutting it with him anymore. He is forever referred to as little Timmy or just Timmy, a name he despises. Today he is taking home a bit more than his average belongings. His pack is filled with thick books, miscellaneous notes, and lab reports. He clears out of the lab room and hastily marches through the halls. He doesn't feel like walking his typical path all the way to the stairwell in the front of the building, so he instead uses the closer one, which is right past the gymnasium entranceway.

Without any warning, he exits the stairwell and suddenly sees a flash of red. Then he finds himself lying on the floor, staring at the ceiling, dizzily. He tries to regain his composure after what felt like running into a brick wall, he starts to hear dark laughter just above him.

His vision quickly clears up, and he sees three large jocks leering at him. *Steroids must be their primary source of nutrition*, he thinks. All three guys are wearing varsity letterman jackets for Franklin High, which was weird considering how hot it was outside.

That just proves the coat is more of a badge of honor than a meaningful piece of attire.

It quickly dawns on Timothy that these weren't just any jocks standing over him. These were the Death Pack boys. Franklin High's meanest, crudest, most celebrated front lineman and the most feared bunch in the whole school—Eric Hottman, Craig Knightly, and Carlos Melos, the official starters of the offensive line of the Dueling Dragons.

"Hey! Twinkle toes! What's wrong with your eyes man?" Eric boldly address Timothy, "Considering you have four of them and all?"

Timothy tries to overlook the insult, stands, and comes face-to-face with three boys. Timothy has a slender, yet well-proportioned frame, even though he is only five-foot-seven and a hundred and twenty-five pounds, when wet. He has a natural fattiness to his body, soft in some spots but muscular in others.

Eric, the slender of the three big players, bouncing in at Buck-ninety-five-pounds of purely cut lean muscle. Craig is considered the biggest of the trio, weighing 365-pounds of brute bulk and stout. Carlos is averaged between them at Two-hundred-thirty-fives-pounds, stoutness like a Brahma bull. He is pudgier around the gut, but he has solid thick arms and shoulders. Both, Craig and Carlos tower like giants over Timothy, each being two-to-four inches over the six-foot mark.

Mocking the fact that Timothy has a head full of dark, luscious brown curls and huge puppy dog eyes, "Hmm ... Curls! I can see how you would get such a name!" Eric's voice deeply resonates.

One might think Timothy treats his hair with products. Nevertheless, it's all natural, thanks to his basic homegrown genetics. Unfortunately explaining his latent prepubescent issues, while in his adolescent growth stage. Timothy's smooth, golden caramelized skin reflects his Latin roots, given to him by his late father's side of the family. His thick, long eyelashes are the gifts from his beloved mother's side, with their Celtic and Jewish ancestry.

Studying Timothy closely, Eric senses the little man's oozing fear. This brings Eric much pleasure. He looks around and sees that everyone has finally cleared the halls, leaving no one in that section of the building. He steps up closer to him.

Somewhat fearful, Timothy starts, "I didn't mean to bump into you guys, honestly!"

Meanwhile, at the opposite hall diagonal to theirs, Jason emerges from the restroom and sees the three guys lurking over Timothy. He also notices Timothy's books and belongings scattered all over the floor around him. Wanting to see what was going on, he decides to stand back and simply observe for the moment.

Eric giving Timothy a good once over, "Hmm! You know? You're not wearing the school's regulated uniform, Curls?"

Timothy sparks in defense, "In the labs, we don't have to wear the school uniform. We're allowed to wear comfortable attire under our lab gear."

"Oh, you are one of those ... little geeky ass kids upstairs, huh?" Eric sounds eerily seductive.

Timothy's gut is screaming, *Danger, danger!*

He begins pleading with Eric and the others, "Please! I just wanna pass and go home. Okay?" Timothy points to the front of the school, "My ride is waiting for me out front."

Eric grunts while firmly grabbing his own bulging crotch, "Don't worry little man! I got a ride for you right here. You want to try it out? Must warn you, it may be a bit of a rough ride."

Timothy steps back, hitting the lockers behind him, "Uh! I am not homosexual guys. Please stop handling yourself like that!"

Craig steps to Eric's side, "What gives? My boy was offering you a ride, that's all! You think we're queer? ...Ha! Big laugh!"

Timothy shaking his head, *No.*

"It hurts to think, you think my boy Eric here, maybe ain't good enough for you or something? Am I wrong in thinking this?" Craig's question feels more like a demand, to Timothy's ears.

"Look fellas! I am not huge like you all! I am a guy who wishes to be respected as a guy!" Timothy standing up for himself, which isn't easy for him to do.

Carlos laughs. "Ah Man! I remember this little taint now. The browned sausage is plump, I admit. But to call him a man? (Pftt) Not hardly."

With a twist in expression, Craig glares to Carlos with heated confusion, "What are you f'ing talking about Carlos? Your scopin' out the kids, Willie, and beans?"

Carlos aggressively clears his throat, "Dude! It wasn't anything like that, Yo! Winnie sport had to come down to the locker room one day. Some dork accidentally lit a F'ing stink bomb up in the labs, last year. Little homie here was reeking with the stuff. They brought his ass some clothes and made him take a shower. I saw baby wonder showering, not that I was looking and shit. It's funny though. You would think with all that thick curly stuff on his head, he would be a hairy ass little monkey, right? Surprise, surprise! Mui Chicca here is completely bald south of the border, Man. Even his ass crack is squeaky ass clean."

Craig looks very perplexed at Carlos, for knowing something so intimate about the kid, "How da fuck did you know what's his ass crack was, Melos?"

Carlos laughs again but harder. "Dude, I wasn't checking his freakish little rump out. But the kid slipped in the showers on that cracked tiling. You know the one?" Craig nods fully aware of which one, for he was the one who broke it the year before, after a big game.

"Well, he tumbles over, lays spread fucking eagle right there on the floor, legs bent upward in the air, exposing his whole bottom spread, rosebud and all, like a baby getting a pamper. Dude, he had the cleanest little hole I never wanted to see on a dude. His junk was everywhere. He has a sausage, but no hair, man. Craig bro, I could have sworn it was a young girl's bubble booty if it wasn't for the deli department slinging around."

Timothy's eyes start to flush with embarrassment and shame. He knew the incident all too well, but he never knew there was a witness. All three guys start laughing together. "Is this true? You mean with all that curly action up top, there's no carpet to match downstairs?"

Craig gets close to Timothy's face. He has a scary feeling that these guys are not going to stop at jokes. Craig moves to Timothy's side, trapping him between him and the lockers, breathing heavily, the scent of day old corn chips all around his neck. "I wouldn't mind seeing it, Curls! You wanna show me?"

"Show you what?" questions Eric defensively.

"I want to see if he's really all hairless and shit."

Both Eric and Carlos step back while looking at each other, confused.

"Excuse me? I don't think so. Please … I want to go home. Please?" Pleads Timothy.

Craig leans in closer and grabs hold of Timothy's chin with his massive hand, his palm almost the size of his face. "Look, pretty boy, if you want to keep this face pretty, you best do whatever the fuck I tell you." Craig becomes more aggressive, pressing Timothy's head hard against the lockers.

Timothy is unable to slip away from Craig's secure grip on his chin, which is extremely painful. Eric knows something isn't right with this situation. Craig is taking the practical joke to a criminal level, and Eric tries to edge his friend back; however, before Eric can talk to him, Craig reaches his head over and forces his mouth over Timothy's. Then he presses his tongue deep inside of Timothy's unwilling mouth as tears form in the boy's frightened eyes.

Timothy fights hard to break free while being forced to taste Craig's vile tongue. While pressed against Timothy's trembling frame, Craig's take the advantage and thrusts his thick course hand down Timothy's stretchy waistband, past his underwear, to the flesh. His meaty grip, tugs around Timothy's very soft fleshy butt cheeks.

Timothy is rudely awakened when Craig forces his middle finger, with a long nail, up Timothy's clinched puckered opening. Timothy screams without a sound escaping his lips. Craig starts licking the outside of Timothy's face like an ice cream comb on a hot summer's day and painfully nibbles on the boy's tender lower lip eventually drawing blood. Timothy screams out in agony, just wanting the thug to stop, hurting him.

Eric and Carlos stand idly by in total utter shock, too stunned to move or say a word. Neither have ever seen Craig like this, sexually abusing a scared boy right in the middle of the hall.

Never meeting Timothy personally, Jason always knew the boy admired him from afar each day. He knew Timothy didn't deserve to be humiliated and abused like some piece of meat.

Eric tightens his fists. He knows something like this will destroy a kid's sexual innocence. Even he, can't stand by and allow such a perverse thing to continue. He marches boldly toward Craig and abruptly slings Carlos to the side.

Equally frustrated with what he is witnessing, Jason tightly clenches his fists and thrashes his feet to the ground with an electrical discharge. Jason zooms across the long hall corridor, leaving a trail of surging static energy in his wake.

Meanwhile, Timothy's ultimate fear of abusive jocks consumes him. He isn't aware of the pain rising from his broken arm because of the impact against the locker. His lip is bleeding, and he passes out in Craig's massive arms. All the while, Craig's fingers are still very much deep inside of Timothy. He releases a monstrous grunt of victory.

Eric's eyes go dark as a loud metal crashing sound rings throughout the narrow hallway. It's Eric's face connecting with the hard metal lockers. He instantly falls unconscious from the impact. Eric topples over to the ground, out cold. Before Craig and Carlos can figure out what is going on, they suffer the same fate.

At that moment, Timothy drops to the floor with a thump, his head smacking the ground. Jason stands alone, looking at the three bullies around him as if daring them to get back up, but he's also hoping and praying they won't because he hates violence.

With pain in his heart, he turns to see his violated admirer lying on the floor. He sees Timothy's shorts pulled halfway down along with his underwear, exposing his bare bottom. It's apparent from the blood that Craig's ragged nail has cut Timothy's sphincter.

Jason panics slightly, thinking about how it will appear to anyone who walks onto the scene, seeing three jocks down and a smaller kid with his shorts halfway down, with a hairline drizzle of blood coming from his bottom. Even stranger to him is the realization this is the first time he has used his unique gift of quantum speed in an open environment, and for some mysterious reason, he is incredibly drained of energy. He feels severely nauseous. It's not just from what he witnessed either. Something is wrong with his power.

Can't stand to see Timothy so exposed. Jason's not comfortable touching an unconsciously naked boy. While straightening his shorts and briefs, Jason accidentally sees Timothy's not so boyish floppy circumcised Johnson, stops and analyses it healthy girth for a blink of a second before covering it up.

He then looks up and observes Timothy's innocent teary face and the blood dripping from his lips. His heart just pops. In his thoughts, Jason questions, *Why you little lad? I was going to say hi to you today. I can't believe this happened to you.*

Without hesitation in the blinking of an eye, Jason ran to the bathroom and back. With a damp paper towel, he quickly cleans around Timothy's visible facial bruises. Dabbing his forehead near his right temple, from hitting the floor. He then moves on to remove the blood from Timothy's plump bottom lip. Jason gets an awkward sensation in doing so—a feeling he isn't at all too comfortable with. He sees that Timothy's lips are full, round and moist. Something of which he isn't familiar with in boys, nor has he ever really studied before.

Cautiously, he looks behind him. Luckily, the jocks are still unconscious. Not wanting to doddle, Jason gently taps Timothy's soft cheek, trying to wake him. He gives no response. He tries whispering, not wanting to be loud.

"Yo lad. Wake up. Come on. Snap to it." He continues to whisper while putting his warm hands on the sides of Timothy's face. While trying to regain a sense of the world, Timothy feels the warm, gentle touch on his cheeks and a soft, mumbling voice. It seems as if he is waking from a deep sleep on the morning after a long night of working at the lab.

Timothy tries to open his eyes, but he realized he has an excruciating headache. He squints with pain. Jason sees a look of pure shock on his face. Jason is not sure what is happening to him. "Hey, are you okay? Can you talk?"

Timothy can only hear Jason's concerned voice as an echo while trying to open his eyes. He can only visualize blurry images of light and dark shadows. There's a figure staring at him, but the image is unrecognizable.

Timothy detects the complexion of the person conversing with him, is very fair. There is a hinting of red hair coming into focus. Jason acknowledges Timothy struggle to see, and remembers the

boy wears glasses, with light gold trimmed frames. Looking aimlessly around, Jason discovers the location of Timothy's eyewear.
Only a few feet away on the floor, near a row of red lockers, Jason
retrieves them and gently places them on Timothy's dazed and
confused face.

"Are you okay Lad? Ye understand me?" helping Timothy to
gather his wits, he can't help but wonder how much Timothy saw
before passing out. Timothy is flooded with the memory of Craig's
painful violation to him, and lashes out subconsciously. Timothy's
fist nearly strikes Jason's face, if it weren't for Jason's super reflexes
to dodge the attack.

Jason sparked out in defense, "Whoa! Laddie-boy! Chill! I am
here to help you!" Hearing a strong accent, Timothy realizes the
guy is obviously not Craig.

The Scottish lilt in his savior's voice brings about a new fear.
His vision is clearing slowly, but when he sees his helper, he cringes.
"Please don't look at me. I am disgusting."

Confused, Jason says, "What are ye, glaikit (foolish)? What're
you saying about yourself? Get up, Lad! We've been here too long!
Must go!"

Hearing the urgency in Jason's voice, Timothy suddenly realizes
he's lying on the ground. Gathering his wits, Timothy recounts in
his mind the three brutes for whom ambushed him. Fearing they
may still be within proximity and remembering he was stripped of
his clothing, only brings a humiliating scare to him.

CHAPTER 7

Finally, building the courage to open his eyes completely and face whatever is lying before him. Timothy quickly acknowledges with relief; his shorts were repositioned onto him. The blow to the head was a bit too intense. He manages to make out the image of Eric, Craig, and Carlos on the ground not so far away, all three seemed unconscious.

Soon after, with a rattled grunt and groan, a voice emerges, "What the f—?" Carlos's words are heavy and garbled, "What just—!" Carlos starts regaining his senses sooner than Jason would have liked.

"Kid? You— all right? This is really serious."

To Timothy's humbling surprise, the caring voice belonged to his great admiration Jason, in the flesh. Timothy instinctively flinches in fear, shocking Jason with suspicion. Timothy wonders, *how much did Jason witness? Was he involved in the dressing of me? Did he see me naked? OMG!*

The thoughts mortify Timothy terribly. *Out of all the possible people on the planet, why would Jason be the one to see me naked, or worse, dress me?*

"Lad! Move your arse! You went for a wee bit kip (sleep). But it's time to go! We can't stay here!" Kneeling before him, Timothy sees the light ginger fur along Jason's meaty calves. Examining further, Timothy notices how short Jason's breathing is, almost hyperventilating. Somehow Jason appears drained and weaker then he used to. Climbing to his feet, while his head throbs in agony, not to mention his raw tender bum-hole. He nearly falls twice.

With an in-depth look of worry on his face, Jason glares unswervingly into Timothy's eyes and asks if he's all right to move. He tells him that he will carry him if necessary. Timothy tries desperately to explain the confusion away and get a grip on the situation.

Without warning, Timothy is suffering excruciating pain in his head. Jason sees him struggle and takes hold of his arms. Instantly Jason is forced to let go hearing Timothy scream painfully out. Not noticing the bruises on Timothy's elbow and forearm before. Hearing Timothy's pitchy voice brought chills to Jason's soul, as he fears there is severe damage to Timothy's arm, like a sprain or possible fracture.

Timothy calms down enough to look on the floor. He sees Eric facedown, but Craig is leaning against the locker, slowly moving around.

Timothy start, "What's happening? What happened to Eric and—"

Jason is hushing him, "Don't worry about those bangers. Got to get you out of here now. We need to go!"

Timothy sees the bruises on Jason's knuckles. "Your hands. What did you do? How'd you—? Are you hurt?"

Can't seem to remove his eyes from Jason's raw knuckles. At the most inconvenient moment, Timothy expresses his firmly imbedded nurturing spirit— always looking out for the needs of others over his own.

"Dude, stop with the poofter shit. I am just dandy, Aye? (now begging) Please, just snap it! Let's get the—"

Jason's unable to finish his plea when his body is thrashed up against a line of lockers near Timothy. The sound echoes clearly to the far side of the empty hallway. Because of his weakened state, Jason crumbles to the ground, nearly unconscious. Shocked and confused, Carlos doesn't understand how Jason is able to absorb such a direct hit like that.

"Carlos, stop! Don't hurt him!" Timothy pleads with the oversized upperclassmen. Carlos stands over Jason, begging for him to get up. He then turns his attention toward Timothy. With an angered expression on his face set to kill, Carlos squints his eyes.

"You're the sneaky piece of shit! Sucker punching people and shit! Well candy top, you've messed with the wrong fucking crew, Dawg! (turning to face a frightened Timothy) Your bitch-ass boyfriend is about to be turned out! He thinks he is a super ninjin and shit." Carlos huff's seeing Jason is slow to move.

Timothy's autocorrect kicks in, "I really think you meant to say, ninja!" Timothy questions himself for even saying such a thing.

Dazed and gasping for air, Jason can hear Carlos yelling at Timothy for correcting him. With no time to waste, Jason uses the last ounce of his energy to spring to his feet. He sprints in Carlos's direction and delivers a massive punch to his jaw with the screeching speed of a cheetah. Timothy couldn't even begin to calculate Jason's speed, but he knows it was clearly superhuman.

With the flickering of red from Jason's shorts, Timothy witnesses Carlos dropping to the ground, hard and out cold.

"Oh-God, is he dead? How the hell did you do that? I mean, you were so far—" Before Timothy can turn back, he hears Jason whimper as he drops, face down to the floor like a ton of cement. Twice, Jason has been targeted without any sense of the attacks, which is wrong in his mind. Another trait of Jason's ability with speed is a three-second alert sense of impending danger. Yet, today? This isn't the case.

Timothy watches as Jason reaching for his own back in assured pain.

Craig takes hold of the back of Jason's neck and pins him facedown, wailing into his back and sides with his fists. He then tosses Jason up in the air and over to his back with one movement of the same arm. He clutches Jason's throat while pounding him in the ribs and obliques, and drop kneeing his thighs. He hits him several times in the sweet spot underneath the rib cage, stunting his breath.

Timothy hates every second of the ungodly abuse and is compelled to help his fallen hero. Maneuvering his way to help Jason out, Craig incidentally sees his approach coming. Not allowing such an action to be had, Craig picks Jason off the floor by his T-shirt, ripping a portion of it in the process, and mercilessly thrusts him down to the ground like a ton of bricks, smacking the back of his head to the ground. Timothy could hear Jason's bones buckle from the impact.

Wasting no time, Craig grabs hold to Timothy's face using his giant oversized hand and locks him in place.

Looking down at Jason with Timothy in his possession, Craig spits out, "Look Curls, your pretty boyfriend thought you were going to save him? Ha! Ain't happening, sweet lips! Not today! So, sit your little weak candy-ass down, until I am ready to play with it!"

Using only the one hand, Craig thrusts Timothy off his feet. Timothy's body is hurled through the air and abruptly slams into the line of lockers on the opposite side of the hall. He too crumbles to the floor, in a dazed state of shock. Timothy can't move his body for the sheer force of the pain.

Helpless to move, Jason looks over to Timothy with rage in his eyes. He can't imagine how bad this is going to get, and he can't do anything to help him.

Why did my power leave me when I needed it most? Jason wanting an answer.

Craig spits directly into Jason's face, as he glares down at Jason's bruised, limp body.

"Yeah, bitch! (addressing Jason) Your pasty white ass is mine, Brodie! Your little punk friend is going to see me put my size fifteen's all up that wannabe Braveheart ass of yours." Craig chuckles hard.

"But since you were brave enough to sucker punch me like the little pussy you are! I will be all gentleman about this and give your ass, two options! You either beg for mercy like the little faggot you are? …or I will just have to enjoy pounding curls after I dismantle your ass all over this fucking hallway." He takes a stern breath and releases a hardy grunt.

"So- What say you, pussy? If you cry like the faggot prick I know you are, I may go easy on your plump red ass. Yes …the booty is sweet, I can definitely see this."

Jason's swallows hard, for he knows exactly were Craig is going with all of this. This hurts Jason to his core, never wanting to be any man's plaything ever again.

"I may have to eat out the both of you. (chuckling deep and greedily) … Funny! White and dark meat. Hmm, who'd have thought? But, to save you from such a humiliating act from in front of your little virgin friend there, one tear is all required from those big green puppy dog eyes of yours, Reds! …or just call me your fucking master, Bitch!" Craig sinisterly snarls.

For Jason, crying is never the option! He obstinately refuses to do such a thing in any public venue. It's the true Kinsmen way. Never understood why there are so many sick and demented people in the world, even as young as Craig, bewilders the likes of Jason. With his beady eyes, grinding teeth, and the perspiration dripping from his short, dirty blond hair—he appears more like a demon from the depths of hell, than an adolescent boy.

Craig wastes no time kicking Jason solidly in his already blackened ribs. Jason's rib can easily be heard cracking. "Ah, you feel that Reds? That's just a sweet payback for that gnarly sucker punch earlier!"

Craig drops to one knee and reaches in-between Jason's thighs; grabs firm to Jason's genitals. Compressing his testicles, Jason grunts in horrid pain. Timothy hears this and feels his own blood boil. He desperately wants the torture to stop, and is ready to do anything possible to do so.

Jason catches Timothy grinding teeth and clenching his little fists tightly. As tears run down Timothy's long sorrowful face, he fumbles to erect himself. The crippling pain of his arm makes it impossible to rise onto his feet. Jason is aggressively shaking his head, trying to get him to stay put and not advance.

In Jason's mind, he feels he can endure whatever brutal torture Craig can dish out if he doesn't have to worry about Timothy's safety.

Craig's hand clenches Jason's tender bulge. Timothy notices Jason's unspoken command, and he retreats his advance with unbearable shame.

Still lying on his back and groaning while trying desperately to breathe, Craig grins and nods his head. "Damn, you have some big kahunas, Red. Really plump and full!" He chuckles. "Your twig is huge." Craig sees the gland of Jason's penis peeking out of the leg portion of his loose shorts. "Why are you not wearing any undies Reds? Were you hoping to get laid today? (Craig points to Timothy) …Maybe by your little sissy-boy over there?"

Craig turns his attention to Timothy and gives a demented chuckle. Timothy is deeply frightened by his dark sneer.

Craig finally releases Jason's throbbing package, and Jason

instinctively reaches for his crotch. Craig stops him from doing so by slapping his arm away. He fondles Jason's thick, floppy bulge. "Red, this floppy piece of meat—right here belongs to me now." Craig laughs as he punches Jason square in the chest, knocking all the air out of him. He jumps to his feet and stomps the heel of the shoe into Jason's gut as hard as he can. He works over Jason's exposed body—his legs, calves, and outer thighs—with harsh kicks just so he can see the instant bruising on his porcelain skin.

Jason holds back all his resolve. He bears down, grinding his teeth. Blood starts to trickle out, and he grunts in pain. Timothy hears grunt after grunt with each blow.

Craig slams his massive knee into Jason's lower back several times. He stands up and gives him one good kick in his ribs. They all hear a crack. Jason screams out in pain as blood spurts from his quivering lips.

Craig is amazed how much abuse this guy can take and still not cry. This kid could have easily been a good battle buddy for him, but that was a fleeting thought. The kid was going to either cry or pass out. Jason screams with each blow, all the while he never loses sight of Timothy. That gives him hope that he is still strong. Timothy yells at Craig to stop before he kills him. Nevertheless, Craig is in rampage mode, and he'll have none of it.

"Why aren't you like your, bitch-boy? He is sobbing like a baby for, you!" Craig taunts him.

Eric regains his bearings in the background and stumbles to his feet. Craig finally realizes Jason is never going to give in. He then yanks Jason's shorts down, exposing his severely bruised buttocks. "Wow, your ass looks like Christmas, Red."

As he cackles, he forces not one, but two probing fingers inside Jason. He thrusts down hard as Jason's squirms helplessly. He pulls out his fingers, and takes a prolonged sniff, and taunting Timothy, who is watching in complete horror.

"Look, Junior. Hmmm, smells and looks like teen boy spirit, doesn't it?" he scowls with great enthusiasm, as he wipes his fingers clean on Jason's ass-cheek. Craig thankfully pulls Jason's shorts back over his exposed bruised ass. Timothy grinds his teeth, allowing his blood and drools to flow freely from his quivering lips. He prays the abuse is finally over.

Unfortunately, things get worse. Timothy searches for Jason's face to see if he is okay; however, Jason refuses to look in his direction. Timothy watches Jason's body tremble. Craig spreads Jason's legs apart and stands directly between Jason's knees.

"Here you go, sweet cheeks!" Craig unleashes a relentless front kick, striking Jason's partially exposed testicles, causing him to curl up into the fetal position. The pain is so intense that Jason releases a silent scream as his body goes numb.

"No, you don't, pretty boy!" Craig thrusts him over onto his back, lifts Jason's head off the floor by a handful of his hair, and slaps Jason's soft face with his free hand. Jason's eyes begin swelling with tears, which delights Craig, but Jason feels himself slipping away fast.

"I'm … sorry, T-Tim—" Jason flinches before he turns his face away and passes out, leaving a single tear in the corner of his eye.

Craig doesn't like getting cheated out of a victory. He takes a firm hold of Jason's limp body, grabbing his throat with both hands, and he pulls him off the floor and dangles him in the air. It's like a scene from a Marvel movie.

Eric turns to see a defenseless boy sobbing and calling out for help, and now he's watching Craig strangling a redhead boy. Eric yells, "Craig, what the fuck are you doing? Are you trying to kill that poor kid?" Lying helplessly on the floor, Timothy nods.

"I am going to kill this little-redheaded fagot, he's the one who got the drop on us all. The little shit is fast. He thought to kick me in the junks was a good thing to do…" Craig peers down on Jason, "Didn't you Red?"

Timothy springs into action and forgets about the intense pain. He charges Craig with everything he can muster and starts pounding on him. He strikes his beefy arms and back, but his blows have no effect on Craig.

Timothy and Eric can see the pale color in Jason's fair skin turning from bitter red to a shade of blue. He was clearly being choked to death. Timothy pleads for Eric's help. Somewhat dumbstruck, Eric soon realizes the gravity of the situation. He knows what must be done regardless of his friendship and loyalty to Craig.

Eric takes a linebacker's rushing stance. "Craig, let the kid go bro! You're going too far asshole!" he shouts out. Scott and Kyra both faintly hear the shout several halls away. Scott springs into immediate action. He quickly dashes toward the scene, Kyra not far behind him. However, Kyra feels an odd energy surging. She springs forward, darting past Scott, who is at his full-on sprint. He is knocked unknowingly into a passing stairwell, and down a flight of stairs, knocked unconscious. He never knew what flew passed him.

With no more warnings, Eric charges Craig straight on with every ounce of force in his thick body.

Kyra zips around the corner within a wink of an eye, confused about her speed. She isn't sure what she passed getting there. She couldn't make out much of anything while running. Nevertheless, she arrives just in time to see Eric charging at Craig, who is holding her newfound redheaded friend by his throat.

With deadly precision, Eric hits Craig with precise force, breaking Craig's death grip on Jason. Jason slams onto the hard floor after Craig releases him. This time Craig also slams down to the hard ground with Eric on top of him. The hit was damaging enough to knock the wind out of Craig, rendering him unconscious.

Timothy scrambles, using this moment of opportunity to scuttle to Jason's side. Eric climbs off Craig's unconscious body. Timothy thrusts Craig arm away from Jason's limp body. No more Mr. Nice Guy. With an aggressive grunt, Timothy delivers a swift kick to Craig's squishy soft crotch. He can feel the brute's pelvic bone in the follow-through. Even in Craig's unconsciousness state, his body instinctively jolts from the mighty blow. The twinge in Craig's body gives Timothy a sense of satisfaction and a startling sense of remorse. The pacifist in him is trying to come through.

Kyra says nothing to startle her beloved classmate Timothy. She never would have imagined Timothy would possibly be capable of that kind of a violent act.

CHAPTER 8

Timothy looks at the dark bruising all around Jason's throat. Examining Jason swollen, partially shut eyes, Timothy only thought is to get his fallen hero away from Craig's clutches. Not concerning himself with the obvious girth difference between him and Jason, Timothy grabs hold. Wrapping his arms, albeit in sheer pain, around Jason's broad torso, Timothy clamps down tight. Like a child reclaiming its toy from an older sibling, Timothy tugs Jason free from Craig's motionless body and pulls him to the side.

Timothy examines Jason's multiple wounds and bruises, he notices that his new friend and protector is not breathing. Without hesitation, Timothy administers CPR. Using mouth-to-mouth, Timothy acknowledges how Jason may have broken ribs, and didn't want to compound them further with compressions. Fortunately for Jason, Timothy knows exactly what to do. After administering the first few breaths, Timothy yells for Eric to go get help.

It takes quite a few repetitions and gentle pulses for Jason to feel a sensation of hot air entering his sore throat. He slowly feels very soft lips pressing firmly against his.

Gradually regaining his awareness, he sees Timothy's tearful face hovering directly over him, and he can barely make out the words he is yelling. Jason desperately tries to tell him that he's awake and that he can stop kissing him. Nothing is working. He can't speak or move. Kyra is praying for Timothy to revive Jason.

Jason clearly sees Timothy placing his lips firmly down on his, and feels the rush of warm air entering deep into his throat. He really wants Timothy to stop. It feels wrong to him, like a gross unwarranted act.

Timothy's tongue can be felt entering and exiting his mouth with each push of breath, yet Jason's body fails to respond. Unable to move any physical part of his body, the only thing that appears to be operational is his tongue. Jason runs his tongue upward directly into Timothy's unsuspecting mouth, wrapping his tongue around Timothy's, and rubbing it tenderly.

The slithery sticky motion gives Jason a strange sensation, an oddity he can't identify nor understand. He should feel disgusted by this abominable act. Nonetheless, he gets an overwhelmingly warm desirable tingle inside.

Eric watches Timothy selflessly care for the unconscious red-headed boy with such compassion. Unfathomable to Eric how Timothy would willingly be a participant in such an act. Considering its only minutes since Craig's emasculating abuse on him. It's just unbelievable. He is shocked when Timothy is seen springing back harshly and wiping his mouth vigorously with wide-eyed disgust.

Kyra wonders, *where did Scott go and why is it taking him so long?*

Jason starts coughing, regaining his breathing pattern, once more.

As his eyes focus upward, he sees Timothy trying desperately to hide his tears, wiping them away with his shirt. Unaware. Timothy exposes his soft light brown smooth belly and tiny round navel. Jason understands exactly what Timothy was attempting to do in saving his life and he playfully taps Timothy's soft tummy making him wince, and retrieve his shirt back down over his stomach.

With pain, Jason cracks a smile, while coughing. "Wow, you actually saved my life lad." Jason thanks him, while still gasping for air.

Although spitting blood with each coughing breath, Jason still finds it necessary to be cocky…

"Maybe less kissing next time, Aye? At least have some mood music."

Jason starts a round of uncontrollable coughs.

Timothy knows Jason is trying to ease the tension between them. Nevertheless, he can't help but admire Jason's strength through the severe pounding, and never shed a single tear. Timothy feels like a poor excuse for a man in light of his sobbing in front of others. He only wishes he was centered as Jason appears to be. Having pure fortitude, Jason stood his own ground, even in the face of uncertain and possible bodily harm.

With some awkward assistance from Timothy, Jason sits erect against a row of red lockers. Eric is still dazed by the blow from earlier. In fact, he never went to get help after seeing Craig losing all his humanity, fearing what would have happened if he left the scene.

Eric takes the movement from both boys as a comforting sign, and then he asks, "Who was the one that sucker punched me?" Jason and Timothy look over to Eric in disbelief.

"I mean, I don't remember seeing shit, just a fucking red locker blasting at me!" he exclaims, though he already knows the identity of the puncher. "I don't know you, kid." He looks directly into Jason's swollen eyes. "But you sure have some big balls to crack my jaw the way you did, and… rightfully should have. Taking Craig and Carlos down as you did was crazy as fuck, bro!"

Jason just nods. Nevertheless, he's still royally ticked over the whole ordeal. "Dude, seriously, you should be on the JV squad with fucking moves like that, man?"

Jason lacks physical strength but retains blistering fire in his bloodshot eyes. "Why, so I can be surrounded by pervs like you and yer fucked-up dickhead clan? I think not. If I get my strength back, I am going to kick all of your fucking asses!" Jason growls with bitter rage, grunting while trying to get to his feet. Timothy desperately tries to calm him down. Confused, Jason questions, "Why? Why the fuck not? Did you like Craig jamming his fucking finger up your ass, digging for God knows what? The asshole was laughing at you crying and squirming to break free, and he didn't bother to move a damn muscle to stop that ass wipe from—"

"Stop, Jason. Please! Forget about him. He isn't worth your energy. It is over and done!"

"Lad, I saw the whole fucking thing man. He (pointing to Craig) … was going to let that fuck-face beast … sexually assault you. Don't you know that? Don't you care about your own fucking life laddie? You don't deserve this shit, none of it!"

"I said stop—Damn it!" Timothy slams Jason up against the lockers behind him as tears pour uncontrollably from his eyes and down his quivering lips. Timothy is mortified. "You must stop this. Please. He was the one who helped save you … when I couldn't." Jason wants to attack Eric with everything in his heart, but Timothy's pleading stops him.

"That's my point, lad. I am a man, and so are you." He points a stern finger at Timothy's chest. "You … don't need to be saving my ugly rank ass, knowing you are possibly going to get yourself killed. I'm spazzing. I don't understand why my body totally failed me today. I can't understand this freaky mixed-up day. None of this crap ever should have happened. It's only because of those rank bastards we are even here."

Nervous, Eric steps forward. "He is totally right—little one. I deserve everything your friend just said."

"Shut the hell up. I don't need you speaking for me. You know damn well that your batty buddy was messed up from the start!" But then Jason immediately feels something deep down inside, a desire to care for Timothy's needs instead of his own. He starts to calm down for the sake of a boy he hardly knows.

Eric turns his attention to Timothy. "Look, I am really sorry, kid. It wasn't my intention to physically harm you, especially in any sexual way. I never believed Craig would go so far."

Jason looks to Timothy, and Timothy looks to him.

They're silent

Eric breaks the awkward silence and starts, "We were told to scare you a bit as payback for jerking Jake's chain in some science class. He told us how you and this girl jacked his chain in class earlier. So, he gave us the heads-up when he found out your after-school schedule this evening."

Eric avoids Timothy's eyes as he addresses him, "Your friend has every right to berate us. We deserve it. It's a good thing your buddy came to your aid when he did. Not many people will do that for someone, even best friends is a rarity. Unless the person cares deeply enough about you. Many of my buds would have never taken on Craig or Carlos. I am sorry, Dude. It is unforgivable, I know."

"You're damn straight!" Jason lashes out bitterly before Eric finishes.

"It's not forgivable. Bullying is the work of cowards, and Craig is a perverted demon that needs to be put out of his misery for good."

Eric sighs. "I should have told Jake to screw himself, instead of playing this ass-backward prank. If you want to report the guys and me, I won't stand in your way. I'm going to report myself for my part in all of this, I won't mention your names, to keep you out of the headlines."

Carlos steps up and pushes Eric's shoulder hard. "What the fuck! Report? Report hell, Eric! You out of your damn mind, bro? We are freaking seniors, man. Craig was your homeboy, and you are going to shit all over him now? So, you just gonna roll like a little bitch because our boy went a little psycho and shit?" Carlos exclaims with fury in his dark inset eyes. He continues to mumble some profanity in Spanish, which only Timothy can translate.

Timothy and Jason gaze upon each other with gratitude. Jason wipes some of the tears from Timothy's face in a rather soft and loving manner. He knows how much Timothy's arm is hurting him.

Just as Craig stumbles to his feet, he turns to Eric with a look of disbelief, holding his crotch very tightly.

Scott finally sprints to Kyra, not sure how she passed him. She just stands there in the distance, not even breathing heavily. Scott sees what looks like Eric and Craig squaring off in the distance. Scott yells out with authority, "Eric? Craig?"

Eric along with all the others look back to see Scott and an unfamiliar companion standing next to him. Scott approaches quickly, pointing at Craig and Carlos so that they'll stand down. Surveying the scene, Scott witness a traumatized dark curly haired boy holding his arm, kneeling beside a severely bruised Jason Brodie. Scott sees the signs of trauma around Jason's throat, the blood on his shirt and shoulders, the black eye, and huge black bruises all up and down his legs.

On the opposite side, he sees Craig holding his sore junk while mumbling under his breath. He also notes the fear in Eric and Carlos's eyes and the expressions on the faces. It's apparent to Scott something wickedly bad has transpired. Kyra knows something unthinkable was happening when she arrived.

Scott has strong words. He sees the scared look in Eric's eyes as he gathers the other two players. Something is mentioned to both

Carlos and Craig. Timothy observes as their demeanors seamed to change instantly from venomous to compliant, as they retreat away.

Seeing the bigger guys back down so easily to Scott, Timothy is amazed. Somehow when Scott speaks directly to either of them, they immediately prostrate and obeyed him. In his observational deducting, Scott gives an impression he had the power to make people do whatever he tells them.

Meanwhile, Jason regains his breath. Eric and his crew are gone now, and Scott asks Kyra to give him a minute with the guys. Kyra understands a situation such as this must be handled delicately. Rippled with compassion, seeing her friend Timothy and the new acquaintance, Jason from earlier, both in physical trauma, steps away to the double metal doors to await Scott's cue.

Neither Jason nor Timothy could help but to notice Scott's hardened stare on Kyra's retreating strut. His attention is undoubtedly focused on her butt, with great intensity.

He turns his attention back to the guys. Scott steps close so that no one can overhear their conversation. He examines the boys, giving each of them a good once-over. Scott's eyes fill with rage.

"Jason—dude, what happened here?" His voice sounds authoritative and direct. The anger in his voice reveals just how much Scott cares about, Jason. "I need to know what started, this? (Jason shies away from Scott's big brother-like stare) Hey, don't look away from me, Jason! You need to tell me something! How physical did this shit get in here? I do not like what I see from you or the Kid."

In his defense mode, Jason reverts to his wittier charm. He's acutely aware of what Scott is asking about, but he doesn't want to go there with him. "You mean we ain't cute anymore, Scott-man?" Jason redirects with humor, yet Scott's patience or humor isn't to be tested.

In Scott's mind, he knows there is a sure positive way of getting the answers he needs, but seeing Jason as a dear friend, he chooses not to go such a route.

"Look, I understand you don't want to rat on anyone. I get that—believe me. But, this isn't a laughing matter. I know you're tough as nails! Hey, if not for you— What about your buddy, J-man? You guys truly don't have to go this … alone, Jason."

"I dinnae ken (I don't know), Scott. Your friends be a bunch of bangers … must I point that out to you? Especially the Craig bloke! Nothing but a severely twisted bent bastard he is!" Jason's wit evaporates when he sees Timothy with his head hanging low, grabbing loose papers scattered all over the floor, only using his one good arm.

Not comfortable with Jason's wording and tone, Scott tries to clarify to his younger friend how the three players and him, are not friends, but mere associates.

"J-man, those goons are not my friends! As the quarterback, we play together daily, nothing more. I don't necessarily approve of what they do off the field. Thankfully, it's their last year."

"Oh great! So, they can torture another level of students in college, Aye!" Jason kicks a locker, which hurts him more than the metal object. This forces Timothy to look up and back to his meaningless task, to appear busy. Jason doesn't have a response for him.

Afraid of Scott possibly learning too much of what had transpired, Timothy willingly avoids him as much as possible. Unfortunately, Scott's suspicion is greatly triggered by Timothy's act of avoidance. This too is highly exaggerated, by Scott acknowledging a dried hairline trickle of blood, which seemed to have run down his inner thigh at some point.

If what he thinks is reality, Scott wants Timothy to be forthcoming, in fact, he needs him to be, just so he can physically, take action.

"This is it, guys! Painfully uncomfortable as this may be? I

CHAPTER 9

Well, it appears you guys are cool enough to take it from here and get some help, I think," says Scott. The boys nod in response.

With a shift in his tone, to a more relaxed one, Scott started. "Yo! Since I know J-man already! I would like to get the scoop on, you. (directing his attention to Timothy) I'll start by telling you what I do know. How about that?"

Seeing Kyra in the distance, Timothy can only assume, she may have given him some insights about him already.

Scott starts, "I happen to know you're one of the mega brains within the SciTech building's Star program, and that's wickedly cool being underclassmen and all!"

Timothy's amazed someone of Scott's social ranking, would even have an inkling of who he is. However, being ridiculously modest, Timothy return. "I am okay. (a glimmer of a blush occurs) I'm not all that! How'd you learn this about me? Was it my friend and laboratory partner Kyra, over there?"

"Whoa- Let me get this!" Jason learns some vital information.

"You know Kyra, and she's your friend? Dude, she is a senior to boot?" Timothy nods to confirm, shocking Jason in the processes.

Timothy glances at Scott and sees the excitement in his eyes when mentioning Kyra to him.

Scott snaps a charming smile. "Actually, she didn't have to say a word. I've seen you hard at work up in the labs. Mostly by yourself, I've noticed. I visit often and chill with my friend Demarco, before heading down to the after-school practice."

"Ellie? Demarco Ellie? I am aware of him and his work. I've helped him a time or two. He is the only senior left in the program, and he's pretty smart."

"Well, he tells me you are the real talent up there. You and my beautiful friend Kyra. He did say that you were a dude of very few words though."

Jason butts in, "Dang Skippy he is! He's a super ... techie wizard. Don't you dare be fooled by this scruffy lad? His name is none other than Timothy Daniels! Top of his class, in the Sci-Tech championships thing-a-ma-bob. He is super advanced in human dynamics, electromagnetics, engineering, photo spectrum array analysis, and one hell of a human physiognomy biologist." Timothy unable to wrap his head to the remarkable knowledge by Jason, as he continues, "Plus he is labeled the kid who is going to earn the Nobel something or other, one day by his fellow classmates."

"You meant the Nobel Prize, right?" Jason makes an evil eye at Timothy for daring to correct him, but he quickly blazes a cheeky wide-grinned smile, revealing his blood-stained teeth to reassure him he is not upset at all. "See, he's a wee bit of a canny arse too, Scott-lad."

Timothy is dumbfounded beyond belief, and rightfully curious about how he knows so much about him, and finally, he asks out loud.

Jason wraps his sore arm around Timothy's neck like they're

old friends. "Bro, I thought it was best to know, the young guy who seems to refer to himself as my biggest fan by your lab instructor, Aye? I see ya be spying on me from your lofty lab tower, while I'm taken much-needed laps."

Timothy's eyes pop wide open. "Yet, I admit, it was a bit freaky at first, seeing a nerdy bloke checking me out all the time. But bumping into your advisor Jamerson, after last bell today. He gave me a quick Four-one-one on you. I admit it was very flattering what he had to say about you. How you had such an interest in my running and not up there ogling me sexy butt, while I am doing me crunches." Jason cracks with witty humor.

Timothy's face turns flush, embarrassed, and in an unspoken language, Jason gives Scott the wink, meaning they can change the subject.

"Well, J-man, it looks like you guys are cool as far as all this is concerned, but you seem banged up. I can get the nurse before I take off. You really need to be looked at! Both of you!"

"I would, but you know blokes like me don't have—" Scott raises an eye in shock. He stops Jason abruptly by coughing. Jason, not thinking, was so relaxed around Timothy, he didn't reflect on what he was about to say in front of him or the beauty, Kyra.

Scott faced Timothy and reached out to shake his hand. "Well, it's cool to meet the great, Mr. Daniels, as J-man like to put it. Once more! Don't worry. What happened here stays here … unless you want to pursue something. I would like for you to think of me as a new friend." Timothy nods as he shakes his hand. Scott peers to the lovely Kyra and back to the fellas.

"Now before this gets too mushy, I've got to take a lovely little lady home." Timothy smiles, and Kyra blinks her eye at him with a caring smile.

The boys watch as Scott and Kyra exit the building together. Just before leaving, Scott pauses and looks back, "Oh, J-man, I'll catch up with you later." He throws a thumbs-up to him.

"Yeah, gotcha, Scotty!" And then in a whisper, he says, "If you ever really could."

Airing some things out among themselves, Timothy and Jason talk about understanding and getting to know each other. Just as they start to bond, Jason slips. "Timmy! I don't know— How can my boy Scotty snatch the sweetest flower in the garden, you know?"

Timothy is struck by the fact that Jason referred to him as Timmy, a nickname which is usually very problematic to him. While he was growing up, it was cute hearing little Timmy here and there, but as he is coming into his adolescence, the name sounds mean. Bigger kids and bullies along with overbearing and jealous professors would love to belittle him with that alias. "Wouldn't you love to get a peek in that garden?"

Timothy takes a little offense and says, "Hey, Kyra is a great friend, probably the only one I will ever know. Don't talk like that about her, okay?"

"Okay, Timmy, I gotcha!" Jason glimpse over and sees Timothy's expression and immediately regrets using the belittling nickname. How emasculating it must sound after such an ordeal.

"Look, bro, my bad! Honestly, I have no right calling you out of your name. I won't—"

Timothy intercedes abruptly. "No Jason, it's alright honestly."

"Are you sure Lad? I don't want to be—"

"You are okay, Jason! It's just a pet peeve from my past. It has had some negative connotations—stupid bullies, thugs, and mean adults in my life, like belittling me with it." Timothy clarifies with mixed emotion.

"Sorry Lad! Clearly, anyone should see you are coming into your manhood. I still got you, height-wise though." In his attempt to chuckle, Jason's lungs and chest have other thoughts, force about a string of coughs. "I won't be dissing on you Lad, by calling you—"

Once again, Timothy stops Jason cold. "Don't! Like you, I am not made of glass. Yes, I don't know how to control my emotions at times, as you may have noticed. Nevertheless, I am tougher than I look. Honestly, it's cool when *YOU* are the one referring to me by such means. I honestly don't mind, at all."

Jason feels rather weird as the word *you,* apply to him directly. He is instantly reminded of the mouth-to-mouth encounter earlier.

Timmy starts. "So, if you want to call me *Timmy*, that's fine. Not wanting to get too psycho about it, but I'm comforted when it's you say it." Jason remembers the naked boy on the ground and his yearning to watch and protect the kid, Jason deep down, likes the fact he did comfort him.

Timmy continues. "Plus, I can tell the difference. You aren't belittling me at all. Of course, I am just rambling on again. Don't pay any attention to me."

An unexplainable warmth comes over Jason like an enormous furry blanket. The feeling of complete acceptance is new and daunting. And the submissive party isn't a beautiful young girl but a sweet, kindhearted, young lad. Jason shakes his head in disbelief. He knows beyond the shadow of any doubt that he is unquestionably heterosexual. Nevertheless, he can't help wanting to nurture Timothy. He even feels a tingling in his loin.

Following his gut as always, he steps closer, reaches out, takes hold to Timmy's bruised arm, and examines it. "How is your arm, Timmy?" Jason felt the strong overwhelming need to be protective. "Yer guid? Just a wee bit sore?" Timmy responds with a yes. Timothy stretches it out and is alerted by pain. In return, Timothy reaches out to touch to tap Jason's highly blackened rib. Instantly a surging spike of pain travels up and down, Jason broken body.

Flinchingly trying to deny the sensation below his beltline of a growing erection, Jason tries hard to mask his pain and his loin from Timmy. Timothy sees through this façade, still marveling how Jason can shun his torment so well.

"Jason? You okay? You look like you are in such pain. Don't worry about your, thingy down there. It's natural reaction to abuse, I've read." Jason looks at Timothy with the biggest puppy dog eyes, feeling assured by Timothy his semi-erection isn't weird.

"The pain is nothing! Like I told Scott." Jason maintains his macho bravado, not willing to show weakness. It's a trait he acquired over the years of being on his own. Timmy does not believe the ruse. "I don't know, Jason. It could be severe, you know? Are you sure?"

"Look! I am not a poofter! I can take care of it." He feels a shot of pain.

Jason wishes Timmy would stop showing such concern for him. It's making him weak inside. He feels that his protective shell is melting away, forcing him to lash out.

Timothy is not backing down this time. "Enough of your macho bullshit. Don't stand there and try to lie to my face after all this—! I know you are hurting and in significant pain. I also know you feel severely violated too. I am not a freaking idiot! I am nowhere as strong as you—I get that! You're no fucking armored tank either!"

Jason's jaw drops as Timothy harshly rips into him. "I've witnessed the terrifying blows Craig dished out on you and the immoral act he performed on you. (Jason turns from him) Even with your powerful physique, you couldn't have taken such damage and simply be okay! When Craig sexually—" Timothy's voice fades away as the overwhelming discomfort of pain builds up inside Jason's internal organs.

Jason clutches his side now with both of his hands, compiled with an unnerving sensation deep within his own anus. Timothy doesn't finish his thought seeing Jason toppled with unease. Jason does not want to be any man's victim ever again. To show pain and fear is a weakness, not befitting a kinsman. The pain builds exponentially to a point even Jason can't deny it. He has no witty comebacks or rejoinders.

Timmy naturally assumes the role of caretaker and protector. "You need a doctor and not a damn school nurse Jason! I will take you myself. I will have my driver take us both."

Jason shakes his head quite adamantly. "No, no money or insurance, bro!"

"What are you talking about? You don't need either for an emergency and believe me, that's what you have! There's plenty of free clinic's in the area with good doctors. I know the nurse here won't be able to do much to help you. We can call your folks, and they can meet us there." Timmy catches a weird glance from Jason when he mentions his parents, but he continues, "Plus, I am twice the medical technician than our good nurse here at the school." Timothy shows renewed confidence in his own abilities, but he sees a shame covering Jason's facial expression.

"I can't go —." Whispered Jason under his pain-stricken breath.

Timothy's stunned and confused. "What? What are you talking about? You can't what Jason? You can't go where? The medical clinics? Why not? The only thing you need is your name, age, and a known living address!" Jason can sense Timothy's elevated aggravation.

"Just let it go, Bro! You can go—" Jason returns fire. "Take a good shower! Get your shit together, and I'll be right as rain! Promise you that, Aye?"

Timmy shakes his head with skepticism, as Jason doesn't back down. "Like you said earlier to me, I am not a wee frail thing needing such attention either! Just be me Lad and leave it be, Aye?"

Caught off guard, Jason hears a statement, stabbing him like a knife at his heartstrings. "You don't have a— home, family, or loved one to take care of you. Do you?" Timothy, appealing to Jason so delicately and concerned, Jason's eyes pop with utter shock, as his very silence validates him.

Timothy's compelled to justify his statement. "I remember Scott saying he would see you later. Even earlier than that you said—and I quote— "…blokes like me don't get…" just before Scott stopped you from finishing."

"Timmy, what are you doing man? Are you anal-ing me, Lad?" Questioned Jason, feeling scared and sincerely terrified.

Timothy wants to laugh at such a horribly inappropriate mis-use of Jason's vernacular, and unintentionally corrects him, "I am pretty sure you meant to say analyzing you—I would fair to think. The other way may prove very uncomfortable indeed."

As Timothy's classmates would often refer to him when he is in such a corrective mode, Timothy the robotic grammar Nazi. "I deduced, Scott with an Angel of Mercy complex, helps out at the seniors' home on Third Street. Every other Friday after practice, I believe. He too coaches a minor youth group at the Youth Outreach Center. Sometimes referred as the Y.O.C. The home for displaced youth and adolescent runaways. This he does Tuesday through Thursday. Scott is a severe creature of habit. He never misses a day and considering what today is, he's most definitely gearing up for the Y.O.C. tonight."

"Blimey, you little twit. How could you— Scott? I mean se-riously! How stalkily perverted are you? A serious poofter going around spying on blokes so thoroughly isn't cool, Lad?"

Timothy doesn't acknowledge the degrading and crude insult. "School paper, if you need to know. I tend to memorize what I read. They refer to that as photographic memory. I think of it more of a sensory recall. I retain more than just optical memorizations. I do it with smell, taste, touch, and sound. Anyway, they had a big article about him a few months back before spirit week, making him the most sought-after teen bachelor in this school. Kyra, the girl with him, is my longest friendship in this school or outside of it. She is quite equivalent in her studies. Yet, Kyra's the prettiest flower in the garden, as you have so eloquently put it. She's been his secretly admiring fan for quite some time. Who the hell could ever compete with perfection? Outside of someone like you."

Timothy immediately wishes he hadn't said the last statement out loud, seeing the reaction on Jason's face.

Timothy continues, "Simply put, invisible guys like me aren't blessed with charm and great looks. We don't stand a chance with girls like Kyra or most girls for that matter. But that's another subject of irrelevance. To get back to my question, are you … homeless, Jason?"

Jason wants to lie so badly that it pains him. His physical pain is overwhelming his senses, and the nurturing look in Timmy's eyes won't allow him to keep up his warrior persona. He soon realizes a lie will doom what appears to be the makings of friendship. If he lies now, any chances of growth will die before it even starts.

CHAPTER 10

Jason wants this friendship to be a real one. He wants to be completely honest, even if it means losing him because of the truth.

"Jason? You know I mean you no harm, right? There is no need for shame. Saying what is true is all I ask for. No judgments here, okay? I like you, Jason, I care about—"

Jason can't allow things to get too emotional and abruptly grunts, "Okay! Shit, shit, shit! Okay, Timmy! Yes ... I am. Okay, damn it!"

"What ... what are you saying, Jason?" he asks with a calm tone.

"Yes, I'm a bastard homeless, fuck! The trash you find and laugh at when passing by on the streets. The scummy scrub no one wants, in their lives, not even my own peeps." Jason's eye's filled with heavy saturation. "Okay, you satisfied, Timmy? Are you? Is this what you're after? Proving I am a nothing to nobody, and want to see if I can cry, too?"

Timmy doesn't like the self-loathing and abuse Jason is placing on himself at all. "Jason, stop! Don't you ever put words in my mouth!" Timothy's tone is equally enraged. "I've never—, and I really mean never—thought of you in any such way! You need to get off that shit and stop talking about yourself in that way too, Jason! You are much too amazing for any such as that! Plus, I never want to see your handsome face in tears!"

Jason pauses long, reflecting on his words, and kindly nods.

They stand in silence.

They stare at each other's broken spirits—breathing, staring, breathing, staring.

"How long have you been over there at the Y.O.C.?" Timothy breaks the awkward silence between them.

Shrugging his shoulders, Jason also softens his tone considerably to match Timothy's. "I've only been there for a few years, I guess. Time moves funny when there is no one to come home to, aye? We got homeschooling, thanks to Mrs. Prescott, the boss lady. The rest of the time ... nothing. Always alone, the one thing I could always count on, being alone!" He pauses to catch his breath, which is torture with each inhalation. "I really don't want to talk about this anymore, is that okay?"

Jason's armor is quickly breaking away. He feels his emotions rushing through him like an unstoppable tidal wave. The last thing Timothy would ever want to see is the strong man he admires breaking down in front of him. He wants the bold, cocky Jason, not a broken, little boy.

"I understand you don't want to talk about something that hurts. I just want to know if you are being cared for—that's all. Like does anyone else know your living situation here, at the school?"

"No. Scott-boy is the only one who knows anything about my shitty situation. He is the only one who seemed to give a shit, Aye? He will stop by the center and play with the young lads outside. Then there are times he will chill with the teens, just to bullshit around. It took some time before he was able to gain me... trust. Which wasn't easy for him."

Timothy smiles, liking the openness of Jason, now.

"He's the one who got me into this school, actually!" Glimmering smiles appear on both of their faces. "He told me about the amazing running track they have here once he knew I loved running. He's pretty dope for a senior and the closest thing to a … Um—friend." He looks deep into Timothy's eyes. "He told me the story of his accident and how it changed his life, which inspired me to come." He smirks. You know, even to this day, I can't talk to him half the way I am talking to you right now. I don't want to be, you know … that kid! You know, the whiny poofter-type."

Timothy's eyes pop open, feeling bold enough to question, "What is that? You've said it quite a few times now! —poofter?"

Jason cracks an odd grin, forgetting his Scottish slang isn't always common to everyone else.

"Oy! my bad, me Lad. I do say it way too much. It's uncool of me, I admit. It means—homo, queer, bent, twat, or sissy-boy. Got it, Aye?"

Timmy's eyes narrow and veer away from Jason. "Oh, I get it!" Jason hears Timothy's tone sharpen. "You are another jock who hate gays too, right? You feel okay justified in calling people—weaker, smaller, more sensitive than you, this sort of name, regardless of their sexual orientation? Like Craig, Carlos and few others around the school? Hmm?" Timothy nearly demands a response from the silent Jason.

With his jaw hitting the floor, Jason was never aiming to have such a conversation today, by a long shot.

"What about me? Jason!" with fire and tears in his eyes. "How do you see me?" Timothy staring long and hard into Jason's scared eyes.

"When I resuscitated you, seriously you thought I was a poofter—vile, detestable, abomination to mankind? You needed to mock me or test me? Slipping your tongue into my mouth, to gauge a reaction from me? Did I pass the faggot test? Even though I was so scared, I nearly defecated myself, thinking I may lose someone too special, to lose?"

Jason remains silent and staring, but the twinkling in Timothy's eyes, grow brighter with each word.

Timothy's words sting Jason deeply, much more than Jason would have ever thought it could.

"All I could think, at that moment— Was wanting you to live, regardless of how you may have felt about me." Timothy's voice cracks hard. "I should have known you are no different! All of you, jock-boy types, are the same!"

Timothy pauses, sniff's ... and continues further.

"I like to believe, I'm not so different, you know? I lost my father really early in life, so I never had the strong male figure to guide me; brave, loyal or mentored."

Pounding his chest with his working arm, releasing his inner rage for the first time in his life. Timothy continued.

"My father didn't show me anything before his passing. Like— how to be one of the guys. There was no set instruction in his passing to help me figure all the shit (tears falling) out! He's gone now. I have his intellect and loving desire for the sciences! I never learned to acquire what you have, and I really want to be a good man and not a scared boy for the rest of my life."

Timothy begins to sob. For it was the first time he has let go of everything buried inside him.

Jason seeing Timothy's vulnerability wishes he could remove everything he mentioned, which brought the boy before him into so much pain. With desperation, Jason stumbles closer to Timothy.

"Timmy-Lad, I am not as strong as I play it. I lived in halfway homes, foster dumps, and the nasty streets since I was nine-years-old. I was a scrawny, freckled face, pale-skinned, redhead. None of which did any good for me growing up. I was taunted daily. Bullied by bigger blokes and prodded to see how fast I would bruise. I really won't get into the other shit I had to endure. Besides, (Jason needing to take a long breath) …after shit today! You of all people will be the most receptive and understanding."

Timothy opens wide, seeing something in Jason he didn't see before.

"I hide this shit, deep within myself, Timmy! I forced myself to flee situations, to jump into the dark unknown. I need to survive, anyway I could. The streets, became my new mom and dad, for some time, Until the Y.O.C."

Timmy can't believe how open Jason's becoming with him, and he understands why Jason speaks the way he does. "Is this why you work out so relentlessly on the track?"

"I have one goal in life, to be able to take care of myself! Dealing with the streets? No one is going to be there, to help you when things get rough. My running was always my best defense and normally comes through for me. Today is an odd exception, for I still don't understand what happened."

"Well, I was blessed you decided to be there for me today? The tongue thing—if you want to know the truth, wasn't all that bad. (Timothy blushes) You were my first human kiss. Excluding my mom."

Jason scrunches his face tight. "Eww! Seriously little Bro? Another guys lips and tongue shouldn't be your first experience. Especially from a gruesome mug, like mine!"

"I am just saying—in a scientific, theoretical way. That's all."

Jason smiles. His teeth are marred with streaks of blood. "Hmm … Fine! I'll be candid with you, too! For a wee bloke, you weren't too shabby for your first nip, of the Ol' tongue. I honestly have nothing to base this comparison on. You were my first bloke, too. But I can say with some certainty, you had the softest lips I've ever felt for some time. Never would have thought, for a bloke! You rival some of the sweetest lassies I ever had the pleasure of tangling my lips and tongue with. For future note? Try not biting your future love's tongue, like ye did mine, Oy'? That's a deal breaker for sure, Laddie."

Jason laughs out to soften the tense mode in the air, which his ribs didn't like.

Timothy gets the revelation, of his knee-jerk reaction in biting Jason's tongue during the CPR session. "Oh-wow! I'm so sorry Jason! Didn't mean to bite you! You scared me!"

"I know, Timmy! It was my own dumb fault. It's a really shitty thing to do to such a sweet guy. You saved my bruised arse. You can see how all of that working out turned out? My ribs are seriously fucked! My legs bashed to hell. God knows how bad me bruised banger and jolly knockers are. They feel like scrambled eggs, right now. They're hurting something fierce, hard to walk. And there is no use telling ya about me, bum-hole! Pretty sure you already know. Unfortunately, I hated how you had to see him do that to me, so up close and personal like. You should have never been forced to witness such a vile act, Timmy-Boy."

Timothy cringes just thinking about how forceful Craig was with Jason's butt.

Holding on to his sore arm, Timothy inquires, "Can I say, the way you move is nothing short of miraculous. Today your speed was superhuman, unlike anything a human is supposed to be capable of. You aren't scrawny anymore, that's for certain. Have you ever really seen yourself—"

"Sure … when I step out of the showers naked. Not a pretty sight, mind you. But it's all I was blessed with."

"Jason, you have an amazing body. There is no other way of saying it without sounding like…"

"Poofter?"

"Yeah! But I really mean it. You are amazing … in my eyes."

"Um, okay. I think?" Jason gives Timmy a rather peculiar look of unease. "I still got my arse handed to me by a prick."

Timothy shakes his head. "Please no more arse puns. Please! Your hairy arse … saved my not so hairy one. And I couldn't thank your wonderful arse enough, Mr. Brodie!"

Jason can't overlook a chance to be his wickedly humorous self. Slightly turning his aching body around with his butt towards Timothy, he generously grabs both his royally bruised cheeks and starts flipping them open and shut. Unknowingly Jason exposes far more cheek flesh than he realizes. Mainly because of his missing underwear.

"Okay, Timmy-Lad. You can always thank me by bending on down here and giving's me a wee bit of a kiss, old chum."

Timothy wants to laugh with repulsion, but he's too deeply intrigued. He is unable to turn his eyes away from Jason's exposed flapping cheeks.

Jason peeks back over his shoulder and sees how Timothy is deeply captivated by his animated buttocks and not shying away like most boys would. He senses Timmy might be physically attracted to him as well. His bantering is only fueling the confused, fragile state of Timothy's sexuality.

"I really need to cut this out, little bro. It's not right to do that to you. It's foolish of me." Jason smiles and tousles Timmy's soft curls, arousing a sense of pleasure. Timothy doesn't seem to mind Jason playing with his hair.

"You were a beast, little dude. Damn, yer freaking locks are so soft and smooth like silk, little bro. I can play with your shit all day."

Timothy smiles. "I am five-foot-seven. I am not *that* little." Without warning, Jason gives Timothy the cheesiest smile and hold the sides of Timothy bewildered face.

"Little bro, you're the best! But I feel you might need this right now."

Jason comes in extremely close, allowing Timothy to inhale Jason's musk, drawing him even closer. Timothy can feel Jason's thick bulge rubbing tightly against his stomach. To Timothy's surprise, the pain in his arms seems to vanish as his cock springs to life in his shorts. He is electrified with arousal thinking about Jason's girth mashing against his soft stomach. Jason hugs Timmy like he has never hugged anyone before, and he gives no sign of releasing him.

Jason then whispers lovingly into his ear, "Just for you, Timmy. There is nothing small about you, me boy. You shouldn't ever be ashamed of what you've got. You are me, kinsman, now. Both proud and true!"

"What are you doing, Jason? Someone one will see us and think—"

Jason whispers, "Don't care, idiot! I am embracing my real brother today for the first time. And if he cares any at all for me, he will hug me, too."

"But you don't want people calling you a poofter, you said."

"Again! Don't care about any of that right now. You're nae alone anymore. Besides, we already went beyond first base, remember? So, stop fiddling about and give your kinsman a burly hug. It'll be cool. I don't bite like someone I know." Timothy feels the bass in Jason's chuckle.

Deeply conflicted with Jason's sudden change of heart. The strong embrace of Jason's arms is very inviting indeed —warm and protective. It's a fatherly type hug, Timmy has missing for so long.

Timothy cuddles into Jason, unlike anyone he has ever hugged, including his beloved mom and Eileen, the house cook. Timothy completely submits his entire being to Jason's care, even with pain coursing through his body.

While Timothy's usable arm is wrapping Jason's waist and his fingers slip deep within Jason's Butt cleavage. His busy fingers reach deep and find Jason's taut sore sphincter ripples. Instinctively, Jason's anus clinches tight the few times Timothy's investigating tips massage upon it. Timothy's finger is only denied entry into the thin fabric of Jason's shorts.

Enduring the not so subtle intrusion or awkwardness of Timothy's probing, Jason understands the emotionally sweet, distraught Lad is probably well overdue, for an uninhibited embrace. Even if is a mildly sexualized one. Ironically, Timothy's advance doesn't feel vile to Jason, like the abusive encounter with Craig.

Whispering gently between kisses to Timothy's tender earlobe and forehead, Jason nurtures the boy.

"Timmy-boy, it's okay to let it all out. You are safe now. No one is here to harm you anymore. You are my hero today, too. You are— … beautiful, kid." Jason swaying Timothy from side to side helps calm the boy greatly. Continuing to rummage his slender fingers through Timothy curly mane, allows Timothy's emotions blossom. He moans deep into Jason's firm pecs. Jason says nothing but holds him dearly for as long as he needs to be held. However, hoping Timothy doesn't realize how to slip his fingers under his shorts and have full access below.

Neither boy knew Eric was secretly eavesdropping the entire time. Learning everything there is to know about their innermost tormented secrets, Eric observed all from the confines of the open stairwell. Seeing the boys deeply affectionate hug so boldly, in the center of the hall— amazingly with no regard to anyone possibly catching them? Spoke volumes to Eric.

Being the stereotypical homophobe and womanizing jock, Eric's heart is softened somehow by all that has happened today. Is it their need for acceptance, compassion, comfort, or maybe … love? He couldn't tell, and at this point, it didn't matter. Seeing them only makes him regret and rethink the way he views the world.

Two young skateboarders crash into the building just behind

Eric, their boards in hand. They see Eric staring at Timmy and Jason's loving embrace. After a double-take, the two Skaters start snicker among themselves.

"Dude, seriously, tell me that ain't, J-man Brodie!"

"Shit! it is, dude. What the fuck—! Is he snuggling a goober kid?"

"Fuck! Man, he is! The kid has his fingers all up ass crack, dude? Eww—"

"Yeah, major gross! Didn't know J-man swung, like that."

"Me either. I thought he was seeing some new girl."

Eric overhears their whole berating conversation, with true discord.

Seeing things differently now for himself, Eric turns to negate the skater's hostility with ferocity. Being cautious in not wanting to disturb Jason and Timothy's much merited personal moment.

Laying deep into the young skaters, outraged but in a hushed voice. "You little butt wipes got anything else stupid to say about those guys? It is their own damn business, and they don't need two skid marks, judging them." The skater kids feel nervous and threatened by Eric's aggression.

"The guys you are joking over? were viciously assaulted and beaten. So, the last thing they need is your shit. The thugs were pricks just like you two skid marks! (Eric points to Jason) See the bruises on the one you call J-man?"

The boys nod while examining Jason's horrid bruises, leaving them speechless.

"And the f'ing jerks are going to pay. I guarantee this!"

Eric concludes, seeing the fear in their boy's eyes. "If either one of you half dicks says anything to anyone about this, your asses will be buried in the woods. Got it?"

The skater boy's apologies and scramble out the door, fearing Eric's wrath.

Timothy dries his face after their long embrace. The hug was exactly what Jason said it would be. Totally relieving the much pent-up emotions from Timothy and even from Jason. Timothy persuades Jason to go home with him, so he can look at their wounds and get an awesome homemade meal. With wide bubbly eyes, Jason accepts the invite.

Eric, on the other hand, marches himself directly to the counselor's office for a meaningful one-on-one, to clear his conscious.

CHAPTER 11

On the silent journey home, Kyra sits uneasily in Scott's car, pretending to listen to the radio. His car is a flashy '65 Mustang in two-tone black. It has dual chrome pipes, letting everyone know that there is serious power on the road. Although Scott is fixated on the path before him, he can't seem to help, but sneak peeks at Kyra from time to time. The wind from the open windows dances gracefully through her flowing hair, which seems to glow golden in the sun. He's mesmerized.

Kyra laughs at herself. What has she gotten herself into this time? She's supposed to be on punishment, and now she's coming home with a hot senior. Her father will be overjoyed at seeing this. *Not!* But the more she looks at him, the more her affection blossoms.

Breaking the awkward silence in the car, Scott turns down the radio and asks the first question since they climbed into the car, "So why haven't you ever tried any of the athletic programs?" After her skillful maneuvering through the congested hallway at full throttle, he was genuinely curious. Somehow, she had soared right past him.

Kyra snarls at the thought of after-school sporting programs. "I just don't get into the whole sporting thing."

"Funny seeing how athletic you truly are. Seriously, no one had passed me by in a full-on sprint like that before, except Jason, the kid you met today."

"I guess you could say there is history. I had years of martial arts, dance, and gymnastics since childhood." Scott looks over to see if she is wearing a strap. "I guess I am just not really into that old team spirit thingy. That sprint was purely a shocker to me today. It must have been pure adrenaline kicking in."

Kyra hears Scott chuckle. "Hmm, I see. Excellent belt three, I must say." He points to an actual belt around her waist, forcing her to check it out for herself, which makes Kyra blush. She slugs his shoulder with his sarcasm. "Ouch! You know you sounded a lot like Jason just now."

"Oh, I see. I seem like a steamy, hot, young, sexy babe magnet with a Scottish accent? The one with the deep sexy voice who thinks you are a super-cute hottie … for a bloke?"

Scott says, "Say what? I sincerely hope not." Kyra chuckles. "Yeah, that's him. He is the fastest kid I have ever seen other than you. And yet … he doesn't want anything to do with the sports programs either. And I am like, seriously? Why is that? He trains in secret just before the after-school teams start their workouts."

Kyra remembers how he was shaken when she accidentally bumped into him by the stands. "What was that all about?" she inquired.

"I don't know! It's like he is always running from something. He confides in me only partially. He is still pretty tight-lipped about most things that are really personal, and I try not to meddle that much."

Brushing her hair from her forehead, she says, "I met him today for the first time just after your practice, and you went to shower. He appears to be really sweet, very polite, and a little nervous around the guys from the team."

"Really?" he asks.

"He has the cutest accent. It appears, he and Timmy somehow know each other."

Scott breaks in, "That's right Timothy, the little brain-trust is your friend, too, right? I heard his family is really loaded, moneywise?"

Kyra responds. "I've known Timmy— Oops, I should correct that. He gets so upset when people call him that. But I've known Timothy for a couple years. We teamed up last year in the regional SciTech trials. The kid is like … the next Einstein of our time or even better. The next Nikola Tesla would be more precise. He is amazingly smart, cute, and so shy."

Scott's smiles. "Hmmm, and from the way it sounds, so are you. Not shy. I mean you're really smart."

Blushing, she responds, "I am okay, I guess."

"You are just modest, Kyra."

"Enough already. Let me finish."

"Sorry, my bad. Go on."

"Well, as I was saying, today was different. He doesn't show or express basic emotions normally. Like he has Asperger's syndrome. Super high brain functioning but low on the social scale."

"You never see him really laugh, cry, giggle, or anything like that?"

"He might awkwardly smile, but that would be it. Somehow, today I saw anger, fear, and shame all at the same time. When Jake and Ben maliciously taunted him in chemistry class today, he had an outburst."

"Jake and Ben from the track team?"

Kyra nods. "After seeing him up close and personal today and not just a lab brain, I realized he is a very attractive guy, but I never noticed his attractiveness before. All the stuff they were saying about him missing puberty and being completely hairless really got to him."

"Some guys are cruel. A lot of young guys mature faster than others physically. That by no means makes them any smarter or more masculine. Timothy is a great kid, and I really hope he is okay. He will eventually hit his growth spurt, and feel better about himself."

"I hope so, too. It would be great for him to find someone special in his life, someone who can boost his self-esteem. Because the truth is that not all boys grow hair all over if that is what he is counting on. Just a fact of life."

Scott is a little uncomfortable with the direction of the conversation. He doesn't want to be designated to the dreaded friend-zone, not with Kyra.

"Never mind about all that, Kyra. Timothy is okay for a young guy! I don't really check out fellas, I hope you know?" Kyra giggles, catching his hint. "I will agree! underneath those silky locks lies a massive brain."

"Hmm! Don't check out the fellas, huh?" teases Kyra, with a sparkle in her eye.

Scott cracks a smile. "Hey, the kid has great hair. Can't knock a fact."

She laughs and quickly agrees with him.

Kyra's curiosity grows exponentially, and she inquires about the hallway scene. Scott shrugs, slightly tilting his head to the side.

"I don't know, Scott! It just looked to me that Timothy was terrified, and I could plainly see he was injured when I was helping him pick up his gear. I've never seen him in that state of mind before. And Craig looked really angry." Scott could not deny that Kyra was more observant than he realized, especially since she arrived on to the scene much sooner than him.

"There's no way of putting it nicely. Eric and his goons are nothing but bullies and thugs. I also think they may have gone too far in humiliating the underclassman. I can't prove how far they went because the boys are trying to move on. All I could do was simply offer my support as a senior."

"Do you think they will tell the school's authorities?"

"You know, I really wish they would. But I don't see that happening. I'll be keeping my eye out for them for a bit. The last thing I want to do is make them feel like victims. However, I truly think it was a good thing that they found each other and made a new friendship."

"What makes you so sure of that, Scott?" Kyra says, curious still.

"I don't know. I just see it in their eyes. It was in the way they were looking out for each other. You can only sense something like that when two people have nothing to hide and open themselves up to the support of others. I know Jason has been on his own for some time, and from what you've told me about Timothy, he may be in the same situation. Going through whatever hell they just experienced forced them to open up and rely on each other completely. They have made a bond, a brotherhood.

Kyra settles back into her seat. "Well, I really hope it all works out for the best. Those two boys need to have a happy ending." When Scott hears the term *happy ending*, he feels awkward. He wishes now that he didn't know the alternate meaning of those words.

While riding home, she gazes out the window, reflecting on the prior events. She thinks of Timothy giggling in the class. Scott, however, thinks of fun times he's shared with his redheaded buddy. Watching his buddy's eyes pop when he visited the center, was magic to him. He knew he was taking Jason away from his gloomy life, for an hour or so. His presence seemed to make things a little easier for him at home.

CHAPTER 12

Not far from Kyra's home, Julie stops by her house after leaving the Library, assuming her friend would already be home. Nevertheless, she wants to be certain. She thinks maybe Kyra's brother might have grown a heart and taken her home after missing the bus.

She rings the doorbell several times without any answer. She starts to worry a bit, considering it is almost an hour and a half since school let out. She decides to wait on the swing on Kyra's front porch. She didn't want to be rash and jump to conclusions. But Kyra's parents not being home throws her off a bit. Kyra could be out with them. She slips in her earbuds and listens to the jams on her phone.

Meanwhile, not too far from home, Scott builds up the nerve to ask Kyra out. "Maybe we … I don't know … can get together and hang out?" Although nervous, Scott speaks very smoothly.

"Really? And do what exactly?" she responds in more playful banter.

"Well, I am helping my wacky cousin Joel at Mr. Bowman's farm and the fairgrounds this weekend for the Harvest Moon Fair.

If you'd like, I could spot you an all-access pass for the day and free popcorn."

Kyra smiles as her heart races like a stampede of prize-winning stallions. "The fair? I haven't done one of those in … like ages. That's something my father would have done for Kyle and me. Oh, I don't know." Scott waits with bated breath for a reply in his favor. "I admit that the popcorn is tempting though."

"C'mon, you love torturing me, don't you?"

She knows how this is eating him up. "I am sorry, I just can't decide. But if a nice caramel apple is added to the tally, then maybe."

"Kyra? Fine … caramel apples all night long. How about that?"

Kyra smiles, "We'll have to see about that Mr. Tanner. I am under lockdown at my home. But, if by a miracle of a chance my sentencing is reduced, I would be honored to be your chaperone. If you promise to be a proper gentleman, that is?"

Scott glazes, with rosy cheeks.

Kyra continues, "I guess it would be cool. I also have an exhibition that weekend. You can support me, while I support you, sounds fair don't you think?"

Scott nods, "Wow, that would be awesome! Unfortunately, I promised Mr. Bowman to help him Saturday and early Sunday morning, prepping the fair."

"It's no biggie, really. There will be other events. By the way, (she places a finger on his firm chest) what about your escort of perky vixens all over the school?" camouflaging her true question, Kyra tries to learn Scott's relationship status. *Is he or isn't he available for dating?*

Pulling up to a streetlight, Scott pauses and looks down into his lap. He taps the dangling keys hanging in the ignition.

Kyra's concerned. *Did I ask too much?*

"What's wrong Scott? Did I say something wrong or out of place?"

"No, of course not!" He slowly turns to face her and gaze into her caring eyes. "It's nothing you said, Kyra. It's something I seem to be dealing with a lot lately. Sometimes way more than I really want to."

The light turns green, and some horn beeps twice behind them. Scott isn't paying attention to the signal lights at all, but then he pulls the car past the intersection and parks on the side of the road. Kyra feels unease. Why did he stop? She isn't that far from home. He turns the ignition off, and the rumbling pipes go instantly silent. Scotts shifts his body toward Kyra to give her his undivided attention, and nervous, he runs his hand through his hair. She in turns unbuckles her seatbelt and faces him.

"Kyra, I am not going to lie to you. I like having fun at the school. Strangely, people sort of expect it from me. You can understand, I am sure."

She nods. "What is this about?" she inquires.

"I am about to explain some things you've got to understand. What you see around the school—that's not the real me." He pounds his fist against his chest, with emphasis, on the word me.

"I can understand that, Scott. Yet, why are you so weighed down right now?"

"Kyra, I don't want meaningless dates with pretty faces. I want more out of life than stupid parties and girls throwing themselves at me. I know everyone says that I am dating this one and that I've been with that one."

Kyra knows very well all the circulating rumors involving Scott Tanner. "Yes, I think I may have heard a thing or two from time to time. I always looked at it, as you being majorly popular. You are so athletic and attractive. But I never judged you in such a manner."

Scott's eye perks like a child in a candy shop, with a free-for-all ticket.

"Oh, so you think …I am attractive, huh?" He responded with boasting cockiness.

Kyra can't believe he would stoop so low, looking for self-glorification. She shakes her head, with a quarter grin to the side, "Hmm! I would say of course, but I feel you! Mister Modesty, may already know such an answer!"

Scott plays coy to her assumption.

"I can't think of one female who doesn't think you're anything, but mad-heat in cleats, Scott! You broke the hottie meter some time ago."

Kyra is totally crushing on Scott's amazing bashfulness. It appears Scott values her words and reels in her compliments. "Wow! I don't know what to say. I don't usually get such compliments."

"Boy, what are you saying? You get compliments every day!"

"Mostly superficial people trying to get close to me, only to catapult their popularity meters." He considers her eyes once again. "I want to tell you something a little more serious and personal. I just hope you don't feel slighted by it."

"What are you talking about, goofy? Serious? There is nothing you can say that would slight me. Go-on speak your mind!"

"I'm … lonely Kyra. (he takes a huge sigh) There I said it."

"Whoa? What are you talking about Scott, you are surrounded by people every day?"

"Have you ever been a store during a mad sale like Black Friday or a concert with a horde of screaming fans all around you?"

"Yes, I can relate … more than once."

"Well, that's my life, Kyra … every second of every day."

"Oh! Wow! That bad?"

"I am seriously seeing no one right now, and I haven't in the recent past!"

Kyra is trying to wrap her head in what he is saying, "But you have been dating, right?"

He smirks. "Not really. They were more like arranged setups for appearances at parties, venues at school functions, and cheerleaders wanting to make a name for themselves. But just between us, I am so sick of the useless drama. I understand that drama is a huge part of the brand. But I've had enough of it."

"Oh, wow, I never imagined it was so chaotic."

"It's funny though. I really miss the fact that only six years ago, no one knew me. I was simply an unknown skateboarder loser sitting at the front of your bus in middle school. I was too shy to make eye contact with anyone, especially the prettiest girl on the bus or at the school."

Kyra thinks back to the sixth grade. They were at Andrew Jackson Middle. Magically, she remembers the image of a boy with shaggy blond hair and messy boy bangs covering his blue eyes, wearing thick glasses and toting a Legendary X-men backpack. She remembers how he would never look anyone in the face back then.

"What the heck happened? You are like the god of the universe at school now?" Kyra is completely amazed at the total transformation.

Scott blushes. "It was an interesting twist of events actually. The summer before my last year at middle school, I was skateboarding down by Milton's Mall with my cousin Joey and his friends. A huge white SUV swung out from around the corner and struck me. My cousin, eventually told me how it looked like I was somehow targeted."

"Oh, my God! That's crazy!"

"Yeah, you tell me! I was told, I was laid up in a coma for more than two weeks, barely alive. I had flatlined several times, I was later told by my doctor. But my cousin and family said I was seriously jacked up. They said all the bones in my legs were splintered or broken. My spine was messed up. My right shoulder was crushed. My left forearm broke into three sections, and they said I had several severe head fractures in my skull. The doctors initially said something to the effect that I may not come out of the coma alive, and if I did, I might suffer serious brain damage and trauma. I went through three intense brain surgeries and finally came to a few days later."

"Oh, my God!"

"I went through a lot of therapy and surgeries afterward. It felt like forever. I had no one at my side except my mom and her new boyfriend, Stephen. He wasn't so bad. A bit pushy, but way better than my old man for cutting out on us altogether."

"What happened? If you don't mind my asking?"

"O' Nah, it's chill now! My old man left my mom for his co-worker and part-time golfing buddy. It was when we found out my pop was living on the down low, for some time. If my Dad having a guy for a mistress wasn't enough, the guy wasn't that much older than me. Michael Stone was the punk's name, and he a pompous jerk to boot! You know the saying— all gays are jolly friendly people?"

Kyra nods.

"That's bullshit. Pardon my language." Scott continued.

"Don't mention it," Kyra responds clearing her throat.

"Michael was the evening manager at the bank where my old man worked. I haven't seen them too much since they made it official. The most recent attempt was a couple years back. Ironically, I was totally cool with him being gay and with a guy only ten years older than me. When he did finally come, he saw just how much I had changed in the few years he was gone. My Dad's male partner seemed a little too interested in my social life for my taste. It was so creepy and weird, especially with the way he would ask. It only got worse when my dad wasn't around. He kept looking me over, like merchandise on a rack. But worse still, he had this insatiable need to touch me at awkward moments in conversations, whenever he was talking to me. When he placed his hand on the small of my back just below the elastic of my sweat shorts, I literally freaked. I chose to stay the hell away from him, the remainder of their visit."

"Wow, that's super creepy, Scott! That sounded like he wanted to—."

"Yeah, I already know."

"Did you at least tell your Dad about his Perv of a boyfriend. Seeing you were such a minor?"

Scott smirks. "No, I didn't. I didn't want to cause a scene for a holiday. I was a big boy, and I knew how to handle myself if it came to that. Plus, I figured that creepy ass-grabber would be gone soon and out of my life. I really wanted to have time to hang out with my father, and that's what pulled me through."

Changing the subject slightly, Kyra softened her tone and asked, "When you were in the hospital recovering, you did have at least a few friends visit, right?"

Shaking his head slowly, Scott explains. "No, not-even-one. (breaking his words down with emphasis) Everyone thought I was a walking disease after all the rumors had spread about my old man. Mostly about him being a major pervert and how foolish my mother was for being fooled for so long by him. There was only one exception—Madame Levette."

"Madame who?" Kyra sparked, never hearing the name before.

"The sweetest angel who entered my life, Emilia Levette. She would stand outside the old McGruder's movie house, to smell the fresh popped-popcorn. She really loves the stuff. One night, while I am in really bad shape in the hospital, my mom was making it routine to be late in visiting me, drowning her griefs and lack of a life, with her new friend Jack Daniels and Wild Turkey."

"Never knew it was —."

"It was a growing experience, for sure. Anywho, Madame Levette visited my room that night, while my mother was off

stumbling aimlessly around the hospital. She was being detained
for wandering around and calling the vile staff obscenities."

"Wow, your Mom went off the deep end. And this Madame
woman just walked into your room unchecked? You were a vulnerable minor."

"Yeah, it was rather unusual, considering how everyone thought
Madame Levette was a mental case. They figured she was a crazy
old black woman with funny-colored braids all down her back.
It only brought to light how much racism was still lurking in our
so-called nonjudgmental little town. It never seemed to bother
her much, she said. She was originally from Louisiana, outside the
French Quarter. When she came to my room, she walked up to my
bedside whispers. '*You're going to need this, my young whisperer.*'

"Whisperer? What's that about?" Kyra squints her brow.

"Had no Clue! But, she pulled something out of her bag, held it
close to her face and spat on it. She had some mumbo-jumbo words
and placed the object in my swollen hand."

"Eww! Sounds like a hygienical nightmare."

"Honestly, I thought so too! I was more frightened of her than
the tiny object. It was a weird copper coin, she placed in my hand.
I asked what the coin was for? She told me to keep it close to my
heart, and repeat the following words, '*I am my own healer. I am my
own servant. I am here to help many, and I will be strong of mind.*'
She told me to say it three times before falling asleep and not to
forget it. After that, she walked out of the room."

"That's very odd. Did you do what was asked?"

"Well, she freaked me out so much that I dared not to."

"What happen?"

"Everything, really. That night was the first night I essentially
slept in weeks, for fear of going back into a coma. When I awoke
the next morning, it was like everything had changed inside of me.
When the doctors came that day and ran some test, they couldn't

believe the results they saw. They did even more test. They immediately called my mother in. Surprisingly, she was sober. The doctors informed her that my brain had completely healed, and my fractures had completely restored themselves. It was nothing short of a miracle, the staff kept saying, while people kept coming in and spying on me until I was released."

"You think she had something to do with—?"

"I like to think so. Not long after I came home, I found the Madam down by McGruder's theater. It took a week for me to build up the nerve to actually talk to the woman."

Kyra is fully engrossed in his story now.

"I finally did. Well, actually, she did." He laughs out.

"I was hiding behind the dumpster, snooping on her. I thought for sure no one could see me. She stared at the sky and said."

'Boy, you know it is not right to be spying on old people. Yes, I am talking about you, Mr. Tanner. The boy ... behind the dumpster. Come now, boy. Don't keep me waiting! It is rude. I have been expecting you.'

"I literally had no choice, but to come out from hiding, to see her."

"Say what? Are you kidding? (Kyra smirks in disbelief) You mean to say, she just called you out?" Kyra laughs more, "Wow, kind of reminds me of Julie, this Madame Levette."

Scott perks an eyebrow, when Kyra mentions Julie had a likeness to Levette.

"We went to the Starbucks, and she bought me a chocolate shake while she got an herbal tea with two lemon wedges. After we were settled, we started talking. She told me of her great shop in the south. It was a place where she and her family told fortunes, cast blessings, and sold trinkets and other wild stuff to superstitious tourists. She said she only gave happy fortunes to strangers because people didn't want to know the true readings." Scott chuckles.

"And she managed to get in a room and visit you?" Kyra asks in disbelief.

"Exactly, but it was our secret because only the family could visit. After the first few nights, I learned that she just had a way with people. Surprisingly, no one ever seemed to stop or question her."

"So … what happened? How did she get this far north?"

Scott straightens his face. "Well, she told me she owned their shop for generations. It was passed from her great-great-grandmother to her grandmother and then to her mother and then finally to her. But the true readings were only reserved for her immediate family and locals. One day, unfortunately, an arrogantly young, cocky, rich white man, demanded a true reading from her, and not the BS they peddle to dumb tourists. Feeling threatened, she agreed and gave the man a fake reading to trick him, hoping to satisfy his demand."

"So, what happened?"

"To her surprise, the man didn't like the reading, called her a charlatan and demanded a real one. He was no ordinary white man, she said. His eyes were like that of death itself. She could see pure darkness in the man and told him to leave and never return, but he refused. Seeing her fear, he knew she was what he was seeking, and he told her to read or die."

"What did the man want to know?"

"That's the thing. It was all about a key, a very special key that was broken into several parts."

"A key? A key to what?"

"That's just it. He wouldn't say. He just went on to say it was made of a special green crystalline stone. Maybe, Jade, he thought."

"Jade?"

"Exactly. sensing a power emanating from within the man, Madame Levette thought maybe she should do what the white man asked. As she took hold of his hands, she could feel centuries of darkness and chaos flowing through him, but it wasn't his, she said. She could see the key in question, and she noticed that the key was not just a jade stone. It was a jade-encrusted living crystal heart much like a human heart made of flesh. The stone heart pulsed with power. She said as she tried delving deeper into the reading. She saw the heart was broken into five parts—two of equal size and three much smaller but no less powerful. He was getting rowdy, and he tried to kill her after she explained to him that the key was lost in a place, not of this world."

"What did she do?"

"She wore an ancient talisman that was passed down through the centuries. To think about it, it was the same one she gave me the first night I ever saw her. She said when he touched the talisman, something very dark and evil left the man that very moment. She believed it was a great dark spirit of fire and ash, and it left the man convulsing on the floor. While he was in the clinic, he lost everything—his business, his family, and his dignity. When he lost the money he somehow swindled from the mob, he became a marked man. Soon the flood destroyed his nice home, his yacht, and his family, who were all asleep on board, while he was out gambling the night away. He was later found fatally beaten, bleeding out while dangling near death from an old tree, completely stripped of all his clothing and possessions. He was just off Bourbon Street for all to see, she said."

"Oh, wow. And you say all of this really happened? How'd you know?"

"A little later she warned me about the graphic nature of a video that was captured by locals with their phones. It depicted the event just before the flood came and destroyed almost everything. She showed me the video of a naked young white man tied upside down to a tree by his broken ankles. The footage showed people prodding, poking, spitting and molesting him while he cried out for mercy, swearing that he had been possessed by demons.

All in all, it wasn't something I ever wanted to see at that fragile age then, something so horrid being done to another human being, and unfortunately, I will never forget it. The clips told of many horror stories and showed me how dark the world was after those deadly floods. Madame believes the city was cursed by that dark beast as a testament to its power."

Kyra shakes her head in disbelief and starts to access her inner thoughts. *This explains why Scott's so watchful of Timothy and Jason. In many respects, those boys are exactly like Scott, from his past.*

Nonetheless, without any provocation, thoughts of her best friend, Julie, spring to her mind. She is getting the same sensation as she did with her teacher's wife's dire situation.

If Kyra didn't know any better, she would classify this sensation as a type of early warning system. She wonders if this Madame Levette may have some insights, to perhaps help her with the strange things happening around her.

Kyra abruptly asks, "Is your friend a witch or voodoo priestess?"

With an expression of alarm, Scott says, "No, no! She is nothing like that. She says her family was granted certain gifts by a very powerful source—some lady in white, I think she said—because of an alliance that was forged against a dark foe or something like that. There are no dark spells or any beastly deities that I have ever noticed. Ironically, she is a true born-again Christian worshipper, but for the upcoming fair, she is doing an homage to the old pagan craft of fortune-telling. You should really check her out. I mean, she is really cool once you get to know her."

Kyra sees the excitement in his beautiful blue eyes, but she doesn't have the heart to tell him she really doesn't follow all that sort of stuff—psychics, mediums, or sorcery. Because of his excitement and feelings, however, she feels compelled to say yes.

"Maybe we could make it a date?" Kyra's eyes pop, and Scott

sees her expression. "Not a date. What am I thinking? Oh, my God. I was only saying—"

Kyra smiles, seeing him struggle with his words. To her it's adorable. She can't bear his suffering, so she relieves the tension. "I think we can manage a nondate date … this time." Unexpectedly, at the time, Kyra gets another subtle vision about Julie at her house and darkness around her.

CHAPTER 13

Back at Kyra's home, Julie also gets an unsettled chill that tickles the light hairs on the back of her neck. This feeling is nothing new to her. Conversely, when something's wrong or out of place or when something serious is about to occur, she receives unexplainable vibes. Her vibes come in several forms. Her senses of smell, taste, and hearing will often play roles. However, other times it's stronger. She'll have visions of things yet to occur or events that have already occurred. Sometimes she sees situations from someone else's perspective. She doesn't bring most of this up to Kyra, knowing she's a serious skeptic. Very Ironic considering, Kyra's families lineage is rooted in folklore and suspicions, on both sides of her gene-pool.

Julie instinctively starts to dial Kyra on the phone, when she suddenly senses the need to investigate around Kyra's place. She halts from tapping the last digit of Kyra's cell number. She maneuvers the full length of the front porch and peers into the oversized bay window of Kyra's huge Victorian-styled home. Gazing thoroughly in the window, everything appears in its rightful place, and there are no lights or sounds out of the ordinary.

Just as she is about to step away from the window, out of her peripheral vision of her right eye, she glimpses a peculiar shadow moving at the top of the stair

Without haste, Julie takes a running start, leaps into the air, and rolls into a forward flip, clearing the banister railing and landing with a tuck-and-roll to her feet. She dashes toward the side of the house, not missing a single step. Confidently springing into action, she swiftly climbs the huge oak tree stealthily up to the second level, where she can access Kyra's bedroom window. Her agile movements are like that of a bobcat with total precision and speed. Kyra's window is partially open, but the lock is somehow not broken. As she climbs through, she hears the sliding doors to the backyard downstairs in the kitchen.

Trying to get a visual once again, backing away from the window, she sees a figure walking across the yard, dressed all in black with a hoodie and a black ski mask.

"Hey, you!" shouts Julie to catch the attention of the stranger. She is hoping to get a glance at the intruder. The stranger pauses but never looks back, and the figure raises one hand high in the air. Julie's senses start tingling. The mighty branch supporting her weight starts to crack.

With no time to think, Julie uses her ninja-like skills and reflexes and maneuvers through multiple branches of the tree, tossing and flipping her way down to the ground. She snaps her neck to the side like a wrestler on prime-time television and cracks her knuckles.

"I don't understand what the hell that was about, but … you picked the wrong house today, scum!"

The intruder sharply turns. Only its eyes are visible from the mask. It shakes its head, impressed by Julie's dazzling feats of agility. The stranger patiently stands as Julie charges across the well-groomed lawn. It thrusts its hand outward, with the palm facing toward Julie, like in a stopping gesture. Shaking its fully masked head, as if being left no choice to do what needs to be done.

Julie feels the wind rush out of her lungs as she is pushed back many feet through the air. However, though bewildering to the intruder, Julie is quite masterful in her learned abilities. While freefalling to the ground, Julie contorts her body in a way that allows her to twirl. In her rotations, she manages to flip out of the freefall into a rather skillful landing, tuck-rolling back to her feet in the end.

The intruder tilts its head to one side and nods slowly, showing their respect.

"Look! I don't know who or what the hell you are. You don't know who you are playing with, for I am Shira-Kami! We can play this little game all day!"

Without a word, the stranger reaches into its pouch from around its waist and pulls out a hand full of sharp daggers. Julie looks on with wonder. The hooded stranger holds its hand upward, and six daggers begin to levitate.

"Okay, nice trick!" Julie says, trying to sound braver than she currently feels.

The hooded intruder lowers its arms to its sides as the deadly daggers start twirling slowly and then circle the intruder's body like a shield. Julie whispering to herself, *I don't like the look of this little game.* The intruder nods its head, and a dagger breaks its formation and flies in Julie's direction like a bullet. Julie isn't expecting such an attack, and the knife grazes her neck just as she dodges. Not believing what just happened, Julie checks her neck and feels a trickle of blood from a small cut. When she sees the blood on her finger, she realizes she can't play with this person.

Taking a deep breath filling her inner strength with mystic-chi, Julie begins to channel her mastery of the mystical warrior arts. Putting her body in a monk-like prayer stance, her body starts surging with tantric energy. This technique is very unique to Julie and was taught to her under her tutelage in Japan. It is steeped in a rich tapestry of a long-forgotten art form, lost to the modern-day era of science and industry.

While eyeing the intruder, Julie's hair becomes light and flowing with unseen energy. The irises in her eyes blister with a white glow. After years of tedious studies in the mystic shinobi arts, Julie is channeling her higher innermost state of awareness, which opens her natural psychic abilities to a heightened point of prowess. The intruder guides the daggers to all fly toward Julie. A more focused and mentally stabled Julie is ready for the extreme challenge now.

With a deep state of mental acuity, Julie moves purely with instinctive grace, avoiding the daggers at every turn. Her fluid motions are like that of water and air. She twists, dodges, spins, leaps, and tumbles her way clear of each passing blade. Her sleight of hand is smoother and quicker than the attacker's visible line of sight. Managing to corral one of the blades back with dazzling swiftness, Julie catches the hooded person off guard, as the dagger slices through the attacker's outer thigh. In a surprising octave pitch, the criminal cries out in bitter pain.

The outburst came in the form a young female, adolescent primarily. She could tell by the voice. Now Julie is one step closer to learning the mystery woman's identity. With agonizing pain, the intruder rips the protruding dagger from her outer thigh, blood starting to quickly trickle out. She tosses the dagger to the ground and holds her hand against the wound tightly.

"Like I said, we can do this all day, bitch! I am hardly afraid of you and your little parlor trick!" All the while, the intruder realizes Julie is more of a contender than she originally bargained for.

Julie becomes boastful. "Why are you here? Why my friend's home? Who the hell are you? Just take off the stupid mask." The stranger remains silent, trying to think of her next move to escape.

"You are aware I am about to kick your miserable bitch ass all up and down this damn street, right?" Julie taunts the unknown person, even though she has not quite figured out how she is going to do that yet. Without warning, a car's deep rumbling sounds from the front driveway of the house. The noise catches Julie's attention, which is just the distraction the intruder needs.

Then the intruder exacts her psionic attack with the full extent of her power. Julie's body is slammed with the force of a demolition ball swung at full thrust. The telekinetic punch is so strong that it completely smashes her lungs in as her body slams into the side of Kyra's house with a bone-cracking force. There's an audible crashing sound as her body bounces off the wall and plummets into the oversized hedges. Such an impact would usually kill or severely injure the average human, but thanks to her intense physical conditioning, the fall renders her unconscious, which allows her attacker to escape, wounded and unseen.

Julie has seen chi masters perform masterful works in Japan. Unfortunately, it was never quite like this. The whole matter leaves her utterly confused when she wakes up. Quickly, with much pain, she climbs back to her feet after she wrestles free of the prickly branches. She looks around, but the stranger is clearly gone. She wipes the debris from her tattered clothing. She slowly makes her way to the front yard, staggering at times for balance. The impact of the wall and fall was more damaging than Julie originally assumed, but it's nothing for the Shira-Kami within her to handle, with proper rest.

She's hoping to see one of Kyra's parents' vehicles home from work, but she's utterly dumbfounded when she sees a beautiful Mustang at the end of the long driveway. Unable to see who was in the car with tinted windows, she continues to make her way toward the front of the house.

Meanwhile, Scott spots a girl standing in front of Kyra's house and questions Kyra, "Is that Julie from school over there in front of your house?"

Kyra squints her eye. "Uh, yeah! She's my BFF, but she looks a little—" Without finishing her thought, she turns sharply back to Scott, and with a beaming smile, she says, "I can't thank you enough for bringing me home, Mr. Scott Tanner."

Scott gazes deeply into her eyes. "For such a crazy day, I am glad I met you. It is my pleasure driving you home, Ms. Kyra Mathews."

"Oh!" Kyra fails in her attempt to hide her flagrant blushing. "You know, Kyra is just fine." To avoid any awkwardness, Kyra quickly hops from the car. She bends over to wave goodbye. She steps back so he can pull out of the driveway comfortably.

Watching him drive away in a dreamlike state, she is harshly interrupted by Julie's sudden presence at her side. With an intense expression on her face, Julie visibly shows signs of distress. There are several scratches on her face and limbs, and there are twigs tangled up in her bangs and hair.

"Seriously, Julie, I am going to put a cowbell on you, girl. Stop doing that Shinjitsu stuff." Still, within her excited state, Kyra acknowledges Julie's visible state of distress, "Anyway … What happened to you? Your seriously looking jacked right now."

Julie shakes her head slowly, and with as calm a tone as she can muster, she says, "Look, your house was just broken into. The little twerp managed to get away." A look of petrified horror is clearly visible on Kyra's face.

Devoid of any words, Kyra grabs her cell and calls her father to explain the situation. He replies and alerts the authorities. Julie explains to her in detail, all the events leading up to her and Scott's, timely arrival. Julie stresses to Kyra why they shouldn't say too much to the authorities about the invader. Kyra loves Julie. She's her best friend; hitherto, she often feels Julie has an active imagination and a flair for the dramatic, at times.

Julie knows Kyra all too well and sees the look, which is all too familiar planted on her face. The look says, "Seriously, Julie? Are we going through this again?" Julie leads a charge to the rear of the house, and Kyra follows in a confused state.

Once on the side of the house, Kyra sees the remnants of the confrontation.

"What the—!" Kyra exclaimed while observing the garden tools and daggers on the ground and stuck in the tree. She sees the disheveled bushes near the house that cushioned Julie's fall. But the most impressive sight is the huge branch in the middle of the yard.

"I don't know what that bitch was after, but she wasn't exactly all that normal if you get my drift?" Julie explains the stages of the battle to Kyra.

"You saw the attacker's face?"

Julie shakes her head. "No, I did not! She was wearing a ski mask."

"A mask? So how do you know, it was a … a woman?"

Julie didn't think about the question, in detail. What could she say, to bring a sense of believability? She can't just say, "The sleuth spirit within me dictates the criminal is female and young with assured certainty."

"So how do you know it was a woman?" Kyra asks more intensely, determined to get answers.

"Actually, it wasn't a woman!"

"Huh? But you just said—"

"Excuse me, Sista-girl. I never said a woman. I said that bitch! Anyway, it wasn't a woman I was fighting. It was a girl—teen like us. Her movements, her breathing, and her voice showed all the signs of an adolescent female. But she had a unique scent about her, like hard metal and cleaner solution."

Kyra is slightly amused. "You mean you had the time to stop and sniff the chick?"

Julie simply sneers and playfully slaps her shoulder.

The description Julie gives her brings something back from earlier in the day. She encountered such a smell herself. Not wanting to alarm Julie, she keeps her thoughts to herself about what she suspects. The new girl in school today had passed by her in class, and she remembers a similar scent from her. But she also remembers how something wasn't quite right with that new girl. Her attention and her stare, while Timothy was talking to her, was intense.

Julie suggests, "We should see if anything is missing from the house."

"No, my father said specifically not to enter the house right now. Wait for the authorities to get here first."

"Well, I am here with you, and you have nothing to fear." Julie clutches Kyra's hand tight.

A few hours later, the last of the local police department officers finish up examining Kyra's family home. A middle-aged officer steps up to question Julie about the suspect in question. All the while, considering what she is saying or not saying. In her statement, she gives a slimmed-down version of the confrontation she had with the masked intruder. The officer explains how it appears nothing of any monetary value is missing from the home, after a thorough inspection.

"It is really odd. Out of all the belongings the Mathews have, nothing was snatched."

Julie agrees with the officer. "I just wish I could be more helpful to you," Julie adds.

"Don't worry, young lady. You have been quite helpful, especially taking on such an intruder the way you did. You know how dangerous that is?"

Julie nods, understanding his concern.

"All that to the side, you may think about going into law enforcement one day."

Julie smiles. "Maybe … just maybe. I know how to handle myself after all."

"Oh, I believe you. By the way, I am Potter, Lieutenant James

Potter. I know very well who you are, Ms. Thompson! I have seen you in action at last year's Young MMA Expo and Competition. My nephew was in it too." He laughs harshly. "He didn't get too far. However, you were in a league of your own. I was beginning to believe you were holding back on the boys. Seeing the backyard, I think I may have been right. Something epic happened back there!"

"Oh, really? I didn't really take too much notice, I guess." She wants to change the subject.

"But don't worry your sweet little head. We'll get to the bottom of this mystery."

"Oh? Hope you do, Lt. Potter!" Julie salutes him.

He salutes her with a slanted smile and says, "We will! I have a good eye for things not normally obvious to others."

Julie feels there is a hidden message within his soft-spoken words. She says nothing but smiles and allows the officers to finish up with, Mr. Mathews. Then she returns to Kyra in her room, where Kyra is steadily picking up all her belongings tossed about the room, and putting them back in their rightful places.

Darkness starts to settle outside of the Mathews' home as Julie and Kyra sit in her room, talking about the day's events. Kyra talks about her adventure with Scott, and Julie mentions a nice guy she met in the library named Adam, who graduated the year before. "You should really meet him. He is a beautiful Native American guy. He is also a fusion martial arts specialist of mixed, Japanize and Native American cultures."

Kyra peps up with excitement. "Sounds amazing. You always did like the worldly guys." She giggles along with Julie.

Seeing no need to hold Julie hostage in her home any longer, Kyra releases her best friend. "Thanks again, Julie! Being on the scene and being my bestie in all of this craziness."

"Sure thing! I will always have your back, K-girl! Just don't get too distracted, our exhibition tournament is coming up fast."

Kyra brushes back the hair from her face. "Can't forget that, thanks again!"

"I just wish your father would let you spar this year. You are amazingly good."

"Me too. But that day will never come with General Dad on guard."

"Agreed!" Julie sighs.

As she is departing, Julie snaps around and says, "Whatever that girl was looking for, your room was the main target. Just be cautious. I think it may be something very unique if someone like her is here to look for it."

Nothing else the house except her bedroom was ransacked. None of the locks were forced open, and it was peculiarly strange how her locked window wasn't forced. It appeared that it had been opened from within. The top-of-the-line security system was never once triggered, which was also very strange. Kyra agrees. She wonders if Julie wasn't overexaggerating her story. Just maybe something freakish and inexplicable is happening.

After watching Julie leave, Mr. Mathews says with a fatherly tone of concern, "Are you sure you are okay, Bumpkin?"

A smile lights up her face. "Wow, Dad. You haven't called me that in like … ages."

He smiles softly. "I know, sweetie. It's only because you are growing up so fast. Even though I see you blossoming into a beautiful young woman, I do worry about you … always."

Kyra smiles while reaching in for a hug. "Believe me, Dad, I get it. I understand. I also appreciate it, even if I don't say it. I will always be glad to be your Bumpkin." The warm smiles and tight hug lasts but a moment but also seems stuck in time. Kyra slowly walks back to her room to inspect her things again. She's still curious about the motives of the intruder.

CHAPTER 14

Pulling into a private gated estate, Jason can't believe the size of Timmy's elegant, old English-styled brick home. The three-story house is very long, and too many windows to count. There's a massive turnabout driveway up to the front entrance of the home. Surely this home has been featured in the Lifestyles of the Rich and Famous. Jason tries to take it all in.

For him, homes like this are only found in films, mostly of romantic tales. He has never visited one, up close and personal such as today. Anxiety suddenly overruns him, with the worry of his inadequate attire. Unfortunately, aware of his own rankness from the sweat, blood, and remnants of urine, has him apprehensive of any chance encounters. His initial instinct is to quantum-speed his butt out of there before anyone has a chance to see or get close enough to smell him.

Realistically, in his current physical state, it wouldn't be advisable. He wouldn't make it past the length of the car they're riding in; Sprinting down the long windy driveway, is virtually impossible, without landing splat on his already bruised face. He doesn't want to give the impression he's a bum or a wuss, in front of the beautiful driver and Timmy. It's clearly obvious in Timothy's observation of Jason, the boy is infatuated with Susan. Jason's wondering eyes, appeared to be most busy on the drive, checking out almost every breathing female along the route home. Jason is a sex hound, for sure, Timothy quickly gathers.

"Seriously, lad? This is your crib, bro?" Jason inquires as he steps clear of the shiny Land Rover limo.

Timothy follows, admiring his cute ass, "Yes, actually. This is my home, and my lab is on the adjacent end of the pool and rock garden. That's where we will be."

Jason doesn't know what to take in first. Everything is larger than life here. Gathering their belongings from the vehicle, Jason takes Timothy's stuff. After all, he can't really carry it himself with his sore arm. Timothy releases Susan as the boys stand before the extra-wide, solid oaked doors.

With no need for keys, the front doors open as they advance. A mature male servant named Mr. Eduard Lee Frank answers the door with smug, English accent. "Good evening, Master Daniels." He eyes the nervous Jason. "Hmmm, it appears Ms. Susan didn't exaggerate about you bringing home a— guest, I see." Mr. Frank's eyes cut harshly at Jason and back to him. "Is everything okay, Master Timothy? Did you injure your arm?" He shoots another wicked eye at Jason, who is badly bruised and beaten too. "Should I contact your—"

"Ah no! Mr. Franks that won't be necessary thank you! I can handle things from this point. Besides, there's no need to worry my mother, over a scuffle at school."

"Oy'!" Jason tries to be supportive even when his ribs hurt. Mr. Franks is obviously holding his distance from Jason.

"Very well then, Mister Daniels."

Timothy and Jason advance their way through the narrow corridor, later filtering into the main atrium of the home. There is a massive skylight far above their heads, letting in much radiant natural sunlight. Mr. Frank clearly detests the strange Mr. Brodie, but he gathers their belongings, nonetheless, bringing them into the house.

"Sir, should I inform Ms. DeVoe you'll be having an afternoon snack for two? In your laboratory, I figure presumably?"

Timothy's squarely caught off guard, by Mr. Frank's statement. Realizing suddenly, Jason is the first house guess ever to visit the home for him and not his mother.

Jason's eyes are in sensory overload by all the spectacular wealth abound. The floors shine brilliantly, like glassed marble. A dueled southern-style staircase lines the outer surrounding atrium walls, leading up to the next level, with an impressive water fountain feature in its central core. The ceilings were at least twenty to thirty feet in height, over the tiering of stairs. Timothy delights in seeing Jason's awe-struck expression.

This was the first time Timothy could see how beautiful his estate truly is—only through Jason's mesmerized eyes. He never gave much thought to his home before, but seeing someone, he adores marveling it, tickles his inner core.

Timothy gently wraps his arm around Jason's waist, helping to escort him slowly through the massive house, while passing servants along the way. Making their way through the massive country-style kitchen, which could be a house within itself, Timmy sees Ms. Eileen DeVoe, the house cook, hard at work preparing in the kitchen. Timothy calls out to her. "Hello, Eileen? I am home."

Turning about to face the boys. Her face shows signs of utter shock, "Oh Dear Lord, Timmy. What on earth happened to you, sweetie?"

It is obvious to Jason, Ms. DeVoe seems to sincerely care for Timothy. Watching her rush to his side to examine his face and arm.

Mr. Frank beeped ahead of you two, saying you were heading

down to the labs, and to bring your snacks down for two. Is this still the plan?"

"Um, Yes ma'am," Timothy answers with sweet tenderness.

Jason witnesses the gentle connection between them, like a mother and child sort of bounding.

Ms. DeVoe, a slightly older African-American woman, with a southerner's drawl in her speech, is pleasing to Jason.

Eileen wipes her hands on her apron, gives the boys a good look over, especially Jason. Seeing this was her first time seeing the new face. She warmly greets him with a beaming smile of southern charm.

"Hello, young Sir. I am Ms. Eileen DeVoe. I handle all the cooking needs of Timothy's family home. It is a delight in seeing another young face in the home."

Taking a further breath to acknowledge the onslaught of bruising's, coupled with the nasty black-eye on Jason's young face.

"Dear Lord! What on earth did you boys get yourselves into? I mean, it is always nice to see a new face, Albeit, by the looks of things, someone didn't seem to agree. Are you boys okay, should I have Mr. Frank call someone?"

A bit hesitant at first, Timothy sees Eileen as a second Mom. He explains, in short, the events of the afternoon… obviously omitting key points in the retelling.

Jason is a bit overwhelmed by the immediate attention. He simply smiles and nods his head, not able to speak on his own since he's so choked up emotionally. When she asks for his name, he can't speak. Timothy chimes in on his behalf, exclaiming his full name. Eileen assures Jason that he is in very the masterful hands of young Timothy. Jason shakes his head in agreeance.

The boys make their way through the kitchen area, Jason leaning hard on Timothy's shorter frame as the crippling pain takes hold.

Finally calmed down enough to speak again, Jason admires Timothy. "Wow, Timmy! You, like have your own staff!" Timothy a little taken by the comment at first. It's never been an issue for him, being surrounded by staff. Not being a big deal for him, he completely understands how different everything must be, in Jason's eyes.

"My parents fought long and hard to get here. They're experts in the fields of science and botany. My father was big in the molecular sciences. He worked alongside the government years ago before he passed. He invented some wickedly amazing things along the way.

My mother, on the other hand, is a chemical photo electro-statics engineer for NASA. She deals with light particles and dark matter in astrophysics. Since both of their jobs were deeply engross-ing, they always had sitters and people looking after me. They were barely home, even for holidays."

Jason takes a seat on a leather bench near the double doors to the pool area. "Wow, that must suck. It looks like you and I aren't so different after all, I guess."

Hearing the pain in Jason's weakening voice, Timothy knows he needs to start treating him as soon as possible. Without any delay, Timothy grabs hold to Jason, anchoring his weight onto himself. Exiting the back of the main house, they step out into the pool area. It's a major surprise to Jason seeing the gorgeous lawns and matching botanical gardens, on either side of the Olympic sized pool, which is already closed for the autumn season.

There are verandas placed all over the lawns and extra water features surrounding the main pool. There's even a heated spa, which is still primed for use, in the nearest veranda. Oddly, one thing perplexes Jason, and that's the location of this supposed Lab. *Where the hell is it?* Jason visually seeks it out.

To the right side of the main house, there's a single-level

bungalow with a cozy front door and two matching windows on either side of the door. The house is slightly bigger than a two-car garage.

"Hey, laddie, this is a cute little crib. Is this your little man cave?"

Timothy smirks. "There we go with the little shit again."

Jason grunts out a laugh, which really aches in his body.

"This is the pool house and covert entrance to our family.'s lab. Just step inside, and you'll see."

Stepping into the well-furnished pool house, Jason sees a quaint space for chilling out with friends and guests. There is a huge couch, a table that converts from a pool table, into an air hockey table. A few pieces of furniture spread throughout the space, giving it a warm, cozy feel, minus any sleeping rooms.

There's a wet bar near the back, a huge Southwestern-themed throw rug on the floor, and a gigantic TV mounted on the wall. There is a mini kitchen separating the two restrooms/dressing rooms, which features standing showers, personal lockers, and dressing areas inside. One is male, and the other is female.

Very confused, Jason looks around. "Dude, don't get me wrong. This is a great little hangout spot and all, but I don't see where you could possibly fit a so-called lab in here … anywhere."

Timothy smiles with childlike joy. "Yeah, I know. This is the pool house. Mom has guests over at times or throws parties for her associates. But the lab is through that door right there." He points to a door behind the couch.

"Oy', is this your way of taking me to a bedroom and having your way with me in my weakened state, Timmy-Lad?" Jason jokes even as his ribs torment him.

Realizing it's only a smartass joke, Timothy subconsciously wonders, *how much of it, is a joke*?

"You would like—Having someone else do all the work,

wouldn't you?" Timothy walks over to the phone on the wall, picks up the receiver, and presses the buttons as if making a call. Then he hangs the phone up without saying a word. Jason is stumped by the useless act of a meaningless call. Timothy grins and assists Jason through the door. There are two long tracks on the right and left side walls and a floor-to-ceiling mirror on the opposing wall of the entrance. Timothy closes the door behind them and locks it. Jason questions Timothy's motives. The room goes instantly dark.

Instantly startled by the sudden unexpected darkness, "What the fuck, Timmy?!" Jason exclaims questioningly.

Timothy grips tight to his waist in supporting comfort to him. Suddenly, A beam of light, comes through the mirror, to scan them with green laser spliced beams. Jason feels a little claustrophobic because of the tight space and all the security measures, as Timothy can feel his trembling. After the initial scan, all is quiet.

"Now what?" Jason whispers.

"Just hold tight, Jason. It's okay." Timothy replies with confident secureness.

"Dude, if we get any tighter, I'd be inside of you, man."

The room suddenly feels like it is moving downward, and a light illuminates the outer rim of the small room.

"What the blimey hell?" Jason grabs hold of Timothy, not caring if he appears weak.

"Don't worry, big guy. You're safe. I promise. It's only an elevator to the labs down below."

Jason catches the word labs, the plural. The labs must be seriously deep underground since the trip takes some needed time to descend.

When the unit stops, the light in the closet turns green, and the mirror wall slides to the side in one complete panel. After his eyes adjust, Jason is completely enamored by what he sees.

Stepping slowly from the elevator, Jason witnesses the most

miraculous sight. Before him is an open space about the size of a football field. It's filled with high-tech mainframes, workstations, and multiple doors throughout the space. It truly is a full-scale laboratory.

Making their way through the open bay area, which only makes him question just how far underground they really are, Jason peeks in one lab with standing capsule and a bodysuit of some sort on a mannequin. Many corridors seem to reach on forever. Many electronic doors line the walls along the way.

Even though they're underground, it appears there's between a good thirty to forty-foot ceiling. They can't even, see the roof. Motion sensor lights activate as they advance inward. Before Jason could say anything, a little white, metallic orb on a wire zips quickly toward them, a single green light in the center. It stops directly in front of them.

"Afternoon, young Master Daniels. Glad to see you are home."

"Thanks, Marc. It's good to be home."

A little gun shy, hearing the automated voice, Jason inquires, "Who's … Marc? Where is the bloke? Is he in one of these lab rooms, somewhere?"

Realizing how strange everything must truly look to Jason, Timothy takes the time to explains things out a bit.

"Sorry, Jason. I should have really prepared you for the lab. Marc! Marc isn't a person, it's a synthetic AI my father developed and built years ago!"

"AI?" Inquires Jason, with a raised brow.

"Yes— Artificial Intelligence, a computer construct. Truly amazing tech, and very state of the art. His name is a breakdown of his functions. He is the multifunctional automated robotic care unit. Marc for short."

"Oy, that's clever."

"Thanks. He helps me out a lot around the lab. Hey, Marc? Can you prep my biomedical lab for a full horizontal scan and anatomical analysis?"

"Why of course, Master Daniel. Is this for you or for your frightened friend? Both of you appear to require some medical attention."

"Hey, ye wee ball thingy! I am not frightened! And my name is Jason, Jason Brodie." Jason tries to convey his dominance.

"Oh, my apologies, young Mr. Brodie."

"Yeah, that's better." Jason feels a victory in his own little way.

Timothy tries not to giggle. Seeing Jason so worked up is hilarious.

"Yes, Marc, we both require the use of one. I need the showers turned to sterilizing cleanse mode." Marc zooms onward to another section of the lab, leaving the boys standing alone. Timothy grabs a rolling chair for Jason, while Jason is trying to balance himself awkwardly, hating his body for not regenerating like it's supposed to.

"Whoa! Did you send the robot thingy to prepare a—? Sterilize? Is this safe, Timmy?" He swallows hard. "I mean, is it going to be painful? (Jason cups his genitals) … the whole being sterilized thing. Are we going to be able to have children and shit, afterward?"

Settling Jason into the mobile chair unit, Timothy tries to contain his giggles. "Um, Wow! Didn't know you felt like that. There is no pain, I promise. You can shit, just the way you always do. As for us having future children—That's something new to science. Your sperm mixed with mine? I don't rightfully see that being remotely supportive of offspring, I'm afraid. (Timothy says with a straight expressionless face) but, it's sweet of you to think our friendship may go so far as to reproduce, little Timo-son's and Jas-othy's."

Jason unthinkably becomes bashful, to Timothy's odd delight.

Timothy gets back to seriousness. "The shower will do nothing to interfere with you physically. It's only a process to stave off, unwanted bacteria and germs."

Jason is relieved and ticked at the same time, for Timothy's latent wittiness.

"Oh, funny little bloke, aren't you? Little prick." Both boys get a good chuckle. Albeit, with the bantering, Jason feels more at ease now.

Timmy's biomedical lab displays flora and fauna of all types, maintained behind tall glass doors. "After your shower, you can put this robe on and come and lay in the biobed over there." He points to a white futuristic unit much like a tanning bed.

"Oh, wow. Is that safe? You said something about scanning me. Is it radioactive?"

Timothy smiles. He knows what is concerning him. "No, it's completely harmless. It is not intrusive at all, and you don't have to worry about your ability to produce offspring later in life."

Jason takes a quick look at his crotch and back towards Timothy, "Oh – That's good to know, Bro! So, me banger is safe, Aye?"

"You mean –– Your junks?"

Jason gives a boyish smirk. "Aye! Me banger." He gestures to his crotch.

With a grimacing stare, Timothy thinks back to the time Jason said *how he had seen his banger* during their playful banter.

CHAPTER 15

"Something wrong, bro. You look a little sheepish." Jason observes Timmy's sudden withdrawal.

Timothy quickly snaps back to reality. "Uh-no, nothing! Sorry. I just need you to remove your clothing…" his voice came across, cold and unattached.

"So we can prep for the full-body scan, needed to assess your injuries." He continued.

Jason turns bright red with embarrassment, "Oh, you mean … down to me bare bum right here in front of you. I thought you might have seen enough of me when Craig pulled my shorts down?"

"No, no … crazy. You are going to take a shower first and then meet back here to do the scan. You will undress in there."

With a dumbfounded look, Jason nods and says, "Oh, right! Forgot the shower part."

"Come on, hurry it along. Put your dirty close over on the table. Just leave your shorts on and head through that door. Remove your shorts, take your cleansing shower, and put the robe on before you come out." Jason complies with Timothy's directions. Slowly and cautiously, he eases himself into the inviting shower of neon blue light and hot, steamy streams of flowing water cascading down. Jason can feel that there's something special about the shower. He likes the privacy of it all. The flashbacks of Craig assaulting him haunt his innermost thoughts.

Jason wraps the robe around him and steps into the room with Timothy.

"Oy, that shower be amazing, Yo!"

Timothy stares at the dripping beauty before him.

"Thanks to my father designing that one. It's a prototype of the one used in the space shuttle program."

"Cool, Yo. Your father was a genius, Lad."

"Yeah, he was." Timothy sighs in remembrance.

Jason feels he needs to help his buddy out. "You know ... don't worry what those jerks were saying about your junk. They were just tools." Timothy looks around, not wanting to make direct eye contact. "It's nothing. I am used to it. I am a slow bloomer, my mom says."

"Please. I don't think so, me lad. Look, I'm not in the habit of checking out dudes. Girls, boobies, and bottoms, on the other hand, I will graciously look at all day long. But if ya feeling down on ye self because of the sausage log you carrying, don't, bro."

Timothy looks Jason directly in the eye. "Yeah?"

"Oy, little man, ye be packing some real thunder down in your undics, bro. Kinda girthy for a stout. lad. Any bloke would be jealous of your Willie Wonka! I count myself. Mine too stringy."

Embarrassed, Timothy questions what brought this conversation up. "So ... no peach fuzz, aye? Who gives a fuck?"

"Seriously, lad? Girls don't! The only blokes who worry about another bloke's grass patch are the insecure ones. You know the lassies like their lads free of tumbleweeds too? Having their men smooth down there makes it slippery fun for them too ... and less pungent. I often wish I was smooth below, but I'm too afraid to trim down there. Too many horror stories."

"Whoa!" Timothy is completely shocked by the direction of the conversation. "I've always been off about people seeing me … naked, especially jocks like you."

"Dude, stop with this sitting in your own shit, Aye? You are handsome as fuck. You have that perfect puppy dog face that girls adore. Between you and me, your body is totally hot, bro. The one who should be embarrassed is me. I was such a wuss that I went and pissed me own freaking undies in front of your cutie friend, Kyra. I don't think she noticed, but what the fuck, dude? What bloke does that shit? It was a really embarrassing moment."

Timothy places a finger under his chin. "I mean, wow! Life is so over, Dude. You have to end it all now!" Timothy's little sarcastic rant is so straight-laced that Jason must do a double-take to confirm that he is really joking.

Loving dry, witty humor, Jason gingerly taps Timothy's good arm. "That's all behind me now, right, buddy?"

Timothy pushes the line and smirks. "I thought I smelled some-thing a little off in the limo, but I didn't want to embarrass you in front of my amazingly cute, twenty-eight-year-old, chauffeur."

"Oh, shit! Please tell me it wasn't that noticeable, Dude? Please tell me she couldn't smell anything."

Timothy loves seeing the panic before him, and he smiles. "Don't worry, big guy. You had to be really close to smell anything, and besides, if she did, she is totally professional."

With a huge sigh of relief, Jason starts. "Way too close, Lad. I had to dump my skivvy's in the boys' leu, at the school, hoping to clean me-self. But I heard a crashing sound, and wanted to check it out."

Timothy envisioning the whole scene turns to Jason grinning. "Hmmm, that would have been something to see. The poor unlucky guy who could have stumbled in there. What an eyeful that would have been, seeing your butt cheeks, with your leg heisted up, trying to air-dry your hairy balls, with the automatic blowers." He can't contain the humor in it any longer and starts laughing out.

Jason chuckles along with him. Timothy turns his back to Jason for privacy. "Don't worry, Jason. I will leave the room to give you your privacy so that you can disrobe and climb into the scanning bed, okay?"

Jason grabs the robe and wraps it tightly around him. Jason's heart aches as he looks at Timothy's unclean back. He remembers exactly what the little guy went through.

"How do you want me to lay on the bed again, me Lad?"

"On your stomach is fine—if you don't want me to see ... your stuff. You know, your banger."

"Oy', Roger that! Someone must close the lid, don't they? You'll be forced to see my naked bum again?"

"I will promise not to look. After the scan, I will clean and dress your visible wounds. Just tell me when you are in the unit, okay?"

With a deep breath, Jason painfully removes the robe, allowing it to fall to the floor around his feet. Completely naked, Jason trembles from head to toe, for fear of what he is about to do, in showing Timothy how he feels about him.

"Okay Timmy," he says with uncertainty, as his voice cracks. "I am ... ready."

"You're completely safe here. Don't worry Jason, I will be very professional."

"I am sure of nothing else, me Lad!" Jason replies. Timothy turns slowly around only to see Jason totally naked before him. Exposed and very vulnerable, Timothy doesn't know what to say or do, for he's unable to look away. To Timothy, Jason is the most beautiful creature in the world.

Dropping his tablet, cracking it hard on the floor, Timothy flinches to its sound.

A single tear rolls down Jason's soft pale cheeks and plops onto his slightly hairy chest. Timothy wants to run away but finds it impossible to do so.

"Please don't be mad, Timmy." Jason pleads with a sorrowful voice, seeing the fear in Timothy's expression.

"W-w-why did you tell me you were ready?" Timothy's voice trembles. "W-Why are you standing there ... naked and crying, Jason?" Seeing Jason's tears devastates Timothy more than Jason could ever know.

A really awkward silence passes between them.

Jason studies Timothy's reaction. "I want to share me-self with—someone who means the most to me in the world, Timmy. You have shared ye-self with me completely, not holding back anything. You have shown and shared so much of your world with me, and I have nothing in return but—stupid humor, bad language, and possibly my body. I could be wrong about the last one, but you seem to like it, for whatever reason. I am not sure why exactly. Just don't be mad at me if you aren't."

Timothy is frozen, speechless, jaw still dropped.

"Never in my life have I ever been completely vulnerable to someone, not even the monster Craig. I will give you my spirit and my body if you deem it worthy. This is my way of letting you know just how much I trust you, Timothy Daniels. You are the smartest, wittiest, and the most courageously loving guy I have ever known."

Timothy does not look away from Jason's eyes, out of fear. His heart pounds like a jackhammer breaking through concrete. He wants to examine every inch of the perfect male specimen before him, but he refuses to give into such a demented longing.

"But why the tears, Jason?" Timothy asks with a heavy heart. "You don't cry!"

Jason tries to stop the tears from falling, but can't.

"Timmy, you are the only person I will allow to see me like this. Not even the girls I've been with, have seen me naked. I'm ashamed of this (he pauses, and slowly points to his chest) …body, because unlike everyone else in my life, you are the only one who truly gave a shit about me. You have such an amazing heart. I mean fuck, Timmy! You treat me like someone special or even important to be around. God knows, I am not. I know you probably never meant to see my disgustingly bruised-up junk, like this. See how you are too repulsed to even look at them? I just felt I owed you something. Exposing me-self to my new kinsman and brother in life is my one true honor."

Timothy wants to cry, for his powerful hero, is sacrificing his own vanity for him.

"If there is any part of you Timmy, wanting to ever see a lad's willy, don't be afraid. Step on up. You can touch it however you want. My body is yours, dearest brother. I am in your wonderful care. You can examine me any and every way you like. I won't hate or judge you. If you feel there is something here for you to love, then it's yours."

"I don't need to f'ing touch you, Jason! (Timmy's voice is sharply elevated) You don't owe me a f'ing thing, especially your innocence. God knows I can't help but to see your; long, slender, veiny, uncut shaft, Jason!"

"See? I knew you admired me. That's why I had to know. I sought you out to see how true it was."

He raises his arms slightly, revealing the little red bush of hair under his muscular arms. Timothy slowly looks and marvels at the crinkly follicles nesting in Jason's deep pits. He can see Jason's perky nipples and his quarter-sized pink areolas and the light rings of ginger hair surrounding each of them. Timmy follows the freckles along his developed pecs.

Jason is amazed, watching Timothy marvel over each section of his body. Timothy inhales deeply with each look. The deep purple bruising all over Jason's ribs and torso compel him to touch them gently with the tips of his fingers. Timothy continues to follow the thin, prickly trail of hair follicles down through Jason's tight rippled abdominals, to his deep inset navel. Crowning the bushy pubes at Jason's pelvic area, his eyes and fingers play in the thick entanglement of dark gingery wool.

Jason moans, out of desire and fear. Never, would he allow another boy to touch him in such a way, especially without gloves.

Looking onward, Jason hears Timothy slightly whimper as he views Jason's healthy male package only a breath away from his own lips. Timothy examines the badly bruised phallus. He notice's Jason's testicles dangle much lower than his eight-inch shaft. He sees a healthy uncut phallus with a slight curve to the left. With each look at the bruises, Timothy hates Craig with a passion. Timothy continues a thorough examination of each part of Jason.

Timothy is amazed by Jason's sheer beauty, even with so much damage. He is overwhelmed that Jason is willingly allowing him to touch him so intimately with his bare fingers. "I can't believe he did this to you, Jason. What a fucking bastard!"

Jason is so scared. He starts trembling. He feels Timothy's fingers gently pushing inside of him. He's applying a slow and gentle approach, far different than Craig's. Timothy is feeling along the ridges of Jason's prostate to see if there is any damage. Jason holds nothing from Timothy. He slowly bends forward, leaning on the scanning bed. Timothy's slips his naked finger deep into the warm orifice. The musky, surprisingly sweet aroma of Jason's ass is intoxicating and fascinating to Timothy. One part of Timothy is telling him to stop, but he can't. He digs in deeper because Jason is allowing him to do so. Suddenly, Jason begins to grunt and moan as Timothy's fingers examine the inner lining of Jason's anus.

Timothy knows that this is clearly a violation of Jason's trust in him and their new friendship. Nobody should ever see their friend's private area unless they are romantically involved. Timothy hears Jason's whimper and feels torn.

"Please, Jason. That's enough. You really shouldn't have done this. It's not fucking right. You allowed me to violate you. What kind of friend am I?"

Jason hears Timothy's broken voice. Shaken, he stands erect, but he's still unable to look at him. "I'm so sorry if I offended you."

Timothy shakes his head. "No, I am not offended, Jason. I shouldn't be allowed to see your body like this ... or touch you like I did. Although you are built like a demi-god— you're a scared kid too. I can easily forget this, with your deep voice and your amazingly mature body. This is very irresponsible of me. You should be protected from perversions such as me. I know you aren't gay! I see, your sphincter opening has never been probed before. I can't help having the immoral feelings I have for you, and I really don't want to lose your friendship, over my weakness."

Jason turned to face Timothy with a renewed sense of confidence.

"All I know—I saw your face when they explained the shower scene in the hallway and how completely vulnerable you looked. I thought it was only fair to share something intimate with you so that you wouldn't feel alone in your vulnerable moments. Plus, I saw something in your eyes when you saw Craig sticking his grubby fingers deep inside me, repeatedly. I saw—love, your love for me."

Timothy's eyes open wide with fear and hinted joy. "Why? You don't owe me anything such as this, Jason."

"Yes, I did. You held such compassion for me – when others would have run for their own safety. Look, I don't know and don't give a shit if you are homosexual, trans, pan, or any other crap name they have out there. I am here for you, Timmy. You've proved yourself by being my brother, unlike anyone else in my life. I will not hide anything from you. If you feel any pleasure in examining, me? Then touch me. I will forever respect you. We're kinsmen for life. My heart and blood are yours, Timothy Daniels. You can't be violated by someone you unconditionally love. I'm willing to allow you to do whatever you want. I am your friend, companion, and whatever you want me to be, as I hope you are mine. Only if you're willing to accept me as yours."

Timothy wipes his tears from his face. Jason steps closer to him. "Timothy? A bloke or not, you are the closest and sweetest person I have ever had the privilege of allowing into my heart and body. You have really touched my heart, and believe me, I have had my share of beautiful flowers in my life." Timothy looks down at Jason's throbbing cock dancing.

Jason blushes as Timothy studies his growing erection. He holds Timothy's eyes up to his own. "Bro, it is all yours if you want it. No questions asked. I really don't mind. You honor me with your touches, Timmy." He shakes it and makes it dance for him as it stiffens. It slaps his own stomach.

"I couldn't. It's so wrong." Timothy is too shy. Jason takes hold of Timothy's functioning hand and wraps it firmly around his lengthy shaft. Jason's cock is very warm and full in his small palm. Jason meets Timothy's eyes, and like gravity, their faces embrace with Jason firmly pressing his mouth to 'n against Timothy's tender lips.

Jason forced his talented tongue into Timothy's receptive mouth. He continues by slipping his long fingers deep into the waistband of Timothy's loose shorts. Fondling, groping and squeezing, Jason explores Timothy's ample male genitals, while maintaining their tongue party with each other.

Emotionally and physically, the boys were becoming one. Timothy strokes Jason's rigid pole, to Jason's horny enjoyment. Having no perceivable knowledge where any of this is going, Jason doesn't care anymore. Gay, bi-sexual, pan-sexual, he doesn't care. All he wants is what's right there in front of him.

An ear-piercing crash of metal slams hard on the desk, a few feet from Jason's hairy ass. Startled out of his skin, and utterly confused, Jason instinctively springs around. Unaware of his state of undress. With Timothy tight behind him, Jason's full erection is on grand display. The bewitched stunned look on Ms. Eileen's face sends chills through Jason's body. So scared, Jason forgets to cover his animated fully aroused penis from Eileen's line of sight. Not understanding why he is doing it, Jason raises his arms in the air, as if under arrest. Seeing where Eileen's eyes are probing, Timothy switch places with Jason, using his body as a shield between Eileen and his beloved Jason, as protection.

Unfortunately, for Timothy, his loose shorts only revealed, he too was sprouting an aroused tent. Ms. Eileen never would have thought she would witness such an intimate affair. With steady calmness in her motherly tone, "Timothy, as requested, your food is ready. You can leave the dishes in the entrance Lab when you are finished. I advise you to not let it get too cold. I won't be bothering—you boys anymore tonight." She gives Jason a sharp eye as she walks out the lab.

"Fuck, Fuck, Fuck!" Jason shouts, both shaken and very frightened.

Mortified, Timothy takes control and tells the hysterical Jason to calm down and get on the scanning bed. Jason now can truly relate to Timothy's prior traumatic situation, dealing with the shower incident. Not much was mentioned between them as Timothy completed the scans and rubbed a special herbal solution on Jason's visible wounds and sores. The meal was quiet and very awkward, afterward.

CHAPTER 16

Kyra can't seem to stay asleep. The events of the previous day continue to haunt her. She remembers Timothy with Jason, both traumatized physically and mentally. Scott Tanner took her home and asked her out after she missed the bus. To top things off, a mysterious burglar attempted to rob her home. What was really going on? Is the world spiraling out of control? If Scott's information is correct, Madame Levette may be the very person to talk to. Kyra senses something is coming, and not in a good way.

Every time she glances at the clock on her nightstand, she sees only twenty to thirty minutes have transpired, which is driving her bonkers.

I wish I knew what is going on with me, she thinks. Her room is eerily quiet except for the ominous tick of her alarm clock. The darkness of the room is broken by soft afterglows of the moon shimmering in the sheer veil of her lacey window dressing, casting gentle shadows on her walls.

In the utter silence, she hears fumbling coming from her closet. She's quite startled, and her vivid imagination runs rampant. *Maybe it's another baby squirrel who managed to sneak in through the window earlier.* She slowly pushes her sheets to the side and calmly slips into her soft plush slippers on the side of her bed. Gathering courage, she reaches over and clicks on her nightstand lamp. Because of the pink transparent piece of fabric resting on top of the small lamp, a rosy hue of light floods the room.

"Hello?" she quietly calls out. She fears it is only her imagination playing a cruel trick on her, and she doesn't want to wake everyone in the house for no reason. After hearing, yet another thump from her dark closet, taking no chances, Kyra nimbly snatches one of the shiny Sai (a single blade like martial art weapon) from the wall-mounted sheath. She twirls the sharp weapon with great precision and skill in her hand. She takes hold of the metal doorknob to her closet. Taking a deep breath, she grips the handle tight and flings the door wide open. Kyra's heart skips a beat, expecting the worst creature known to man to leap forward from the dark abyss.

To her great relief, there's no such assailant or one-eyed slithering beast maliciously waiting in the closet. Kyra takes a much-needed breath just before she hears another faint thump in the back of the shadowy room. Wherever the noise is coming from, it sounds like it's in a box. She cautiously steps deeper into the closet and starts rummaging through her many belongings. Some are hers. Others are her mother's, sister's, or grandmothers from her father's side.

Okay, I need to clean this death trap of a closet one day soon.

She halts when her eyes catch something very peculiar. There is a green glow arising from a pile of her great-grandmother's old hat boxes, deep underneath the collection of shoe boxes. Digging her way through, she finds a hat box that's heavier than the others.

With excited wonder, she removes the lid, which hasn't been opened in years. Kyra had hopes of seeing one of her great grandmother's fancy hats inside. A bit miffed to spy, no hat was inside the box. Rather there's a hand-carved, Gaelic-patterned box. Maybe a box for knickknacks?

Kyra's great-grandma was known to have many superstitious treasure boxes, full of wonders. That's what she at least told her children, who later passes it down to their own children. Unfortunately, Kyra's immediate family aren't so versed in the ways of her great-grandmother's Celtic traditions of mysticism. Thanks, in part to Kyra's mother's strong-willed beliefs in simple reasoning and the practical sciences.

Upon further inspecting, a sliver of green light slips through the little box's crevices, cutting into the darkness of the confined space. Kyra is extremely curious about what can be emitting light from inside, which has been nestled in the back of this closet for more than fifty years?

Wow, this gives a whole new meaning to the slogan ever life-batteries, she contemplates the idea of how a battery could maintain a charge after so many years. Wanting so desperately to believe there is a spark of magic, in a world that's so overwhelmingly mundane, Kyra opens the small box with great hopefulness, to see something amazing.

To her sudden dismay, whatever was glowing inside stopped immediately the moment she unlocked the clasp, to open the huge box. Slowly combing through the smaller objects within, something peculiar catches her eye—her grandmother's antique keepsake box. Kyra's eyes widened with hopefulness. Its outer facade is covered with dark wood and velvet-like pattern. It has such intricate detail for such a small piece that's about the width of a deck of cards.

"How did you ever get in there, tiny one?" she says while examining the smaller box. She distinctly remembers seeing the little palm-sized box, once many years ago. She thought her mother had put it in another box, her great-grandmother once owned, up in the big attic. With curiosity, Kyra reaches over to open it, remembering how her grandmother so loved all the special unique boxes, in her collection. Shaking the box, she hears something bobble within, a fond thought rushes to her, *there's something locked away inside this little box! But What?*

"What are you hiding, tiny mystery box?" Kyra questioned with suspicion.

With no warning, a sudden green spark of light ignites her fingertips with a shocking jolt. "Ouch! How strange. What the—!" she exclaimed, examining the small box.

"Hey! What gives? Shocking me isn't a good start to our friendship, tiny one. Why are you such a bad little box? I just want to see what's inside." Very surprisingly to Kyra, precisely at that moment, the box unhinges itself and slightly cracks open, presenting a mysterious green glow, as if it was meant for her to discover.

Unsure of what to make of the glow in the box, she tries once more to open the top, praying she is not electrocuted anymore. This time without any resistance, she can touch the box and open the top. *Hurray!* she silently cheers. Peeking inside, she sees a dusty antique medallion. It appears very old, and there's strange writing, all around it. It's quite tarnished with a moldy green stain. She's no longer fearful but rather impressed with the find. The medallion has a little weight in her hand. Now she is eager to clean it and have a better look at it. Taking the item out the closet and into her bathroom, she thoroughly clears the gunk off.

The metal is brilliant, and it appears to be real gold. Its shine is eye-catching, and she can't find any flaws. Scrubbing and scrubbing away, Kyra cleans it as if possessed. Once finished, she marvels at its simplistic beauty. It's not too big and not too small. Rather the piece is just right for her taste. Suddenly, she notices a slit along the side edge. "What?" she says, examining more closely. "Are you a locket? If you are, you are a big one. A locket medallion?" Unable to pry it open, she yawns and then says, "Oh, well. Maybe in the morning."

She talks in a voice imitating Sméagol from *Lord of the Rings*, saying, "My precious." The medallion may be holding a picture of her great-grandmother Allaura or another special person.

Kyra places the charm on her nightstand before she turns over. She can feel her sleep coming on strong. Meanwhile, in the middle of the night, the medallion starts to jiggle and opens, revealing a brilliantly bright green light throughout the room. There's a green stone inside its inner chamber, and without any warning, a pulse emits throughout her room.

In the interim of that night, Timmy works diligently with Jason. "Dude, what was that machine you had me in. It was so freaky. Like some sort of alien tech."

Timothy smiles, "Well, it is definitely different, I assure you. But it's not alien, or at least I don't think it is." He giggles with a snort. "It was a particle accelerator and inducer scanner with nanite technology. It helps mend tissue and microscopic fibers in your body at a molecular level. But I have to say. You are an amazing healer in your own right, Mr. Brodie. I've never seen body regeneration happen so quickly before. Your surface scars are basically gone already, and some of your deep bruises are already regaining their natural pigmentations, especially your soft scrotum tissue."

Jason tries not to laugh because of the pain, but he flashes his exposed genitalia. Timothy just blushes. Jason explains, "I guess I should have mentioned that sooner. It's sort of a side effect of my speed. I tend to heal just as quick. Sprained ankles, torn ligaments, and things like that usually heal in a day's time. However, after meeting your friend Kyra, something weird happened, something not normal."

"Weird? In what way?"

"I felt drained suddenly. It's hard to put into words. When we tried to shake hands, it felt like some serious static electricity.

Which was funny at the time, but then the second time, it was all cool. Then shit happened."

"What do you mean?" Timothy inquires.

"Something came over me like a tidal wave, making me feel nauseous and jittery. It's what made me pee myself. But I guess it all sort of worked out, allowing me to slow down for once, which gave me a chance to chat with you for a few enlightening seconds. that put me in the position of being in the school when I'm normally outside. I wouldn't have been there during … you know."

"Yeah, I will never forget, believe me. Do you think the people from the YOC will miss you? We haven't sent any word to them about your situation or your progress."

"I don't believe so." Suddenly, he shakes his head while raking his fingers through his hair. "Oy, Lad, fudge sticks!" he suddenly blurts.

"Something wrong? You hurting? I didn't mean to—"

"No, you are as gentle as a wee lamb, little bro. It's just … I know Scott. And he's surely going to want to check up on me, after all this shit. The bloke actually cares, which is so odd for a high school hero these days."

Timothy smiles. "I can see why. Who couldn't care about you?"

"No, Timmy, don't go there, little bro. No sweet talking. We promised. Just patching and mending, remember?"

"I remember."

"Good, cause I got to be getting back to me running soon, you know?"

Timothy nods with agreeance. "I'll inform the Y.O.C. you'll be staying with us, for a week or so, at the least."

Jason's eyes widen, as his face pales more than it already is. "Say what, little bro? What about your moms? And that cook lady, Ms. DeVoe? She saw all my— (gesturing to his crotch-bulge) I was fully erect and shit bro? Not to mention my tongue down her sweet little Timmy's throat? She must be hating the very likes of me, right now!"

Understanding Jason's concern, Timmy halts his worry. "Don't worry about Eileen. She won't say anything. She's not that type of woman. I do feel a big lecture coming in the morning for sure. But she is more of a protective mom type. My mom won't mind you staying with us for a while if I tell her you are a good friend in need. She will be amazingly thrilled, me having a living and breathing friend period. The closest thing to a friend I have is Kyra! ...and she has never been to my home or seen my lab."

"Or your special instrument, I bet. (pointing to Timmy's male package) Dude, your place is wicked, much like you Laddie. Kyra would go crazy in this bitch, dude!"

"Hey, what did you just say about that kind of talk, flash-boy!"

"Oh! My bad, Doc!" Jason wants to rile Timothy and flashes his flaccid Willie at Timmy once more. He loves seeing Timothy blush. "By the way, you planning on being, you know! A doctor when you get older, Lad?"

Timmy looks at one of the many lab doors. "Actually, I am hoping to do a lot more than just that. I want to make a difference one day and not just try to catch up."

"Cool, but I think you should at least check your wee chubby first. It's been poking at me for a while now, Timmy."

Timothy didn't realize he has fully aroused yet again, and he quickly covers himself.

"Why you covering up? I told you it's cool with me."

"No, actually, it's not. I know you're straight Jason, and oddly, I am meant to be as well. I obviously can't control myself around you for reasons I can't understand. It's not fair to be this way to you, especially since I'm your friend and the feeling isn't mutual."

"Well, don't worry so much. We have a great start to a friend-ship. I am feeling much better, and you made this pure hetero boy uncharacteristically crazy about you as well. As far as bangers go, you are the only bloke I wouldn't mind seeing naked and bobbing around."

Timothy blushes. "Thanks, I guess. You have always been my private admiration because of your muscular build and exertion on the track."

"I know, Timmy. I always kinda knew, I guess. If you ever want to see my meat and potatoes, don't ever be shy." He opens his robe and reveals his manhood, but this time he keeps it open for him. "They are yours. I don't mind." Timothy looks down with a surprise and sees something amazing. Jason looks at Timothy smiling at his exposed genitals.

Timothy firmly grabs Jason's body part, pulling it up and down to get a good look at his testicles. He is throttling his male organ. He uses his other hand to massage and examines his testicles quite thoroughly, and unintentionally, he arouses Jason with the movements of his warm, soft hands stroking him.

"Hey, what are you doing, Timmy?" Jason says and whimpers.

"This is incredible, your scrotum is completely clear of all its bruising. You are completely healed." Jason is unable to speak. Timothy acutely notices Jason's hairy orbs start to retract inside himself. Before Timothy can question this response, he witnesses Jason climaxing right there.

Scared and hyper-nervous, Timothy's never saw a man, or in this case, a boy, project sexual fluids before, except in educational media. The thick flow of creamy white fluid spurted freely.

"Oh, my God! I am so sorry, Jason. I didn't mean to—"

Jason covers his face in utter shame, totally mortified for being so easily aroused by Timothy touch.

What the fuck? is all Jason can think.

Timothy tells him to stay put while he runs to get a clean towel from the closet. Jason can't help but look at the beautiful boy with great admiration. Timothy starts cleaning Jason with such passion like his favorite toy, which makes it worse, for Jason's sensitivity is much too elevated. Each swipe sends tingling shock waves throughout his body. Jason begs him to stop.

Nervously, Timothy stops. Not knowing what to do, as he sees the glow in Jason's eyes for him. Jason's unconditional love from Timothy, makes him blissfully ponder, *Fuck! Maybe Timothy is exactly what I've wanted all along.*

An hour later Timothy makes a comfortable spot for Jason, in one of the lab's overnight rooms, that his father would use while working on a project that he couldn't get away from, and needed to sleep in the lab. Once settled in comfortably, Jason is handed a remote from Timothy. "This is for the TV." Timothy explains, and hands a smaller remote to him, "In case you need anything, don't hesitate to alert the main house with this remote."

Jason appears stunned, at the room and the readiness for the situation they were in.

"There is a button that will beep my bedroom, it is number three. Just hit that one, and I can talk to you directly. The TV is all yours, and if you should happen to want or need me for anything, just buzz."

Jason has never been so nurtured, or seriously looked after with such overwhelming compassion before. Excluding Mrs. Prescott and Scott, for whom show concerning care, but not quite to this level.

With childlike joy, as if learning there is a Santa Claus, Jason's tries to control his elated emotions. With sparkled eyes of wonder, Jason grins to Timmy, "Seriously, Lad! This is incredible. This room is sweeter than any other place I've ever had to shack up in. It feels so homie in here."

"Yeah, it was something my dad wanted to have down here, to keep him sanely human. By the way, there is plenty of food in the lab's pantry station. There's a fridge and a microwave if you should get hungry later. Eileen likes to know I have plenty to eat when working down here alone."

"Thanks, Timmy, for everything."

"No problem! Goodnight, Jason." Timothy replies, but almost wanted to slip, *I love you*, at the end.

"Night, Timmy-boy." Jason too, wanting to express more than a simple goodnight but retains his feelings.

Timothy shuts the door of the room behind him, giving Jason privacy. Jason whispers to himself, with his head up toward the ceiling, which ironically has a standard nine-foot ceiling.

"Damn Timmy. Fuck! Why did you have to be a f'ing bloke, Laddie? I think I have falling' for you, kid."

CHAPTER 17

The morning brings energy for Kyra. To her surprise, her siblings aren't in any mood to bother her. She quickly readies herself for school, excited to see the handsome jock of her dreams, Scott. She prays it wasn't all a weird dream after all. When she's fully dressed, Kyra glances over to her nightstand and sees the medallion next to her clock. She grabs it and runs down the stairs to show her mother the exquisite piece, which was slightly bigger than a silver dollar.

Her mother was surprised. "Oh my, I haven't seen that in years. My mother would always keep it hidden and away. But it looks great. Just needs the right chain to hang on, I think." Her mother looks through her own jewelry stash and finds a simple gold chain.

"Perfect!" she exclaims. "This is just right for a medallion piece." She takes the chain over to Kyra. "Here! Put this on it. And you can wear it everywhere. It is so suited for you, hun."

Like a child on Christmas day, Kyra says, "Thanks, Mom. It's beautiful. You sure you don't mind me wearing this chain or this medallion."

"Honey, they are both yours. That piece is calling your name sweetie! By the way, that's one of my older chains."

Kyra weaves the chain through the medallion's clasps and places it around her neck. She is amazed by its dazzling sparkle, but she feels in her heart that the medallion is like an old friend who has come home.

"Well, I am out of here. I feel this may be an awesome day." The family says their goodbyes as they each go their own directions. Kyra feels her freedom as her punishment is lifted. She takes her sporty 2015 Ford Edge out of the garage and drives to school.

Minutes earlier at the Daniels' estate, Timothy's mom is typing on her palmtop while seated at the far side of the white granite kitchen island. She is casually sipping a tall glass of freshly squeezed orange juice. Ms. DeVoe is busy assembling and moving about the kitchen. She preps and plates Timothy's breakfast—two poached eggs, blueberry waffles, a strip of turkey bacon, which is his favorite, and a small bowl of mixed grapes with a half-cut orange. A short glass of chocolate milk on the side of the plate completes the meal.

Timothy enters the kitchen in stealthy silence. However, Eileen still sees the fear on his face after last night's fiasco. Before he can ease his way out of the kitchen, Ms. Daniels speaks up without raising her head as she does quite often, "Hello, Son. I see you are up and ready this morning."

Timothy responds without taking his eyes off Eileen, "Oh-yes Mom! Morning."

"Honey, I won't be home until very late tomorrow night. There is a very important briefing with a couple of the three- and four-star general's tomorrow afternoon, and I will have to be in town overnight. But I am scheduled to leave for a week in the California Flats."

"Oh, really?"

"Yes- dear. I'm truly sorry about the timing honey. I'm quite aware tomorrow is your birthday sweetie. I will make it up to you this weekend, will that be alright?"

"There is no need to make a big fuss about it Mom. Honestly? It's just another day."

His mother stops what she is doing to give him her undivided attention. Removing her reading glasses, she gazes deep into her son's eyes.

"Mr. Timothy Lawrence Daniels! There is no such thing as this, being just another day? That's malarkey! You're turning sixteen, and soon to be a young man. I adore you deeply, Honey."

"Thanks, Mom. I know you do, even when I am not worth the fuss."

Ms. Daniels gives him a sharp eye. "Now-now my son! Things will get better, I assure you. You will meet many wondrous people, who will make you feel good and wanted, baby. It's tough right now, I get this. You are at a very awkward stage in your developing life, it shall pass. And as for the girl's, it will happen and believe me, they will find you most adorable." She pushes her glasses back, "By the way, your young houseguest is up and stirring this morning."

"Huh?" A dumbfounded Timothy perks.

"Sweetheart, Eileen has told me all about it. It truly amazes me how sweet and caring you are toward others." Timothy's face turns pale as a ghost.

"Everything?" Timothy makes direct eye contact with Eileen and finds it hard to read her expression.

"Why yes! Of course, sweetie. She informed me how you were helping the sweet young man after he stood up for you after school. Seeing he was unable to get treatment, due to his living situation, you decided to look after him. Which I think is a very mature thing to do, and enduringly sweet of you Baby. Are you and this young man good friends at school?"

With a loss for words, Timothy shrugs his shoulders. "Um—"

An awkward silence follows, as mom's impatience's starts to surface.

"Well, is he honey?" His mother wants some clarity from him.

Eileen turns from him to continue her work in the kitchen, allowing Timothy to speak freely. "Um —Yes, he is. He is a really great guy."

"Aw, that is great, dear. Was that so hard for you to admit? Really, I was starting to worry you weren't going to have any friends before you graduated. If he treats you right, that's all that matters. By the way, Eileen took a plate to him earlier before you woke up. She says he's looking much better." Timothy looks to Eileen with amazement. Knowing how disastrous everything could have turned this morning If Eileen were to say something.

"Your friend is welcome to stay as long as he needs to, baby." Said Timothy's mother.

"Mom! I'm not a baby anymore." Timothy exclaims after she calls him baby.

Ms. Daniels smiles, as a mother who is realizing her little boy is growing up.

"You're Right! I do expect to meet this young man when I return! (giving a stern pointing to Timothy) If you think he needs to stay, he's more than welcome to stay in the guest room beside your bedroom, he shouldn't be all alone in the labs by himself. Ms. Eileen says the poor thing didn't get much sleep last night. It might be a bit scary down there all alone, okay sweetie?"

"Um, sure thing, Mom!" Timothy looks to Eileen, but she doesn't say anything. "Thank you, Mom. I will let him know."

"What is his name?"

"Huh-who?"

"What is up with you this morning, sweetie? You are not quite all here with me, are you? What is your friend's name?"

"Oh-right! His name is Jason Brodie. He is a sophomore like

me but loves running with a great passion. He should be on our school's track team! He has to be one of the fastest runners in the region for sure."

"Hmm, he certainly has a nice strong name. Anyway, with you watching over him, I am fairly certain he will be sprinting in no time." She closes her laptop and relates to Eileen she's about to head out, and asked her to be sure to re-dress his loose sling before he leaves out.

"Oh, Eileen, be sure to have Mr. Frank contact the school to make an appointment for me next week. Somethings need to be addressed. I will not tolerate any kind of bullying, while my son is trying to get his education and be someone important one day."

Eileen notably nods, understanding a mother's plight of protecting her young.

Meanwhile, Timothy parishes any thoughts of saying anything in contrast to his mother's unwavering intentions, when it's his safety involved. Watching his mother step out of the kitchen, Timothy slowly sits at the table, confused about where he stands with Ms. Eileen now. She sees the confusion in Timothy and sits next to him. "Why do you look so nervous, boy? Did you think I would do something to hurt you like telling your mother what I walked in on?" Tears start forming in his eyes, and she cuffs a gentle hand on his shoulder.

Sitting next to him, Eileen starts, "Honey, I care deeply about you. Like one of my own. I know how you struggle with your feelings and being around unfamiliar people. I don't judge you, and it is not my place to do so. I only want you to be safe, in your explorations.

I know you may be confused and maybe scared. This may be normal adolescent curiosity or experimentation. You don't need to explain it to me. I don't need to get in-depth about — Him, you, or last night.

However, I feel the need to warn you, baby. Some boys are curious until it gets serious. You just remember that, when you progress."

"Is that what you think this is?" Timothy thinking long and hard about her words.

"Baby ... I don't know what it is, you two are sharing right now. When examining your handsome young friend this morning, I took a good hard look."

Timothy looks up into her dark brown eyes. "What did you see, Ms. Eileen?"

"The boy doesn't show any signs, of a boy in the life."

This was a new terminology to Timothy, *In the life?* Timothy had to question it.

"In the life? Well, it was a term used not too many years back, for young people, who were considered, alternatives to the contemporary mainstream way of living. They were mostly homosexuals, who were mostly closeted or on the DL circuit. DL is short for the Down low, mostly men pretending to be straight by day and on the gay scene at night. This was hidden from regular society."

Timothy gets an education, he never thought he would get with waffles and bacon on a plate.

"Now, I can be wrong. Yet, I will admit, there is a little something off about him. I didn't see any of the tendencies I'm familiar with. Your friend appears straight as an arrow. Which may also be his true nature. I don't want you getting hurt if he should choose to return to the life he's designed for."

A solitary tear drops from Timothy's face. "He is straight, I am very sure of it. I never thought otherwise. However, something happened yesterday. He connected with me in a way, I really wasn't ready —" Unable to finish the thought, he redirects, "My heart hurts, Ms. Eileen! I don't want what we shared yesterday, to be nothing more than a false read."

Brushing his hair with her fingertips, Eileen releases a chunk of air as if exhaling an invisible cigarette.

"I couldn't help but see last night, how connected you two were. Much like you, he was very sheepish, which is something I don't believe he is used to being. I think he is questioning a lot of things within himself. He may be too frightened to pursue the newest revelation in his life; You! So, proceed with great caution."

"Do you think I'm … in the life? Like others have suggested to me recently?"

Eileen's eyes widen, with shock. "Really, someone said this to you? (Timothy nods) … (she paused) Look, I never once thought of you in any sort of way, but the loving young boy I watched grow up, struggling with his own emotions; reeling from the loss of his father.

I guiltily thought you were going to be a loner-type. Someone void of any sexual desire. What they often call; Asexuals! Now, as for last night? That, my little friend, doesn't automatically constitute anything and doesn't make you a sworn-in member of rainbow pride. Even if you find out you are? Don't be afraid. You are not alone. Mr. Timothy, you have people who care deeply about you and will always love you. Except for Mr. Frank, of course, I think he missed the compassion line, in his construction stages."

"Huh? Is that even possible? Being something and never know, what you really are?" Timothy's tears stop, and he is intrigued by the conversation.

Eileen then says, "Answer this, young master. Have you ever had these feelings toward any other boys in particular?" Timothy shakes his head no with confidence. "Oh, okay. How about girls?"

Timothy ponders for a moment and flusters, "There's one, I find amazing and beautiful. I admire her with wonderment, daily. Now thinking closely about it, boys have never been overly appealing to me, until Jason."

"Well … there may lay your answer. You may just be a sensitive boy who is affectionate for another boy, gay or straight. Some call this feeling pansexual. He may be experiencing the same attraction and affection for you, which is a rarity indeed. So, don't question or label it, too fast. Get to know more first and go from there. Okay, honey?"

"Yes, ma'am."

"Good. Now go tell the handsome little friend of yours good morning. I got some work to do!" Eileen plucks the tip of his nose, making her chuckle. This, in turn, makes Timothy ease-up and giggle.

"You're Jason's friend, has been worrying himself to death down there. Make your visit a short one, tho! Ms. Sarah will be waiting for you! You'd best be getting to school on time, young master. I'm going to inform Mr. Frank's to alert Ms. Sarah, and relay your mother's instructions for him and the school."

Timothy swallows hard, in the mere mentioning of his mother meeting with the principle, over the horrid events of yesterday, isn't settling well in his gut.

"You need not worry about Mr. Gingerbread down there. I'll keep a close eye out, while you're in school. Plus, making sure he keeps his clothes on; this time!"

"Thanks, Ms. Eileen. You're the best." Timothy launches from the table not finishing his meal. He gives Eileen a loving embrace and dashes out toward the lab.

Eileen shakes her head. "The kids today and their silly labels. But I do hope Master Timothy thinks long and hard before doing anything too serious, especially in the way Mr. Ginger is packaged down there." She smiles wickedly.

CHAPTER 18

A few hours into the school day, Kyra advances through halls toward her English class. Meanwhile from the opposite direction, Scott struts with a pack. As their paths interact, each eying each other. The world seems to come to a complete stop in time. While engaged with his clustering, Scott smiles a secret language only Kyra has the key to decode. Scott can't pull his eyes away from her luring beauty.

Unable to stave off any longer, Scott casually breaks free from his little pack. His desertion leaves the others totally perplexed. Making his advance in Kyra's direction, she sees this and does likewise. Soon, standing face-to-face, they stare intensely. "Wow, Ms. Kyra. You are even prettier than when I last saw you."

Blushingly Kyra responds, "Thank you. You are always amazing to the eye, Mr. Scott."

His face flushes over. "Hey, you didn't happen to see my buddy Jason or your friend Timothy this morning, have you?"

Kyra shakes her head. "No, not yet. I have Timothy in my next class, AP Biology, then onto Chemistry."

"Wow! The brain trust thingy between the two of you must be amazing. Two science classes, backing each other?"

Kyra grins and retorts a witty response. "Well, because were aliens, from Planet Zaltari! ...Silly human." Yet, couldn't help but chuckle afterward.

Meanwhile, Tiffany while traveling with Trish, sees Scott and Kyra talking openly in the hall and comes to an immediate halt. Trish unaware of Tiffany's sudden stop, slams into her back, which annoys her to no end. Turning abruptly, Tiffany strikes Trish's shoulder for not watching where she was going. While Trish is admitting her fault, Tiffany Observes Scott and Kyra's emitted sexual tension. Ruffling feathers, Tiffany practically blows a major gasket.

First, she grunts and flips her hair. "Oh, my God! I know ... I am not seeing what I am seeing ... yet again!" Tiffany's voice rings with a deep fury at a level that alarms even Trish, who is smacking her gum frantically.

Trish starts, "Oh, are you referring to Scott and the cute brunette again? It looks like they're becoming an—"

"Hush! I say!" Tiffany cuts her off harshly, not wanting to hear how Kyra and Scott are becoming an Item.

"I am just saying, you may be too late, boss lady."

"No way is this shit going to happen, on my watch! I am the head Captain of the Squad! It's my freaking right to be the beautifully adorned queen at his side for homecoming and the prom! Not some unknown nerdy loser princess!"

Trish supporting her BFF. "Yeah, your right. He should have known his place in the scheme of things. Quarterbacks are the sole property of the head cheerleader, no questions asked."

"Exactly! The natural order of freaking high school."

Slicing her way, determinately through the crowd of swarming students, like a sharp knife cutting through a moist piece of chocolate cake. Tiffany struts her way over to Scott and Kyra, parking herself just behind Scott. Taking an extra second to straighten herself up, Tiffany taps Scott's shoulder.

"Hey, Tanner-hun!" the air is charged with adversely sexual intensity, from Tiffany, "Can't wait to see all of you at the rally tomorrow night! Mmm! (licking her lips) You truly bring the heat to our Dueling Dragons, Scott-babe! Just don't forget to bring that super-hot bod tomorrow." While talking, Trish watched as Tiffany ran her fingertips along the crease of Scott's butt cheeks and proceeded with giving his bottom a little sportsman tap, which makes him flinch nervously.

Making a primal predator stare at Kyra, as if daring her to cross-A-line, blinks her eyes and moves on, with Trish, in close ranks behind her.

Too embarrassed for words, Scott appeared confused by the sudden sleazy attention from Tiffany. Not really understanding Tiffany's plot, Kyra is left riddled with confusion, irritation, and anger, toward Tiffany. She's quite aware, the whole seduction sideshow scene was purely meant for her visual acknowledgment. Tiffany, being like the proverbial dog, attempting to mark Scott for her own personal territory.

"What the—?" jolts Kyra, as she gasps at the boldness of Tiffany's rudeness.

"I-I... (shrugging his shoulder) feel so violated right now. God! Tiffany is spiraling on the deep side—. (shaking his head in disbelief) The girl has gone totally cray-cray!"

With her lips scrunched to one side, "Can't argue with that assessment!" Kyra chimed. Scott, blowing it off, reaches in and gives Kyra a gentle peck on the cheek. "You are all I care about Kyra. You are the flame that keeps my soul warm."

Kyra glows. Saying a prolonged goodbye to each other, they gradually go their separate ways.

Advanced biology class has a few minutes before starting, and in strolls Timothy, a little earlier than normal, wearing his arm in a clothed sling.

Kyra's pleased to see him come to school, especially after the mess from the day before. She notices from a distance how well his busted lip has healed after only one night.

"Why, hello Mr. Daniels? You are a bit earlier than normal." Says Mrs. Bridget, while peering over the brim of her glasses at him.

Timothy drops his gear on the workstation. He's in a daze-like funk, with only one thing on his mind, or should say one person. Hearing his name being mentioned again, he finally snaps out of it. "Oh! Yes, Mrs. Bridget! I got to school a bit tardy and was too late for the prior class, so I came straight here."

"Oh, I see. I hope all is well. It's rare to hear you missed any of your classes. Is everything okay?"

Then he blurts out, "Oh, he is doing great!"

A startled Mrs. Bridget perks up. "Excuse me. What was that?" The teacher tries to clarify, "He? He who?"

Timothy quickly realizes that he needs to get his head back in the game and quick. "Oh, I said something? I meant to say that everything is great, ma'am. Just overslept this morning. That's all."

Mrs. Bridget senses something's a little different. "Oh, alright then-" she responds, lifting an eyebrow.

Timothy sighs and sits patiently for the class to begin. Still caught in a daydream-like haze, Timmy recalls his earlier talk with Jason before coming to school. Jason was inexplicably excited to see him, this morning, like a puppy to its master's return. He gave Jason a good once over, which proved, the boy is healing exponentially faster than normal.

Eileen had given him so much food, he couldn't eat it all even with his enormous appetite. Jason told him about the improvement in his breathing. However comfortable, he couldn't get much sleep, like his mother mentioned, Jason was shy at first to admit, he was a little scared being alone. Timothy could sympathize, for it took him some time to be able to stay overnight in the labs.

They made no mention of the intimate nature of the night before. Neither one was ready to go there so soon anyway. Timothy lost all track of time, and Ms. Eileen had to force him to leave. She couldn't help but laugh at the way the two were so happy together. Something she hasn't seen in Timothy for the past six or seven years—a true sense of emotions.

Kyra sits beside him and can't help but see the pure wonder on his face. He's clearly in la-la land.

"Hey, Timmy, you okay there, buddy?"

The sound of Kyra's voice quickly breaks his train of thought. "Oh—" he paused, "Um, yeah! fine."

Kyra senses something new about him. It's as if there's an invisible glow about him. "I am glad you're okay. You're looking good this morning. Have you seen or heard from, Jason?"

He blushes hard, immediately. "Uh, Jason … yeah! He is fine, checked in with him this morning."

Kyra can't get past the sudden shift in Timothy's personality. *Is there a spark of emotion in Timmy's expression? Why doesn't he sound like Robot Timothy today?* Kyra observes with open eyes and sites a little nervous energy in his right leg. "Do you feel up to telling me what happened yesterday, or is it too soon?"

"I-I really don't want to— not that I don't trust you, Kyra. It's still kinda raw. I hope you don't mind?"

"Of course not! Just know, I am always here for you."

"Thanks. Means more than you know. Maybe someday soon, once things settle?"

"You bet."

The conversation's feeling a little off, so Kyra tries to shift the direction slightly. With excitement, she leans in and says, "I just want to tell you how odd it is that both of us met Jason yesterday. And we found out that he and Scott are good friends. I never saw him before yesterday. How about you?"

"Who? Jason?" Timothy is intrigued. Kyra nods.

"Oh, I never met him personally, but I have known about him for a bit—really since he was new to the school before summer break."

"Oh, I see. That may explain why I've never seen him before." Timothy nods. "Plus, he's my class level."

"Well, it's an odd thing how I just happen to accidentally slam into Jason yesterday. Ironically, I was a major klutz yesterday. I somehow managed to bump into both him and Scott at different points of the afternoon. It wasn't my best day. After a minute with Jason, I quickly deduced that Mr. Brodie is quite the charmer of women, I must say. He knows exactly what to say to cheer you up and cajole you at the same time."

"You can say that again!" Timothy whispers under his breath.

"Huh? Did you say something?" Kyra asks, not sure what he just mumbled.

"Um, no. I didn't say anything, but ... do continue." His words stumble slightly.

"Oh, okay, sure thing." Kyra knows he said something, but it's clear he doesn't want to repeat it. After she regathers her thoughts, she says, "That boy is surely going to be a force to be reckoned with at Franklin High. I can see him breaking many hearts. If he hasn't already snagged a few already. That little player has ... game." Kyra can see Timmy's uneasiness as he fidgets with his hands. She continues, "I just hope he is okay and safe. Maybe it would be good if someone special looked at him. With his macho ego, he will tell himself he can handle anything you throw at him and will never back down to anyone or anything."

"I know, right? Such a freaking pain sometimes with all that posturing."

Kyra snaps her head around in shock. "So … you have heard from him since yesterday, I take it? I know Scott would love to hear that. He has been looking for him all morning. He's been worried sick because of his injuries. How is your arm holding up? Rude of me not to ask."

Timothy looks down to his arm and back to Kyra and shrugs. "Meh!" he mutters, but he gives the appearance of wanting to talk about something way more interesting.

"Kyra?"

"Yes, Timmy, what's on your mind?"

Timothy takes a much-needed deep breath and starts. "You can inform Scott, Jason is doing just fine. Better than fine, actually."

Kyra is elated by the news and exclaims so, to him.

"He is being watched and looked after. But please don't tell anyone else about yesterday." She nods, but she replies in a whisper, "Okay, but sounds kinda cryptic, especially for you, hun. What's happening?"

Timothy is comfortable with Kyra enough to simply confide in her. She is the only true friend to him. "Jason is at my house. I am taking care of his injuries in my personal lab. I didn't want him going home alone with no medical attention."

Timothy is playing doctor with a strange boy he just met. He's at a place she hasn't been invited to, even though they've known each other for a couple of years. "That's pretty awesome of you. I know he is in good hands with your knowledge of medicine." Timothy simply smiles.

"So, I take it you guys must have bonded like Scott said you probably would?"

"Hmm—?" Timmy takes an interest in her subtle words.

Allowing a stranger into your home, never fully knowing them, is a bit risky? Kyra thinking to herself, but immediately she is drawn back to Timothy's journal.

"You can say we bonded. I never met anyone quite like Jason before. He intrigues me." Timothy agrees with Scott's assessment of Jason and his bonding. Far be it from him. Timothy can't help, remembering much beauty Jason possessed, from the first time he has ever laid eyes on the boy.

"So, you two really hit it off ... after Scott, and I left?"

Seeing the sweat collecting on Timothy's brow, Kyra senses there's far more to this story of Jason and Timothy. Noticing the heaviness in Timothy's thoughts, Kyra's curiosity too starts to grow and tries to ease his stress, with an assessment of her own.

"Try not to worry so much, Timmy. Jason seems like a great guy, with a great heart. He's a tender soul if ever I saw one." She smirks, reminiscing her first encounter with the boy on the field. She continued. "I think you two will make good friends. Your personalities complement each other so well. One can only hope for the best with any new relationship." Timothy gives her a bewildered eye.

"The boy can be a pain sometimes, so much a lone wolf, type."

"And, your point?"

"Kyra, I just said he is a pain ... sometimes."

"And, other times?"

"He's— (Timothy becomes coy) I don't know! I guess—" Timothy withdraws.

"Special ... maybe? Something completely unexpected ... possibly?" Kyra digs into his psyche.

"Huh? You know we are talking about a sweaty, athletic, jock for brains guy, right?"

"And your point, again? How do you honestly feel about this, Jason? Speak from your heart, and not your head."

She finds it utterly delightful and heartwarming to see the once lifeless child Timothy really cutting loose with such natural joy for once. She wittingly observes the classmates peering at them too. For the first time in the two years of having Timothy as a student, she finds herself in a uniquely rare position. She has a reputation as the crackdown queen amongst the teaching staff, but Timothy is the only child she has never had the privilege of verbally correcting in her class for any reason. With a secret joy, she realizes she can give him something that will make him one of the regular kids.

Almost having second thoughts, Mrs. Bridget just loves seeing him laughing. "Okay! Look here, you two giddy boxes, Mr. Timothy Daniels, and your sidekick, Kyra Mathews. That's quite enough commotion from the likes of you two. If that isn't something you want to share with the rest of your miscreant peers, then I deeply suggest you two pipe it down! Get ready to possibly learn something!"

The class becomes dead silent as they stare at Kyra and Timothy. Suddenly, the entire class burst out in joyous voices and clapping. Timothy's name can be heard chanted out with honor. Finally doing something wrong gives him a sudden hero-like status. Timothy is downright shocked by the cry of acceptance and acknowledges the reason for the teacher's actions. He nods a symbolic, thank-you. Mrs. Bridget gives a secretive wink in response before calming the class down for the actual class start.

CHAPTER 19

During fourth mods, AP Chemistry class tends to be a little dull and uneventful for, Kyra and Timothy. They're still very chummy after their last mod, with Mrs. Bridget. Knowing the type of elements in the class, they choose to keep it basic, less attention. Just before the second bell, mysteriously the back of the room appears to be extremely quieter than normal. It was rather peculiar indeed the avoidance of slapstick humor, taunts, and theatrics, from the infamous bully-boys, Jake and Ben. Neither one is wanting to be noticed by anyone, especially while wearing their dark shades.

For once, everything appears normal in the room—until the new girl Cheryl, steps into the classroom. She is covered in melancholy and with less flair, than the first time she came into the room. Kyra scrutinizes her this time around. The first thing catching her eye is the nude-toned bandaging under the sheer hosiery, on Cheryl's outer thigh.

Strike one! Kyra mentally keeps score.

When the new girl moves past her lab table, she gets a clear whiff of her scent, which Julie described the evening before.

Strike freaking two! Can this attitude freak show, be the one who broke into my home and went through my crap? For what possible freaking purpose? Kyra desperately needing resolution.

As Cheryl resides in her seat, she appears to be avoiding Kyra in every way, not giving any attention to her. This makes Kyra very suspicious of Cheryl now, adding to her mental list.

Strike three bitch! Utter freaking guilt. Kyra feeling confidently convinced, Cheryl is her man, or should say Cat! Cat-burglar!

The teacher demands Jake and Ben to remove their shades while in the classroom, which makes her break her concentration over, Cheryl. Rather reluctantly along with a series of inaudible grumbles, they do as the teacher instructed. Suddenly, a mighty storm of ooh's turns the room of mean laughter into an inferno of vengeful joy.

Kyra and Timothy are simultaneously shocked when they look back behind and see how both guys are sporting ugly black eyes. Jake reluctantly makes eye contact with Timothy as he shows signs of humiliation and remorse, and he quickly shies away. There's nowhere to hide from the mockery of the class.

Even for Timothy, this was not acceptable. "Who would do that to them?" Kyra says, completely dismayed. Timothy wouldn't think something like that could happen to them, especially because of him. Kyra senses something wrong. "Timmy, what's wrong?"

Timothy stands with such a heavy heart, and peers at the boys. Overwhelmed with guilt. "I'm so sorry, guys!" Timothy, exclaims and runs out the room. Jake and Ben are stunned by Timothy's action, leaving Kyra and the class utterly confused by his remark and abrupt departure. Kyra asks the subbing teacher if she can go after him. Before the sub can respond, Jake says he got it and charges out of the room.

Ben yells out, "What the fuck, Jake?" The teacher scorns Ben for cursing out loud in the class and then allows Kyra to go after them.

Several corridors away, Kyra sees Jake standing over Timothy, who is sitting on the floor against the water cooler, his head deep between his knees. Just as she is about to walk up to him, Jake looks at her and demands that she stands back. Kyra doesn't know what to think or say at this moment, but she watches him cautiously. "Don't you … hurt him?" With a wicked eye, Kyra lips her words so Jake can read them clearly.

Jake squints his brow. "I promise I won't!" he mouths with heartfelt expression.

Jake takes a knee in front of him. "Hey, little man, you okay? You don't have to be sorry about anything." Timothy shakes his head. Jake realizes just how young Timothy is to the rest of the seniors in class now. "Look, bro. I am mainly responsible for the shit that happens to me. You have nothing to do with it."

Under his breath, unable to lift his head to look him in the eye, Timothy says, "How can you say that? I know who did that to you. And I know it's because of me. Isn't it?"

"Dude, Eric and his boys are total nutcases at best. But this time Eric was right to do this to Ben and me, even if Ben doesn't think so."

Timothy raises his head. "What do you mean? I am not following you."

"Well, Ben and I were total douche bags yesterday to you and, Kyra. We often play and joke around too much. But sometimes things can go too far like, yesterday. Having the guys go jock on you went way too wrong, from what I understand. Craig, by the way, was expelled from school for what he did to you."

Timothy's eyes light up like fireworks. He doesn't want Kyra overhearing, Jake. "Shhhh! Don't. Please … don't!"

Jake notices Timothy's fear as he looks at the anxious, Kyra. It is apparent to him that Kyra is trying to overhear their conversation from afar, trying to acquire the reasoning behind Timothy's fear.

"Dude, my bad. I didn't know that shit would go down like that! Please, you must believe me, man. Eric told me the number he did to you and Brodie, and I think Jason is a super cool dude for sure.

After Eric took out his frustration on Ben and me for our part in it all, I know we totally deserved it, bro. And we are men enough to say we deserved it."

"No! Not right! First Jason and now the two of you? All getting hurt because of me. Why me? I am no one, to get hurt over!" The crack in Timothy's voice sounds like trumpets clashing in Jakes' ear. *This kid wasn't emotionless, he is nothing but seeping with emotions, we broke him.* Jake tries to rationalize.

Putting a gentle hand on Timothy's slumped shoulder, Jakes softens his tone. "Don't look at it that way, Timothy. Ben and I have learned a true lesson about bullying. We both vowed never to bully again, and that being the god's truth, Timothy."

Timothy stares into Jakes sorrowful eyes, Jake sees the hurt in Timothy, tries to lighten the moment. "See! I knew you were a real boy and not the robot everyone tries to say. You got so much heart in that small body of yours. You even care about two jerks such as Ben and myself. Even after the hell, you were put through yesterday. You show us the true definition of being a real man and what two dumbass dicks like us are. Kyra was completely right all along. You're twice the man, either of us ever was. So, don't sweat it. What went down yesterday is history, and we never have to bring it up to you ever again. I will have your back whenever you need it. Got it? Please, no more worries, Dude!"

He still finds it hard to believe how sincere Jake is, but he thanks him, for being cool with him.

"It's cool. Now wipe your tears, bro. Kyra is right over their worried sick about you. Can't have someone that pretty see you like this, right?"

Timothy nods with a smile. "You bet." Jake tussles Timothy's curly locks, helps him clean his face with his hands and then helps him up to his feet.

With Timothy nestled tightly under his right arm, Jake escorts him over to Kyra. Puzzled, Kyra asks if everything is okay. Jake explains to her that everything is cool now and that Timothy is an amazing, dude. Kyra almost can't believe how compassionate Jake is being. *This is shaping out to be an exemplary day*, Kyra thinks and smiles.

Timothy takes another moment to gather himself. The three returned to their class as, new friends. And no one dared to question anything, not even Kyra, who is still curious about her young curly friend.

The remainder of the class proves to be rather calm. Cheryl stands in the classroom doorway and looks at Kyra with such intensity as to blow her up with the sheer power of her mind. Kyra sees her as she's chatting with Timothy and another very talkative student whose is trying to convince her to register for the homecoming and prom queen elections.

Kyra, on the other hand, doesn't quite feel the excitement of it all. Nevertheless, she does feel a unique intenseness from afar. Casually scoping out her surroundings, she sees Cheryl's cutting stare aimed directly at her. Oddly, it's the same look Cheryl gave to her the day before when she fell gravely ill. But today something is very different. She feels nothing but good. Actually, she finds Cheryl's menacing stare somewhat amusing and starts giggling.

Cheryl's stare turns from intense to disbelief. She looks as if something has gone awry. She truly expected something awful to happen, but somehow the crisis was averted. Not liking the situation, Cheryl quickly departs. Kyra smirks.

Strike four! Your goose is cooked, Ms. Crazy! Kyra taking victory in her mind.

Later in the day, Julie meets up with Kyra in the cafeteria just before the end of lunch. They quickly catch up on the events of the day and update each other on their new suspicions about Cheryl. Julie can't keep her eyes off of Kyra's new medallion, as she compliments her on its beauty.

Kyra tells her how she found it the night prior, how she cleaned it, and how it felt like something that truly belonged to her. While chatting, she starts feeling the odd sensation she experienced with Jason on their first encounter. But this time, it's like her head is tingling with energy. A boy walks near them, and suddenly, Kyra instantly sees him dropping the cup off his tray in front of them. And just like that, she was suddenly back, looking at Julie, who's now holding her head as if she has a headache. Before Kyra can ask if she is okay, she sees the exact boy walk up to them, and as soon as he is about to pass, his cup flips off his tray and almost lands on Julie's head. However, with lightning-fast speed, Kyra snatches the cup in mid-air.

"Oh wow! You have wicked cool reflexes!" the boy blurts out with sheer excitement.

Meanwhile, in disbelief, Julie says, "Thanks!" The boy apologizes to Julie for almost spilling red soda all over her.

"Yeah, girlfriend, that is amazing, seriously! Damn! Didn't know you could move like that."

"You and me both! I don't know what just happened. It was like I knew it was going to happen already. How is your head by the way?"

"No worries. Whatever it was, its passed now. Very strange though." Julie contemplates the timing of her headache and the draining sensation. She never knew Kyra could use a chi-power, or at least, it's what she believes it may be. But there was that evening when she helped the chemistry teacher and his wife. *Very strange*, she thinks.

Julie wants to change the subject quickly. "So ... are you or aren't you going to the Harvest Fair with Mr. Wonderful?"

"I told him—"

"Yes, listening!"

"Hmm, I told him I would."

"All right! Yes, yes, yes."

"Okay, already! We shall see. All right?"

Julie pumps her fist in the air. "You go, girl. My main girl, Kyra, is taking the varsity QB to the fair! Woot woot, holla!"

Right then Kyra wishes she had something extremely heavy to throw at her friend for making such an unwarranted scene. "J-girl, you are so like, cray-cray!"

With a huge grin, Julie places a finger to her own chin. "Hmm, not as much as your highness, who swore she was not going to make a scene in high school. The same girl who said she's not going to be a participant in superficial, meaningless, stereotypical bios of the standard populace. Dare I remind her, Miss All-Around Wonder Girl? Can't get any more intense than this, babe."

Kyra covers her face. "It's not like that, and you know it."

"Well, let's say this, babe. When Cinderella is asked to slip on the glass slipper only to find out it is a perfect fit, what do you think is going to happen around here? Worlds will collide. Stars will explode, and the villagers will run a marathon of murkiness."

"Julie, you always loved the theatrical. You have way too much imagination in that bobblehead of yours."

Julie whispers, "Okay, Momma-K, we'll see. We'll see."

Trish, Tiffany's eyes and ears of the establishment, overhears the ending of their conversation dealing with Scott, taking Kyra to the Harvest Fair. Trish immediately goes to warn Tiffany of the news.

"Oh, Kyra? Don't forget that our qualifiers are this weekend for the martial art exhibition. My partner sounds shaky now. I didn't want the added pressure of a new routine at the last unthinkable minute, you know? Yet, I will be paired this year with unknown challengers, competing in the weapons division for the master class level."

"Well, you already know with your mad elitist skills that the competition had best beware."

"That's the thing. I am not allowed to show my true skills in showy venues, only my mastery set skills. So, no temple magic."

"Aw, that's a shame really! I would love to see their faces when you do the wild things you do."

"Hey, our secret, remember?"

"How can I forget? Oh, great, and powerful Shira-Kami."

Julie looks at her and gives an honorable bow. "It is true. You know me all too well, young butterfly. We shall commence in due time after school."

Kyra responds with a gentle giggle. "Yes, most honorable friend and warrior. It has been planned, and it shall come to pass." They both strike out with laughter and playfulness.

Just before they depart, Julie taps her on the shoulder and says, "Don't worry about the Cheryl girl. I will look into it for you." Kyra feels some relief, knowing Julie is taking everything seriously.

CHAPTER 20

Much later on that very same afternoon before the scrimmage, Eric is cleaning out his personal gear from the football team lockers. Scott just happens to be gathering the equipment roster for the coach when he hears a sound coming from the locker room and checks it out. Rather curious, Scott creeps around the rows of lockers and comes out behind Eric.

"Eric, what are you doing, man? The scrimmage isn't for a bit."

Hearing Scott's voice startles him. He doesn't want to see Scott's disappointment for him. Eric doesn't say anything but just continues his task of packing. Edging up close, Scott looks over Eric's back and sees him packing instead of gearing up. "What's going on? Don't you have Mr. Lee this period?"

With a solemn tone, Eric finally responds, "Hey, Scott. I am not going today."

Scott doesn't understand why Eric hasn't turned to face him. He reaches for his shoulder. "Is everything okay?"

Eric flinches surprisingly hard from Scott's touch. Abruptly, when Eric turns around, Scott stumbles back with a startled gasp. Eric's butchered face shocks him. His eyes are nearly swollen shut and completely blackened. Eric's cheeks, forehead, and lips are ravaged with cuts and wounds. Black and blue everywhere, his face is almost unrecognizable.

"What the—" Scott exclaims in extreme shock

Eric quickly interrupts him before he can swear, "Hey, it's nothing, man. Just leave it alone, please."

"Nothing? Dude, your face looks like it's been through a freaking meat grinder!" Having very mixed emotions, Scott tries to deal with the knowledge of Eric's hand, in what transpired to Jason and Timothy. Nonetheless, Scott can't find it in himself to approve whatever actions have occurred to Eric physically because of his involvement. Scott doesn't believe, violence can be solved with violence.

Eric continues folding his gear into his tote bag. "It's nothing more than what I deserve, I guess."

Scott doesn't like the short answer. "Deserve? You have to come a little better than that, Eric."

"Look, I know you're only pretending to give a crap. Especially knowing the shit that went down between Jason, his little buddy, and the three of us. I can't blame you for, wanting to put more dents in my skull."

"That's low, Bro! You are damn straight! I am freaking pissed off with the three of you. But I don't go around pretending anything! I see your shit is all jacked! So yes, I do give a shit. I'm not perfect, so don't get it twisted. I honestly wanted to snap each of your freaking necks, the way you left those two. No one deserves the humiliation they got."

Eric nods. "It still fucking haunts me, Scott!" Eric smashes his fist into the locker behind him.

Scott, stunned by Eric's anger within himself, backs down and calmly asked what happened to him exactly.

Eric tries to calm his own breathing. "I went to the coach, and we went to the counselor's office to explain the whole ordeal, except for naming the boys in question."

Scott seems impressed that Eric would willingly do such an act, knowing full well what he would be sacrificing.

"I couldn't honestly punish those boys any more than they have been! Setting off unnecessary rumors and shit throughout the school."

"I feel you there!" Listening intently, Scott replied.

"No one! Needs shit like that, following them. Especially two great guys like those two young kids. I mean, the way they had each other's backs, man… was fucking unbelievable!"

Scott inquires further, "So what went down with you and the coach?"

Tilting his head to the floor for a moment, Eric looks to Scott and tells him how the coach pulled Craig and Carlos to the side, at the beginning of school. Later, he was retrieved to join them. The coach questioned Carlos and Craig separately, and later he was put in the same room with them.

"I could see Carlos was scared. He was nearly shitting bricks. Craig kept his eye on me the entire time, silent as crap. When the coach and the counselor came in the room with us, school security came in too. Coach and Craig had words about his violent actions towards the unnamed classmen yesterday."

Scott perks with interest.

"Craig, just lost it, man. Craig's voice was venomous and vulgar and fueled with the deepest rage. Coach told him he was going to be stricken from his playing status immediately."

"I know that didn't go well." Scott expressing his understanding.

"Craig flipped out and thrashed the desk and furniture in the administrator's office, yelling about how he wasn't a pervert. He eyed me dead-on, suspecting I was the one who ratted him out." In a full-on rage, he was cursing and blaming me for reporting him.

He lunged over the desk, started whaling on my face, the side of my head, and my throat. He kicked me in the kidneys with his hard-ass metal-tipped boots after I fell out of the chair. He was all over me. I couldn't see or hear shit. I felt my fucking teeth crack. Coach and Carlos had to use all their strength to pull his fat ass off me. He was foaming at the mouth like a crazed animal. All the while, yelling for them to let him go. I have no doubt, Craig was going to kill me. It was fucking crazy. It was a freaking nightmare!"

Scott noticeably studies Eric's body twitching, meaning he was suffering mental trauma from the incident. Eric continues regardless of his tremor, "The counselor called in the big blue, who were evidently close by. At which point, I was weaving in and out of consciousness. The medics came for me. They forcefully took Craig out of the office and straight downtown for booking."

"Arrested?"

"Damn straight! His ass was slapped with iron bracelets faster than Cindy can pop out of her pink mesh panties. They charged him with assault and battery for attacking me. Because of his hostel behavior resisting the cops, they have him down for resisting arrest, too. I didn't realize I was that fucked until I saw my image reflected in the counselor's family portrait, on the wall."

"Not cool! Especially in front of the coach." Scott contemplates the scene.

"Man, I was hurting bad and kept thinking how quickly Craig turned on me and shit. What hurts the most in all this stupid shit—I allowed such sick fucked up dudes to be my crew. Both him and Carlos are two sorry asses. I don't want anything to do with either one of them ever again!"

"Damn! hope it's over, for good. Craig needs to be locked the hell away … for good, Eric! I knew he was a bit loose, but this is psycho-cray cray."

"Yeah, but all I could think about was how humiliating it was to be beat down in front of a coach like I was his little bitch. Suddenly, it flashed on me what must have gone through Jason's head seeing Craig go Hulk and violating and butchering him. I mean, right in front of his friend. It was pure evil."

"Craig did one hell of a beatdown on him, is all I can say-" Scott says.

"Anyway, Coach thought it best that I remove myself from the roster. At least till after winter break. I'll need to seek some counseling in the meantime. Thankfully, Craig is expelled … and maybe jailed. However, Carlos is suspended from all extracurricular activities and placed on a two-week suspension for his part. His scholarship for Townsend next year is toast, man."

Scotts shakes his head. "I know what went down was stupid and dangerous, Eric. But for whatever it's worth, I always felt you were the best out there. You'll be missed out there, especially with homecoming quickly approaching."

"Thanks, bro! I am deeply sorry for the shitty part I played. It was reckless and stupid like you said. I just feel bad for those little guys. Those two really stood up for each other when most would have left your ass hanging in the wind. If Craig hadn't gotten the drop on the Jason kid, I don't know, man. The badass can throw down with the best of 'em, Yo! I can't say it enough, they make an awesome sweet pair, those two underclassmen."

Scott's ears perk up again. "Pair? A pair of what, man?"

"Oh-um … I thought?" Eric mumbles under his breath, as his hands seem to fidget wildly.

"Thought what?" Scott asked with a hinting of agitation and tightening his stance.

Eric hastens his packing, slamming his gear into his bag. "Seriously, Scott-Bro! Just ignore what I just said, okay? I don't know shit! (his voice pitches with fear) Nobody needs bashing over what they feel, is all I am getting at. I gotta roll. Mom's waiting for me out front."

Eric hustles off before Scott can respond to his cryptic message. Scott is left with more questions than he originally started with. In his hasty exit, a couple walking by, sees the battered face of Eric and questions, what happened.

Eric tells them the student, Jason Brodie did it when he was protecting his buddy from the likes of him, and his goon-squad buddies.

With a cryptic warning, Eric gets up close and personal, "So, whatever you do, don't fuck with the redhead Jason Brodie or his buddy, Timothy Daniels, ever! Unless you want to end up like me, got it! Not a good idea ever. He is an animal!" The couple in horrid awe, not knowing who Jason or Timothy is, nod in receiving the information. Eric hurries in his departure, leaving the couple questioning each other as, spreading the word to some friends passing by.

Not far away on the second floor of the SciTech building, Timothy enters the lab for his routine after-school login. He walks over and explains to Mr. Jamerson how he won't be staying today. The news strikes Mr. Jamerson like a freight train, given how uncharacteristic it is for Timothy to skip lab time.

"Whoa! What happened? What's with the sling and the busted lip? Did someone hurt you?" Mr. Jamerson's concern is overwhelming.

Timothy nods yes. Mr. Jamerson shuts the door behind them, locking it for privacy. The first thing he wants to know is if Jason was the cause of his injury.

"I noticed your friend, the runner … um, Brodie? He hasn't been out there this evening. Did something happen between you two? Do you want to talk about it? Did he bully you?"

Timothy gives Mr. Jamerson a strange stare. "Huh? No, no, everything is okay, Mr. Jamerson!"

Mr. Jamerson is hesitant now. "Well, I shouldn't really say this, but it is only out of concern for you, Mr. Daniels, that I even bother to ask. Your dear redhead came floating by a few seconds after you stepped out yesterday. You were getting your things to leave. He had a lot of questions about you. He wanted to know if you were a stalker type or maybe gay. He was rather intense in his delivery."

"What did you tell him?" Timothy asks.

"Truthfully, it wasn't my place to tell him anything about another student. He was rather nervous and extremely jittery like you are most of the time. Actually, the way you are right now too."

"Huh?" Timothy checks himself out. "Oh!" He had never noticed this before.

Mr. Jamerson smiles. "He asked if you were a good lad and not a perv at least. He didn't want pervs checking him out and wanted it to stop if that was the case. He thinks you were snooping up his shorts when he was doing sit-ups yesterday. He wasn't aware he was mooning you by wearing his revealing running shorts."

Timothy remembers the image, it almost causes him to blush. Fortunately, Mr. Jamerson is unaware and continues, "I felt I should defend your honor … a bit. I hoped you didn't mind."

Timothy shakes his head briskly while thinking to himself, *I'm not a girl though.*

"I told the young man about your research goals. Your admiration for his physical athleticism and perseverance, while requiring no glorification by his peers."

"What did he say?" Timothy is nervous. *How far did this little conversation go?*

"He seemed to be surprised at first, and he started pondering, I guess. You had such a genuine interest in his hobby that I think he was humbled by such knowledge. He got excited and wanted to catch up with you to get to know you firsthand, I thought. He was hooked on every word I had to say about your latest academic accomplishments from the school and some of the great studies you have conducted. I explained how sweet and gentle you were toward everyone, and I told him that there is no malice in your bones."

Timothy cherries over. "Sweet and gentle? Oh, God, he must really think I am a—"

"I think not, Mr. Daniels. I think you made an incredible impression on him—that's all. He left with a joyous smile on his face much like yours right now."

Timothy is flustered. "Thanks, Mr. Jamerson, for talking with him and looking out for me."

Mr. Jamerson sees the color in Timothy's cheeks soften his light tan complexion. "You know where he is, your Scotsman?"

Timothy smiles boyishly. Not wanting to bring more attention than needed, Timothy cuts his response short with a nod of his head and says, "He's okay, actually."

"So, you two did actually talk?" Mr. Jamerson is intrigued.

Timothy had an 'I'll never tell' smirk on his beaming face, and he relaxes with a huge sigh. "Yes, we talked. He is fine, and he'll be staying with my family for a spell until he is better."

Mr. Jamerson's curiosity peeks, but he knows it is wrong to question further and simply taps Timothy of his shoulder, "Well, little one, just be safe, and enjoy your new friendship with each other. Heaven knows, it's tough out there, and friendships even harder."

"Thanks, Mr. Jamerson!" Timothy says as he scurries out of the room.

CHAPTER 21

A short time later, the students scatter for the afternoon buses. Just inside the main exit doors of the school, Julie sees a shiny black Dodge Charger pull up in the restricted bus-zone. She sees Cheryl walking when she hears the car's horn, gaining Cheryl's unwanted attention. With a glare of annoyance, Cheryl is eyeing the muscle car with attitude. Fluffing her hair, releasing a sigh, she approaches the vehicle.

Cheryl unmistakably knows the operator of the car. As bustling youths slow to a crawl to get a closer peek at the super sleek wheels, getting an adrenaline charge from the fierce rumbling of its quad pipes. Cheryl rolls her eyes as she steps up to the passenger window and leans in.

Squinting her eyes tight against the glass of the door, Julie can make out a male driver. The Caucasian male has dark, slicked back-hair. The guy could be a big brother, a family member, or something else. She doubts it's a love interest due to her overall body language.

"You are wanted, Cheryl. You need to report in!" says the driver of the car, Michael Landings, who's also known as Dark Hunter.

"What does the great Dr. Kline want from me? The creep

could have just text! Besides, I don't have the so-called key thingy. Everyone can back the hell off!" Cheryl rolls her eyes in contempt.

"Exactly their point, Star Child! Or Whatever the Fuck they call you!" Michael mocks her in a laid-back, *I don't give a damn,* tone.

"Just be the happy little messenger bitch-boy and tell'em I am still working on it!"

Michael deepens his baritone and gives a more authoritative vibe. "Get in the car, Cheryl! Or I won't give a shit how much of the prodigal bitch you are to Kline. I will kill you right where you stand, you little twit. I am not in the mood for your teen-angsts today! This is not a request. You don't want to disobey a directive, Understood?"

Michael's no-nonsense tone strikes fear into Cheryl. She knows he can truly deliver on what he preaches. Michael and Shihan changed drastically over the past few years with their ongoing treatments in the DH program, transforming their once warm personalities to more sinister ones. They're literal killing machines now, doing whatever the DH wants them to do, also referred to as the Beta Rats. Luckily for Cheryl, her treatments are not as strong. She hasn't yet, been given a Kill-order, by the agency.

She still remembers meeting, the sweet and nervous Michael Landings, in their initial transit to the government-ran DH facility. Surprisingly, her memories before that day, are gone. But, seeing Michael now, he is an emotionless husk of a man with an insatiably deadly appetite.

Cheryl, not wanting to show any sign of intimidation by the man, lashes. "Fine! Just don't get your tight panties in a bunch!" With great reluctance, Cheryl slips into the car.

With quick thinking, Julie zips out her cell, snaps several shots of Cheryl getting into the black car. She also manages to get a blurry license plate as the car drives off the grounds, nearly hitting many of the pedestrians.

At that moment Kyra exits the opposite side of the school. She gets an ominous text from Julie.

> *Hey, Butterfly! Meet me at Spellings Library. W/Got the b'tch! * the text is concluded with thumbs-up and kissy-faced emoji.

Kyra feels the message is a bit cryptic, even for Julie. Tossing her long hair back into a ponytail, she releases some excess air out the side of her cherry-colored lips. She treks her way to her mini SUV in the student parking area.

It doesn't take her long to reach the Spellings Library and hook up with Julie. Julie updates her on the mysteries of, Cheryl Hunters, which she tracked down through the school's student information database. Acquiring Cheryl's previous school history, and other factoids, proved problematic. There is nothing to be attained within the system.

"No class pictures! No, write-ups! Nada! Damnit!" exclaimed Julie, with heated frustration. "There is nothing here, which can physically place her, at her previous school. Nothing is recorded on her permanent school's record at Frostburg High, in Michigan!"

Not giving up on her pursuit, Julie tells Kyra how she plans to get more info on Cheryl's home address.

"How did you get her address? Or should I not be asking such things, Julie?"

Julie lightly chuckles. "Oh, really? Wow! Let's just say, the art of deception is a very crafty and powerful thing. Especially when there's very important information needing to be retrieved." She grins, from ear to ear.

"Okay, I see. But now ... I am really afraid to ask."

"Well, don't be, scaredy-cat. It's actually no biggie. I told Mrs. Krismen, the head receptionist in the main office, there was a mysterious box left sitting outside the lunchroom, and there is no one around to claim it. So, she called for Mr. Raul, the custodian, but he didn't respond. I knew he wouldn't. He likes to sneak cigarette breaks behind the science lab wing, where the intercom is inoperable. I can't imagine why?" Julie winks and gives a sneaky grin.

"So that explains why it always smells so smoky around there."

"Precisely! This leaves Mrs. Krismen the sole task of checking it out for herself. All before the lunch periods were to begin. She, of course, asked me, the smart, sensible, reliable student, to stay where I was, allowing her to retrieve the mysterious package."

"Sneaky! Was there really a package?"

"Of course! It was a box filled with lollipops wrapped in newspaper from an unknown sender."

"Say what? Oh, crap-o-la! For real?" Kyra is amazed at the lengths Julie would go through to get what she wants.

"Yep! And a note inside saying that this school really sucks! With little glitter hearts to boot!" Julie finding it hard to maintain a straight face.

"Really?" Kyra can't believe the lengths Julie went to for this little adventure in sleuthing.

"As soon as she was out of the office, I accessed the school's main computer from her desk and typed in Cheryl's creds. I managed to retrieve her current address and the former school she transferred from."

"Oh, wow. That's scary if our school is that easy to break into and get our info." Kyra bursts out in a laugh, while Julie takes the comment as a knock on her hacking skills and pretends to be deeply insulted.

"What did Mrs. Krismen do? Did she open the box at least?" Kyra queried.

"Well ... that was a hoot, girlfriend. Mrs. K. is all nervous, and she opened the box and found the note and the lollipops. She read the note, and that was it, hun."

"Say what?"

"Seriously, the old bag didn't do squat. I thought Mrs. K was going to freak out or cop a major fit. But nothing. She started giggling. She threw the note away, saying something like, 'So true, so true!' She never showed the letter to anyone. Like it was a secret joke only for her. As she laughed, she gave me a sucker and placed the rest in her desk drawer."

"Oh, wow!"

"Exactly, if anything, I had just brightened that old biddy's day."

The girls agree, they will check the location of Cheryl's recorded residence soon.

Kyra brings to point things that need taking care of first, like the martial arts convention on Saturday, and the Harvest Fair on Sunday. With only a couple days left, they need to stick with their priorities first, so as not to look too conspicuous.

Once home, Kyra settles on the couch and wistfully glances over her study notes from an earlier class assignment. While cramming information into her stressfully overworked brain, Kyra receives an email alert from the school's student body, exclaiming the hopefuls for the homecoming's royal court. Names of the nominated are posted, and voting will begin on Thursday effectively at 6:30 a.m. before school, which is tomorrow.

Although she doesn't normally follow these sorts of feeds from the school, she scrolls through the list of nominees. Scott's name is nominated for King's divisions, in both events along with four others, who clearly don't stand a snowballs chance in Hades. When Kyra scrolls over to the Queen's division nominees, she nearly chokes on her own spit.

The email read her worst nightmare. "For the coveted Queen's position in both, Homecoming and Prom of Franklin High, nominees are as follow Mary Tringent, Kathy Mullins, Tiffany Bowman, and by last-minute submission, Kyra Mathews."

Kyra practically drops the laptop, but with the quickest of reflexes, she catches it, almost shocking herself.

What the freaking hell? I told that girl, not to—! Instantly she catches herself. *Oh, fumbling fudge-sticks, I didn't! I was so distracted with Cheryl, I foolishly accepted the entry, she unnervingly forced down my throat.*

Kyle is strolling past the archway of the family room, catching Kyra's odd outburst as she receives the posting from the school and starts snickering with a child-like giggle.

Seizing the moment to torment his twin, Kyle broadcast into the family room, "All hail, her Royal Fat-Hiny, Kyra, the Lame-Ass Mathews!"

Kyra grinds her teeth and draws her fingers into a scratching claw gesture, wishing she had a reachable heavy object to thrash at his thick skull. He dashes off quickly before she can think up a plan of attack.

Knowing uninvited eyes will be all over her from now until the official drawings, Kyra's fear becomes a reality. She has a great aversion to being in the spotlight. It's Kyra's most dreaded fear.

For hours to follow; emails and texts start swarming in, giving her a huge show of support. Quickly circulating over the entire student body, she remembers the words Julie informed her at lunch, "What do you think is going to happen when Cinderella slips on that glass slipper?"

In the haze of a surfeit influx of congratulatory messages. Combing through, she single's out a singular email which caught her eye, addressed from Timothy. It read, "Hi Kyra... I know this wasn't something you probably wanted to happen or expected. However, dearest Kyra, Jason and I think you are a Queen in every sense of the word. We support you and will be there in any way we can to help you in your victorious campaign. Much love from the fellas. FYI, Jason is drooling over your picture, by the way! The freaking pig. But, I love him anyway. Thanks again."

Kyra can't help but laugh at the cuteness of her young friends, and their new connection with each other. Suddenly, with sparkling joy in her heart, her phone chimes with a text from Scott. Quickly grabbing her phone, she opens the text.

"Hey, Kyra! I saw the student board's message. Wow! It's amazing! I really hope you win. I didn't think you would seriously run, considering your initial feelings on such matters. I would love to be dancing with the prettiest girl in school on Homecoming night and most definitely for the Prom. If, of course, I am so lucky to be the bumbling bloke to win and you'll accept me. Talk soon, Dearest Queen Kyra. Your hopefully smitten King, Scott."

The text sends complete joy to Kyra's heart, making her completely forget the recent outburst from her annoying male twin, Kyle. Nevertheless, she's unable to continue her studies, as her brain is filled with images of Scott and her, gracefully gliding across the ballroom floor. Their bodies, only a heartbeat apart from each other, as music serenades them, and a showering of sparkling lights shimmer down upon them. Scott's longing lips are willing themselves closer to hers, while she is powerlessly lost in his eyes.

Kyle walks in to see if Kyra was still mad, while uncharacteristically wanting to apologize. However, when he walks into the room, Kyra is pretend dancing in the middle of the living room with an invisible mate and trying to kiss the space in front of her. She catches him peeping. Without warning, she dashes over to him and gives him a warm sisterly hug. "Love you, knucklehead."

Kyle tries to retreat from her tight grasp. He can't stand too much physical affection, especially coming from his sister, who knows better.

"What the hell, Kyra? Come on! Let me go! Enough, please! You know what happens when someone touches me too long." He finally breaks loose, looks down at himself, covers himself and retreats hastily from the room, "You're freaking psycho, Kyra! Not cool!" he exclaims while exiting the room with haste.

Kyra stands alone in the middle of the room, gleefully smiling. *So silly, that brother of mine. I do forget about his little affliction about physical touching. Poor thing. A cold shower will do him fine.* As if on cue, someone turns on the shower upstairs.

Miles away in an undisclosed warehouse, Cheryl sits in a poorly lit, dingy office, waiting for Dr. Kline. Michael is eager to be on his way so he can hunt down a mysterious wolf-shapeshifter, not to be mistaken for a mere werewolf, which he easily has hunted and killed through the years. Yet this creature is far more powerful and not the easiest to track.

Michael's eyes crossed, fuming over Cheryl's resistance and rebelliousness. Likewise, Cheryl squinches her eyes back at him and cockily starts, "So, are you going to talk or just look like a freaking statue in the corner?" Michael resents her immensely, and grunts.

"Well?" Cheryl persistently pushing for a response from the cold, militant man, "At least tell me again why I was needed to be brought to this back-ass dump of a place. Seriously, when's the last time this place actually saw a freaking broom or a mop, huh?"

It is obvious, Cheryl is plucking Michael's patience. He turns to her, "Look, pissy little brat! You just need to sit there and shut the hell up! If you know what's good for you." Cheryl feels the heat of his resentment and while deep within her, she knows the man in front of her, isn't the real Michael. Whatever he is or isn't thinking now, isn't in his control. He is nothing more than a functioning zombie for Dr. Kline. A freakily soulless puppet.

"Wow, must suck rocks for you, Purple boy? I can say whatever I want, and there is nothing you can do about it." Michael turns sharply at her, raising his fist in anger, and a surge of purple energy emanates from his fist. Cheryl has never seen him use his power in the open before, and she instantly knows she shouldn't play with him or taunt him too much.

"Okay! Chill-Chill already. Jeez Michael, don't go and turn your tighty-whities all brown, with stress. You are going to have a freaking hernia or something."

Someone opens a door within the facility, and they can hear a man wearing a thick solid heel shoe step in the distance. Michael discharges the energy emanating from his hand and turns to see Dr. Kline walking toward them. He does not look like he's in a happy mood.

"Michael, you may be excused back to your hunt. Any leads thus far?"

"Close but nothing solid, unfortunately. This shapeshifter is very powerful, and Black Wolf's power to hide is unprecedented. In his human form, there is no one way to track him down yet."

"Hmmm, keep at it. Oh, go check on Felix and Mr. James about the new test subjects that will be transported in soon." Without a word, Michael looks wickedly at Cheryl as if their conversation isn't over yet as he walks away.

CHAPTER 22

On Saturday morning just after 1:00 p.m., the exhibition tournament at the convention center in Baltimore is about to begin. A voice announces over the main PA system, "Welcome, all guest and competitors, to this year's regional martial arts expo and tournament. Joining us today are some of the most skilled fighters and exhibitionists nationwide. All divisions will perform for rankings and entertainment showmanship."

"Did you remember all of your gear this time, Julie?" Kyra asked her pumped-up buddy.

"Yes, Mother. I remembered everything."

"Good. You'd better!" Kyra isn't trying to hear anything negative today.

"Oh, crap! I can't believe I forgot it." She starts rummaging desperately through her gear. "How the bloody hell could I have?" Julie exclaims with great fear and concern.

"What? What did you forget? There's no time left."

"I forgot to bring my fear. What should I do?" Kyra gives her a wicked stare that can melt steel, and then she karate chops Julie's arm as Julie doubles over with laughter.

Several days prior, the day when Michael picked Cheryl up from the school, she was once again in the sterile lab filled with test tubes and unknown machines deep in the countryside of St. Mary's county. Cheryl despises this place with every part of her being. She is again face-to-face with the project director who oversees the Dark Horizon project. He questions her about her recent failure and tells her what she needs to do before Mr. Black has a change of heart about her usefulness to the project.

She knows the only way to leave the project is dead.

"Hey, I tried!" Cheryl pleaded her case, only to deaf ears, obviously.

"Oh, you tried?" Dr. Kline not liking such responses, anyone else would have had a bullet to the head already, and Cheryl is quite aware of this.

"I was interrupted by this freakish karate-kid girl, a friend of, Kyra Mathew's."

The director isn't smiling. "You are telling me a simple high school girl thwarted a highly trained, telekinetic agent from completing her mission?"

"Exactly! This wasn't a simple little girl I was dealing with, thank you. You said I would be in and out on this mission. Not!"

"Explain!"

"Fine. First, I couldn't find the darn key thingy anywhere in the house, even with the detector rod. Second, something strange was happening in that house while I was snooping about. I knew I was close to it at times, but it would not present itself or somehow move. And lastly, the super karate chick comes out of nowhere, and I mean nowhere, challenging me on the spot. I hit the redheaded bitch with some of my best kinetic moves. The redhead was able to counter each of my psi attacks like she knew what I was going to do before I did it. She would then counter with a physical response. And her evasive skills are freaking epic. Get this. I sling her through the air, and she lands a twenty-foot dead fall like a panther springing instantly into her fighter's stance. She moves like she is a psychic ninja or something. Seriously, the girl is not normal, which started to freak me out. She even called herself by another name, sounds much like an anime character."

"Really? What did she call herself?" Dr. Kline asks, now quite interested.

"She calls herself Shira something. I am not sure. I had a dagger in my leg, which still hurts like a bitch! Thank you very much for asking by the way."

"She's a warrior you said? What exactly did she say when giving you her name?" Shihan emerges from the shadow and gives his undivided attention to the girl. Cheryl is completely taken aback by the smoky dark tone in Shihan's voice.

She desperately tries to recollect exactly what Julie had said. "Um … yes." She has a moment of pure clarity. "After she made that impossible landing and reverses one of my daggers back to me, she said, 'I don't know who or what you are, but you don't know who you are playing with, for I am Shira-Kami? That's all I can seem to remember."

Shihan's eyes imminent a red crimson glow, "Shira-Kami, you say? Intriguing. That may explain a few things. Where is this Julie-girl now?" Apprehension is deep in grumbled tone.

Cheryl feels backed into a corner, pushes out a palm of her hand to halt Shihan advancement toward her, "Yo, look! I don't know where she is or where she lives, but I do happen to know where she will be this weekend."

Shihan gnarls sternly at her.

"Okay-okay! she is going to be at some martial arts exhibition this weekend at the convention center in Baltimore. She and the Kyra girl are both going to be a part of it at some point. That's all I know for sure."

Without a word, Shihan, who's also known by his warrior name, Ryuu-no-kage, steps back into the shadows behind him and leaves no trace.

Meanwhile, Julie puts on her Japanese-inspired attire. Her white top had an etched design of a white fox on the back, while Kyra fits into an elaborate silky blue and black Chinese Tai Chi pant ensemble, adorned with gold etchings throughout.

"Wow, Kyra. Going with the whole Tai Chi look this year, yeah?"

"Well, silly, I have an exhibition in the Tai Chi style and doing one with Wu-Chun broadsword later."

"Oh, cool. Hope I can see you do that one. I am in a three-stage tournament. Much of the competition is going to be a breeze. But my duo exhibition in acrobatic arts is questionable now. Jimmy, my partner, is a loser and a no-show. I need to have a partner and quick if I want to be a representative of Mr. Braxton's Mixed Martial Arts."

While telling Kyra her dilemma, Kyra's wandering eyes are drawn to a tall brown-skinned boy on the far-off mats; warming up, with stretching and some form of Tai-chi.

The young man's musculature in his stretching shows great strength and flexibility.

While warming up, he practices several moves, showing the fluid extensions of his arms, legs, and feet. His movements are like air, graceful and flowing. His dark caramel skin and pumped pecs and dark exposed nipples lend greatly to his sex appeal. His long, corn silk hair is singularly braided down his back. The tip of his braid features a traditional Native American ribbon and a red feather at the base of the braid.

He is wearing silk-like, white Native American fringed pants, with white tassels nearing the top and the ankles. He's also wearing soft white moccasins, on his feet.

"Um, Julie, who is that? He's tall, dark, and wow!" Kyra pointing out the mysterious young male to her.

Julie literally makes a double-take.

"Oh-my-God! He freaking came? Yes- yes- yes! (practically jumping in place with adulation) My prayers are being heard. Thank you, oh great one in the skies." She raises her hands toward the ceiling. "Thank the most magnificent source."

"Who? Who is he?"

"That is Adam, K-girl. He's the boy I told you about at the library. He is Adam Spirit-Hawk Sparrows. He is the one who is going to help coach next semester. He is the last surviving member of two very different cultures—one Native clan and one Japanese nation. His mother was the last of a lost tribe of the Cherokee nation, but she was adopted by the Piscataway's in her adult years. His father was from Japan. He was raised for the best portion of his youth by the hidden Mazuko Clan, which many believed had disbanded many centuries ago. He doesn't like to believe the folklore about his two families. He believes he makes his own steps in the sands of life and not someone else's."

"Okay, stalker much? That some crazy info you gathered, girl!"

"No, I actually talked to him last year. He is really a great, down-to-earth guy, and he's a freshman in college this year. He told me he doesn't do flashy events like this one because his style and spirit are secret and not meant to be on display."

"Hmm, sounds like someone else I know, right, Shira?"

Julie responds with a snarl.

Seizing the opportunity, she lunges in Adam's direction, but with only a few steps to her target, she is instantly halted by a man completely concealed in Ninjutsu attire. Unlike ninjas, who reveal their eyes, this one doesn't. He wore a concealing crimson scarf across his eyes and tied on the back of his head.

"Honored to meet your acquaintance, Shira-Kami. I look forward to our fun exhibition."

Julie can't believe the man knows her hidden warrior name, and before she can ask about it, he says, "I am Shihan Gamo-Chin." That catches Adam's ears instantly, and he starts making his way over to them.

"You are who?" Just as she completes her question, Adam calls out to her by name. She turns for a second, and when she snaps back, the man, who was only a breath away from her, is suddenly gone without any trace.

With visible concern, Adam looks desperately around her, "Julie, are you okay?"

"Sure. Why wouldn't I be? You suspect something?"

Adam looks a bit worried. He scans the room and then turns back to her. "I kinda know about him. That was Ryuu-no-kage."

"He said he was Shihan Gamo-chin."

"Yes, and he is the Ryuu-no-kage, meaning the Dragon of—"

Julie interrupts, "Shadows! I know the language, remember?"

"Exactly, he goes by several titles and names, but this Ryuu is of the Gamo Clan. He just marked you for death, when calling out your spiritual warrior's name."

"I thought that was an old wives' tale, meant to scare the young pupils, by Sensei?"

"No, it is very true. And from what I just felt, he is of one of the deepest, darkest of the demonic chi! Be very careful, little flower. Your school of study is a mortal enemy to the Gamo Clan. They won't stop till all of you are dead."

"I can handle myself!" Julie feeling self-empowered, of her own skill craft. "Thank you very much, Mr. Adam!"

"I have no doubt, little flower. I sense your chi as well. It is very powerful, but you are still learning, not fully blossomed."

"You know … a lot about this, don't you? Are you speaking from experience?"

"This isn't a place to talk about such things. But yes, I do know. When I was a mere boy, my father, who was a strong and very honorable man, was slaughtered along with his entire clan. They were destroyed by this Gamo clan. They're a ferocious breed of enemy. So, I am the last of my father's blood, and I will hold the training that is inherent within me as a secret for my offspring to carry. I am here today to showcase my mother's side of the sacred spirited arts. I am introducing the spirit walk-style today, for the first time. The committees will have a chance to observe it and possibly give it a permanent standing in the arts community. This will bring light to our ancestor's fusion of spirit, air, and power." Julie finds his story so fascinating.

Julie soon explains to him the situation with her missing partner, and he agrees to be her stand-in. Since there's not much time to learn a solid routine, they both go to a more private part of the gymnasium to practice.

Meanwhile, Kyra puts her final gear away and starts to walk to the side bench when she slams into someone. "Oh, I am so sorry. I wasn't watching where I was going. My little brother is a mess." Kyra looks up to see a beautiful brown-skinned girl with dazzling spiral curls, the biggest dimples, soft hazel green eyes, and a bubbly personality.

"Don't be. I wasn't actually watching where I was going either."

Both girls giggle for a second. The strange new girl reaches out a hand. "Hello, I am Tehya."

Kyra drops one of the bags and reaches her hand out in response. "Hi, I am Kyra. Kyra Mathews."

"Nice name. My last name is Proctor. That is my little bro, Joshua." After pointing him out, Kyra can't help but notice just

how adorable her younger brother is. "Wow, he is really cute …
and quite fit."

"Yeah, he is thirteen going on twenty-one. So please don't tell
him that he is cute. You will have a permanent shadow for the rest
of the day. Just a warning. But he and my best friend, Keith, are
like inseparable brothers. Keith helps with training him in sports
and martial arts. Keith was the all-around athlete in our school,
Douglass High."

"Thanks for the heads-up by the way."

"No prob. Do you have siblings?"

"Yes, a knucklehead twin brother named Kyle and a younger
sister, La Rissa. They are more than likely bored out of their minds
right at this very moment. Rissa is not into this kind of environment, like Kyle and me. Kyle is competing later. He's ascended
third-degree black-belt, in the arts of Jujutsu and Aikido."

"Are you competing?"

"No, just doing swords and the Tai Chi exhibition."

"Wow, you're really smashing in that outfit. It is beautiful."

"Thanks. What brings you here?"

"Oh, I'm here for my brother. I have a conference on the other
side of the complex with ancient historical artifacts and weapons.

"Wow, sounds intriguing. But you look a little young to be a
historian."

"Oh, gosh no! I am only a sophomore at Old Dominican
University. I have an apprenticeship with the National Archives
of Washington. I am under the kind and intense leadership of
Dr. Becker. He is amazing to work with. Considering it's just my
brother and me, I have to step up and secure a future for us."

"Just the two of you?"

"Yeah, there was a family issue, and I had to take Joshua and
become his legal guardian."

"Must be tough." "It is a strain at times, but Joshua is a

wonderfully bright boy, and I get plenty of support from Keith and my close friend Simone."

Just then Kyra's medallion peeks out from her attire, catching Tehya's eye. "Oh, wow. What an enchanting piece you are wearing. I saw something like that in one of my research books. Dr. Becker wanted me to archive it. The one I read about is believed to have great magical properties and has a green jewel inside its socket. The stone was believed to be made from a rare mystical jade stone. The medallion was believed to be about a millennium in age."

While Tehya speaks, Kyra finds herself examining her charm that much closer. "But I will tell you the writing on your charm is exquisite and very old."

Julie and Adam step up at that moment. Julie introduces Adam to Kyra and her new friend. Kyra presents Tehya to them. Adam instantly notices Tehya's Native American features and the strong aura around her. Tehya also senses a strong presence in him and in the others around her.

While Adam is reaching out his hand in greeting and shakes Kyra's hand. Tehya could almost swear she glimpsed Kyra's charm pulsate with a green hue, which instantly vanishes as if it somehow sensed her awareness. Tehya chose to say nothing. She doesn't want to bring unnecessary attention to what she now suspects.

Meanwhile, Adam feels a strange energy drain, while Kyra feels that odd jolt of energy again like she did with Jason and Julie. Tehya's, eyes flicker violet and back, without any detection from anyone, for she senses the energy exchange.

CHAPTER 23

After parting ways, the events of the day move rather quickly. Kyra watches Julie and Adam perform a flawless acrobatic routine with such artistry and skill.

Watching Adam move, she can almost swear the boy was going to take to flight at any given moment. Their movements are enough to catch the attention of Shihan Chin. Tehya's brother, Joshua, shows great promise in his routine with the staff and the broken staff. Kyle elbow hugged the kid, after his routine and got a chance to meet his, friend and mentor, Keith.

Kyra's Tai Chi is effortless and gracefully executed. However, when it comes to her execution of the swords techniques, surprisingly something is different this time. While slinging the blades, her control is almost too easy. Her speed is blazingly fast and much more accurate. In her routine, she normally makes a tumbling pass, flings her long sword into the air, and catches it while doing a split. However, this time she goes for her traditional butterfly backflip layout to catch her sword. She feels a surge in her legs and lunges far into the air beyond the normal limits of an average human. While the sword is rotating in the air, Kyra flies into a series of aerial acrobatics, allowing her to perform a triple somersault instead of a single. She catches the sword while in midflight and lands gracefully. She whips herself into a no-hands backflip and lands in a sideways leg split with her sword in hand.

The crowd goes ballistically wild. Julie, Adam, Tehya, and Shinan Chin watched intensely. Adam nudges Julie, "Did your friend always have such a move?"

Julie is just as shocked, "Um, this the first time me seeing it. What the—!"

Meanwhile, Shinan Chin snarls with discontent, really in the fact something is happening.

Before Julie can ask about her final acrobatic move, an announcement comes over the main PA. "Well, well, to all our wonderful guests. There appears to be a very unique exhibition on the main floor. To demonstrate some of the most ancient styles of combat, one warrior has called out another warrior like in days of feudal Japan. It would so appear that we have such a rivalry today from two distinct clans that no longer exist. Ryuu-no-kage calls out and challenges the Shira-Kami. This should be quite a show, people. Please find your way to the big blue mats in the center arena."

Hearing her code name activates Julie's irises to shine with a bright white hue and flicker back to their natural color. Adam witnesses the flare in her eyes. He knows she is summoned, and she will not back down.

As Julie makes her way to the center arena in a zombielike trance, Kyra watches with a bewildering look. Adam makes a hasty charge toward Julie's direction when Michael appears from nowhere and stands before him with eyes of blazing amber. "Hello, Spirit Hawk. Where are you rushing off to, Chief?"

"Demon, let me pass! I have no time for the likes of you."

"Hmm, funny. I came all this way to be with you, and you don't want me? That's rather rude." With a flick of Michael's wrist, Adam is paralyzed from his neck down to his toes. "You just need to relax, young chief. Enjoy the butchery to come. Don't worry. Yours is coming soon enough." Michael lets out a demonic cackle.

Kyra calls out to Julie, but she can't hear over the chanting crowd. Suddenly standing right next to her, Cheryl looks her over before saying, "Give me the key, Kyra."

Kyra is stunned. Cheryl came from out of nowhere. "Key? What Key? What the hell are you talking about?"

"The Jade, key! Give it … or your friend dies in the arena today!"

"I don't know what key you are looking for or what you think I possibly have. You have completely lost all sense of reality."

Cheryl reaches out to grab hold of Kyra's necklace. Sensing the attack, she dodges clear and deflects Cheryl's arm with a chop to her wrist. Cheryl counters her chop with a series of punches, chops, kicks, and grappling holds. Cheryl is well trained. However, Kyra backs down to no one. Both girls engage in a series of tactical attacks and defensive moves. Clearly, the girls were physically well matched in martial arts. Cheryl uses her kinetic power, summoning a blade to her hand, and aims it directly to Kyra's throat.

Tehya catching the tail end of the confrontation sees Cheryl using a kinetic power, wielding a knife with her mind. While in their heated stance, both Cheryl and Kyra, neither see Tehya off to the side. When Cheryl releases the blade for Kyra's head, Tehya eyes flicker to violet, and takes control of another matching dagger, mentally slinging it in countering motion to Cheryl's, and strikes Cheryl's in mere inches of Kyra's throat.

Kyra with fear in her eyes, of what could have been her death, a large green spark of energy appears between her and Cheryl, knocking them both to the ground, rendering them both unconscious. Surprisingly, Tehya is also struck, making her faint. There's not a single witness to witness the flair or the three girls passing out.

While they're lying motionless, Kyra's medallion starts glowing.

The front plate magically dematerializes, revealing the jade stone underneath. The jade starts pulsating with a brilliant green light. The stone sends a shock wave throughout the entire event, releasing Adam from his mystical hold and slightly disorientating Ryuu and Shira on the arena floor. Without hesitation, Adam punches Michael square in the jaw, knocking him unconscious. Suddenly, everything and everyone inside the building is frozen in time, all except Adam, Tehya, Joshua, Julie, Kyle, and Shihan.

Julie is scanning the entire amphitheater, bewildered. Even the fountains and electronics seem to have stopped in their place. Ryuu ponders the sight and laughs, seizing the advantage. "It is time for you to die, Shira-Kami."

"Whatever witchery this is, you had better bring it, you son of a bitch." She slowly steps into her protective fighter's stance. Ryuu slowly removes the scarf, revealing the dark crimson glow emanating from the holes where his eyes should be.

Julie swallows deeply, raising her fists. "Oh, crap. You did, didn't you?"

The dark warrior snarls and lunges into a volley of extraordinary physical attacks. Julie manages to quickly counter. His arms are like steel beams, twice the power she can usually handle. Julie feels she can't use her mundane skills to fight such a vicious creature of darkness. Holding her stance as firmly as she can, she feels for the first time that she is heavily outmatched. Ryuu strikes with alarming speed and lands a surprising blow to Julie's right shoulder, which hurls her ten to fifteen feet away. She lands roughly on one knee.

"Come, little spirit. Is this the best you got? Where is the Shira-Kami I've heard so much about? I will devour your soul this day if this is your best."

She gets her second wind and regains her confidence after that.

I will not hold back any longer. I must do this ... and do this now!
She looks intently into Ryuu's blazing eyes.

"What is this?" he asks after seeing a brilliant violet hue circle
the iris in her eyes. Then the color suddenly morphs into a bright
blazing white. Julie's body is shrouded in a mystical white mist.

"Ah, it is in there, I see. I will have great joy in eating your
power!" Ryuu exclaims.

"Never!" she exclaims as she flips and spins like an ancient
dance, causing a windstorm in the building. Julie lands a single,
highly concentrated psionic punch to Ryuu no-Kage's heart plate
with the power equivalence of a dump truck loaded with C-4. The
impact heaves his body half the distance of the of the gymnasium's
interior, demolishing a row of vending machines as well as rows of
metal chairs and tables, tossing debris from the tables like bullets
through the air. Some of the objects strike people who are frozen,
severing arms and causing brutal injuries. Two of the vending machines release a showery maelstrom of sparks and flairs, thrashing
everything in their path.

This is the first time Julie has ever initiated her psionic punch.
In her chi stance, eyes blazing white, she is ready for whatever it
is to come, harnessing the power of the purity spirit. Just then an
ominous shroud of darkness fills the building, blotting out the
natural light where Ryuu is buried in the rubble. Julie takes on her
strongest stance, ready. With a deep, beastly roar, every bit of hell-
spawn, Ryuu's "Grrrrrrwwwl" resonates throughout the building.

Kyle, Joshua, and Keith are finally reunited with one another
amongst a building of people frozen in time. Joshua, so scared,
wondering where his big sister is. Keith comforts the kid as best
he can. They're all horrified spectators to an ungodly battle of epic
proportions. Cracks of lightning fill the dome of the building. Bolts
of lightning collided with the floor, scorching the ground with
each electrifying zap. A single discharge blasts the ground with

tremendous force before a swirling mass of ashes and smoke appears, and Ryuu stands there, hidden within his dark cloak.

A figure soars far above Julie's head, somersaulting into a dramatic landing before her. The man stands erect and firm. Julie can't believe her eyes when she recognizes her sparring partner Adam. His back to her, he is extremely focused on the shadow demon before them. Adam's hands pulsate with electrical currency, although he is showing great power, inside he feels weaker for some reason. Hearing the snap and crackle of the fierce discharge, Julie is mesmerized by his beauty and towering strength. Even his waist-long braid unravels on its own and dances with a static shimmer. Julie can't believe what she is witnessing. Nor do the others present who can observe.

"Ryuu, I am … Thunder Clap!" Adam's voice magnifies like a PA system. "I stand before you, demon! Your reign of death and mayhem comes to an end this day! You, soulless abomination, come out of your shadows, coward! Face your destroyer!" as more crackling lashes thunderous lightning clash about.

Adam's voice transcends the hall of the building as bolts of lightning crackle all about him. Julie and Adams's spiritual energies are surprisingly merging as one without each other's knowledge. Adam thrusts his hand out toward Ryuu and throws a magnificent blast of pure unadulterated lightning directly at the shadowed demon. Ryuu deflects the bolt with his massive claw which is almost the size of a human, still within his protective shroud of darkness.

"Not bad, Sparky. But you two, aren't ready for the likes of me, not yet!" Ryuu taunts after misdirecting Adam's bolt into an unpopulated area of the building.

In his full beast form, Ryuu can now see, Julie and Adam's spiritual energies miraculously converging into something new and far more powerful than he is willing to challenge.

"Not this time, Thunder Clap and Shira-Kami, but soon! Very

soon! You will see my true power and die." His voice is transcending the space like Adam's but in a darker, more menacing snarl. When the smoke clears, there is no sign of Ryuu or Michael. However, Cheryl is still unconscious on the floor near an unconscious Kyra and Tehya.

Miraculously, all the spectators throughout the entire event all snap out of their frozen state at the same time. It is as if no time has passed for them. Many are shocked and dismayed by what appears to be an instant displacement of the tables and metal chairs. Questions circle through the building about the rare sight of burn markings all over the floors and demolished vending machines. Screams of horror soon manifest, when bodies show up, ripped apart, missing limbs and blood splattered everywhere. Pure chaos and pandemonium take hold throughout the building.

Some strangers quickly jump to Kyra, Tehya and Cheryl's aid in trying to wake them up. When Julie and Adam reach Kyra, she is already alert and questioning them about what happened. Meanwhile, Julie looks over and sees that Cheryl is suddenly gone, and the people helping her are dumbfounded as they peer aimlessly for the young blonde girl, who was just in their arms but magically vanished without a trace. Tehya has come to and calls out to her baby brother, Joshua.

Kyra finds Kyle shaking with unusual fear, a sight she never believed she would ever see, along with Joshua peering at her in the same likeness. Tehya and Keith are huddling tight to each other. Whatever happened while she was unconscious, has truly traumatized them witnessing something too horrific to speak about. Seeing the destruction in the hall and the multiple injuries, her heart clamors with an aching pain of guilt and anguish, feeling she is somehow responsible, but can't understand how.

Kyra studies her trembling brother's eyes. He has never shown such tangible fear like this before. "I wish I could take away whatever has frightened you, Kyle. I wish I could undo the pain and fear in this building." Then the medallion opens once again. However, this time Tehya witnesses its glaring glow and yells out to Kyra, "Kyra, you have it! You are wearing the ancient key of Ancestria."

A pulse of green energy pulsates outward from the medallion, cascading throughout the entire building once again.

After a blinding light, Kyra opens her eyes to a new group of people who are completely different from those who were there just a second, prior. Kyra's memory of the events fades. The only thing she knows is the fact she has just finished an awesome routine, and Tehya is talking to her about her medallion. She's not sure how everyone snuck up on her so quickly. She shakes it off and smiles, "Oh, wow! You all startled me."

They all look confused by her spontaneous response.

Kyra continues, "Guys? What gives? Why are all of you—" Then she just tosses her hands up in the air. "Oh, never mind?" she laughs it off, not wanting to sound crazy. Instead, Kyra starts with the introductions to get everyone acquainted finally. A puzzled look becomes Kyle, as he is staring at his sister, Kyra.

It appears, all had forgotten the battle and why they were all clustered around Kyra—all except Julie and Adam, who sense that their involvement was more than they should openly reveal to the others. Understanding, it's up to them to do something. Adam, still sees something in Kyle's expression, resembling overwhelming fear. He prays Kyle doesn't remember anything, like the others.

All the while, knowing there is a serious threat on the horizon, a start of darkness to come. In his heart, Adam understood something else had taken root, something or someone was pulling at his power today, and amid the battle, something new was gained, being at Julie's side.

CHAPTER 24

Hey, Scott! Can't really thank you enough kid, for coming so early on a Sunday morning. to help set and prep for today's big celebration. Especially after such a long day of work yesterday!"

Scott's once, all-white snug T-shirt, is now transparent with sweat, with his nipples imprinting the shirt. He grabs hold of another bundle of hay and tosses it up on to the back of the tractor's long bed. "Honestly, Mr. Bowman, it was my pleasure. I like to work with my hands, whenever I am able. Besides, I didn't have to sit around church all morning, when there's good daylight and an awesome day to be had."

Mr. Bowman, the middle-aged local farmer, and proprietor of the land for the Harvest Fair, often rely on Scott when his ranch hands are scarce for big functions.

"Seriously, a good Christian boy like you, ducking the good Lord's word?" Mr. Bowman queries him with sarcasm. Joel, Scott's older cousin, yells from the far side of the truck. "I don't think it's the Lord he's ducking. He is ducking all the pretty little lilies scratching to get to his tenders—"

"Enough, Joel!" exclaims a blushing Scott. "Beware of what you say."

Scott feels restricted in his movements. He removes his sweaty T-shirt, revealing his perfectly tanned skin glistening in the sun.

Giving an odd chuckle, Scott address Mr. Bowman. "No, it's not like that at all, Sir! I have to admit, sometimes the unwarranted attention does get a little annoying."

Mr. Bowman laughs hard at first. He remembers what life was like being single, as a strong, strapping, young farmhand.

"I reckon with your talents on the field and that stud body, kid! You must be the new salvation of many blossoming young church fillies."

Scott is a bit modest. "I guess, Mr. Bowman."

"Hell, most of the guys wish they had just a touch of what that boy has to offer, Mr. B. I wouldn't be surprised if half of those blokes, weren't after our little Scotty's bubble butt, too!" Joel jokes, but speaks partial truths. Joel in his own right loves seeing his little cousin Scott blush, too. Letting him know, his little man, is just as sweet as he ever was, after so many years. Regardless, of the bold, strong man, working so hard in front of him.

Mr. Bowman slows down enough to admire his young helper and his amazingly red bashfulness. From an angle, he also sees that Scott is steeped in heavy thoughts.

Scott very flustered gives a stiff finger to Joel. "Um, thanks a lot, cousin Joel! (hating to blush in front of the fellas, like a little kid) Believe me it's not quite like that, and besides, it's not always the young ones, I'm referring to. Those cougars are relentless, sometimes. As far as the fellas, this bubble butt, is strictly off the market! I'll be glad to direct them your way, Cousin."

"Well, if that ain't the cat's meow there, son." Mr. Bowman lifts a stack of hay and peeps his head around.

"Not your cup of tea, young one? Those cougars you say?" Mr.

Bowman, laughs, "How you reckon I was snatched up at an early age? By a dainty young thing? Hell no! I was swooned in by the sexiest woman I ever saw, Mrs. Bowman. There is something about the church girls and their momma's, son. That's as far as I am going to travel down that road, sunny boy." He gives out an old country hoot as he finishes placing the last bundle of hay into its rightful place.

Mr. Bowman climbs off the tractor bed and tries catching his breath from the heat. The weather is hotter than usual at this time of the year. Over at a table set up for the workers, Mrs. Bowman waves her husband over to get a glass of a minty refreshment. Without delay, Mr. Bowman grabs a tall glass of ice-cold minty lemonade and offers one to Scott and Joel. Scott is eager to delight in some of Mrs. Bowman's famous homemade libations, and while sporting his boyish dimpled grin. Everyone present can't help but see the once young scrappy kid, all full grown now, and unquestionably man, and amazingly fit.

Mr. Bowman looks around at all the progress made in the last few days. The many types of ticketing and concession stands were all built from scratch and placed in their locations. A large center stage with multiple platforms for the various performers are finished. The festive decorations are lively and colorful. Flowers of the season placed, along with the dressed-up scarecrows, which have been placed throughout the massive fairgrounds. Last counted over a hundred of them.

The huge red tractor is tilled and ready for the hayrides to both; the pumpkin patch and very daunting hay stacked labyrinth. Joe Wagler's Traveling Carnival Caravan came and set up multiple rides, with vibrant featurettes, a few days ago—Ferris wheel, carousel, a house of mirrors, a haunted coaster ride, and many shops throughout the twenty-acre grounds.

Mr. Bowman feels very pleased with everything thus far. He turns to a sweaty Scott and states out of concern, "Hey, kid, you have really worked your butt off around here. You are one fine worker. I do hope you manage a little pleasure in your life. You must remember that the fun keeps you young, kiddo."

Scott smirks and says, "Don't worry, Mr. B. I try to fit in fun now and then."

Mr. Bowman makes sure to lower his tone so that none of the other guys can overhear, "I am sure you do. But I have to tell you, the Missus and I have watched you grow into a mature, respectable young man. We are both so proud of you just as if you were one of our own. But the wifey seems to worry a little bit more about you socially, runt. With you being so popular all around town and always out, giving to others so freely. She worries you won't settle and find some personal time for yourself. Find someone special to share your time with while you're young, especially with you being a senior now and soon off to college somewhere. Have you had a chance to find a young friend you can talk to and be yourself with yet, outside to gangly horde that clings to you? You don't have to answer me of course. I know it's personal. But we would love to see you with someone who can look you in the eye and mean the world to you and you to them."

Scott would normally feel uncomfortable with this conversation, but considering it is Mr. Bowman, a guy he honors and respects dearly, he doesn't shy away. The fact he's showing such concern about his social and mental state is something his biological father has never done for him. Scott is more than appreciative and doesn't want to hold anything back from him. Nevertheless, these aren't the things he prefers to talk about so openly.

"Son, we think it's great that you are keeping yourself wholesome for that special one out there. It is not an easy thing to do these days, I am pretty sure."

Scott understands Mr. and Mrs. Bowman's concern for him finding companionship. He smiles with a glow which is very telling to Mr. Bowman. Seeing the boyish glee, Mr. Bowman chuckles hard. "Well, ain't that be all. Some little flower has snagged your drawstrings, young man, didn't she? She must be something special."

Before Scott can yelp a single word out, "Yep, I'll say a little lady has him more than by his drawstrings. Maybe by his big Ol'—"

"Hey, watch it, Joel... I swear!" Scott threatens, fearing what's liable to come out of his mouth.

"Twisted little fuck. Mr. Super Buff. All of us have seen your scrunchy little pecker, more than a few times around this here farm. So, don't be getting shit out of wack, baby cuz. We know there's nothing super big down in your trousers, boy. I was just going to say your big Ol' heart, fool!" Joel chuckles hard, to Scott's utter embarrassment, which too, makes Mr. Bowman chuckle a bit.

"Yeah, right!" Scott gruffs with disbelief, and severely blushing now.

Mr. Bowman asks, "Well, is there someone, kid?"

Joel comes into visible sight now from behind the tractor. He chimes over Scott's bronzed bare chest and tight muscular arms. He shakes his head like he too can't believe the man, Scott has developed into.

"What a freaking waste, Cuz-O. Seriously, if I had half of what you got boy—"

"You'd still be a class-A, asshole!" Scott snaps a sharp response as Joel sneers, unimpressed. Joel senses Scott is reeking awkwardness, and a little shame now.

"Don't fret, Cousin. Still, love you, baby boy!" Joel softens his glare and turns to the fellas. "The fuel to our boy Scott is a sweet little thing full of culture too. Her name is Kyra Mathews!"

Scott instantly turns two new shades of red. Mr. Bowman beams when he sees Scott blush. "The Superman being so coy like Clark Kent?"

Joel stands with his overalls halfway off, nibbling on a piece of straw from one of the haystacks, Scott and Mr. Bowman, sits down on a haystack.

Scott tenderly asks, almost too embarrassed, "Why, Joe?"

Joel starts laughing, gathering how serious Scott is, like the little boy he watched grow up.

"Dude, get over it! Your sweet little friend is nothing to be shy about, Scott. She is … amazingly beautiful and super smart too, I hear. A true prize! Couldn't think of a better match for my sweet hearted little buddy, cousin."

Scott is dumbfounded by the overwhelming warmth and show of sensitive affection. Joel is normally the loud wisecracking asshole cousin, who loves busting his chops. He waits for the snappy retort, but this time, there isn't one, just an awkward silence.

"Wow, really?" Scott asks, in the most tender of voice, can't believe what Joel just said.

"Well, Cousin, I know I BS you a lot. You also need to know I honestly think the world of you, especially after the butt-load of crap, you've suffered through your young life. I always knew you're an amazing, dude. You deserve someone special too. You are beautiful inside and outside, kid. (He pauses, seeing Scott's eyes glossing over) Hey, Kid, I love you, dearly! That's all I'm sayin'. So, don't go getting used to it, you here?" Joel, hearing Scott sniffle, flips him the bird in angst, reaches down and sweetly kisses him on his cheek, walks over to the other side of Mr. B, and sits down.

Mr. Bowman taps Scott's shoulder. "See, Scott! Even Joel knows how great of a young man you truly are. If this girl, Kyra, is that special? You should be happy and enjoy her companionship. Bedding her doesn't have to be your focus right now. Just be there for each other. The rest will happen—believe me."

A seriousness becomes Scott's expression, facing Mr. B. and his statement.

Joel laughs out.

"Squirt, just chill! It's no secret, you are a fuckin' virgin! Cousin, all the fellas on the farm knew this shit for some time now. We don't see anything wrong with our tough-boy Scott, being a virgin!"

Joel sees the scared little boy in Scott's eyes. "Scotty, it's no biggie. The fellas think it is boss. You're your own man. Not a wimpy follower of the pack like the rest of us, Dickheads! Many of us wish we didn't rush to throw away our V-chips so early in the game, to be honest."

Scott is mortified. *How does everyone know about my personal situation? How were they so quiet about it for so long?* He's speechless.

"Exactly! Joel's right, Sunny!" Mr. Bowman says while tapping him on his shoulder again.

There's an awkward moment of silence. Scott finally puts his insecurities to rests. "Well, I asked Kyra to be my guest, and she gladly accepted."

Boastful cheers and rousing playfulness sound out as each of the guys charge Scott with ample hugs, handshakes, and ruffling his hair. It's a congratulatory moment for all. Scott finally had the nerve to ask the girl of his dreams out. Scott smiles and throws his sweaty T-shirt at Joel, hitting him on the side of the head with it. Scott sometimes forgets that Joel is the one true friend he has had through all of life, and he often forgets how he is six years older than him because of his wild youthfulness.

CHAPTER 25

"Hey there, Timmy lad, I am feeling like a boss right now. I think I should really head back to school next week, little bro." Jason says as he jogs on the treadmill at a record-breaking speed.

Meanwhile, concentrating on Jason's readings, Timothy glances over the rim of his laboratory glasses to peer at him, "Sure, you are well beyond the healing stage now, I see no problem with that. But I need to see your physical power at its max, not your quantum boost."

"Now? Are you playing with me?" Jason appears confused. Timothy has constantly been telling him to take it slow and not to overexert himself.

"Yes, affirmative."

"But I thought you said—"

"I am aware of what I said, Mr. Brodie. I am saying this now. If you are going to be out in the real world again and you find that you need to use the full extent of your powers, then I need to know you won't have any unforeseeable complications like blacking out or dying."

Jason feels unsure about the task he is being asked to do. He does fear his ability now. That episode had never happened before, but he puts his faith squarely in Timothy's superior mind. "Okay, me lad here goes nothing!"

Jason bears down hard, surging intense amounts of kinetic energy. With a crackle of lightning, he bursts into supersonic speeds. It's impossible to see his legs moving. "Faster!" Timothy yells out. With everything Jason has, he throws his whole body into his motioning. Jason's body starts to glow with serene energy as the threads on the treadmill undergo overwhelming stress, releasing smoke from the motor.

"The speed tracker has you close to Mach-one!" Hearing great excitement in Timothy's tenor, as he informs him of the great news; however, Jason's body becomes hotter with each second. Jason has never pushed himself so hard for so long without using his quantum force mode. He feels strangely overheated as his eyes begin to grow blurry. Soon he is no longer able to see anything within the lab.

Timothy finally looks away from the monitors and sees that something is terribly wrong with Jason. His body is emitting a strange, unexplainable glow. It appears to be his own life's energy. Apparently, as he runs faster, the glowing aura begins to darken in color, turning from a bright golden red to a whisking blue.

"Stop! Stop!" Timothy screams out. "Jason, Stop!"

Jason can't hear Timothy's screams, for his sense of sound is gone now. He feels very light-headed and immediately starts losing speed rapidly and runs off the machine and crashes into the neighboring wall. His body is saturated with perspiration.

Timothy slams his clipboard to the ground, charges to Jason's side, and grabs hold of his collapsing sweaty body. Jason has lost the strength to stand on his own. Timothy helps him to a chair and rips the cables and sticky probes from his friend's body.

Completely out of breath, Jason's normally rosy lips now show a light shading of blue. Trying to stare into Timothy's scared eyes, Jason collapses into his unexpectant arms. Timothy trying with no luck to balance him in the chair feels it is better to set him on the floor instead. Pulling Jason's limp, heavy body onto himself, Timothy safely lowers him to the floor. He places Jason on his back. Grabbing a towel, he rolls it up and places it under Jason's head for comfort.

Jason appears to be going through a hypothermic shock of some kind. His skin and eyes start to lose their luster and wrinkle, a true sign of severe dehydration. Thinking quickly, not allowing his emotions to take over, he knows he must get Jason's body back to room temperature while replenishing his fluids immediately. He grabs an aluminum arctic thermal blanket from the closet and activates its heating element.

He quickly removes all of Jason's clothing, including his damp, soiled underwear. Aggressively Timothy starts drying him off with extra towelings. He places the heated blanket over his weak body. Fearing the blanket will take too much time, he quickly disrobes, gets under the covers, and covers Jason's cold, naked body with his own. While wrapped tight in the blanket, Timothy hooks the slow-drip IV to Jason's arm to replenish his fluids. Timothy can't help but feel the chill of Jason's body under him. Luckily, Timothy knew he wasn't hurting him with his weight.

After an hour or so, Timothy drifts off to sleep. When Jason regains consciousness, he suddenly feels the warmth and the weight of Timothy's limp body on top of him. He can see Timothy is completely exhausted, latched onto him like a kid with his teddy bear. It slowly dawns on him that Timothy's junk is rubbing against his abs. Timothy is completely naked under the blanket.

What the hell, Timmy? Are we both naked? He mentally checks himself with disbelief. *Why would you do something like this? What if Ms. E. came in and saw us like this, all over again?* He wiggles slightly and determines they are indeed naked.

Reaching his hand slowly around Timothy's waist, he feels the soft flesh of his body. He slowly moves his fingers farther down and surprisingly feels the beginning crease of his soft butt cheeks. Jason can't believe what he is feeling, but he is compelled to explore further for some reason. He examines the full length of Timothy's moist, hairless butt crack.

Jason feels exhilarated. He's not thinking. He just wants to feel Timothy. Jason slowly extends his middle finger into Timothy's plump cheeks, nudging his puckered opening. At this moment, Jason gently enters Timothy's very relaxed, yet tight anal cavity with his middle finger. He inches his finger in, digging deeper into his moist internal warmth.

Timothy is instantly aroused, albeit still in his slumberous state. His body clenches tight onto Jason's finger, which causes Timothy to pop an instant erection between their two stomachs.

Amid the pleasuring of Timothy's receptive body, Jason hears his name uttered, "Jason?" There's a look of dread on Timothy's face, as he peers down onto Jason. Understanding how wrong his probing is to Timothy, Jason retracts his finger from Timothy's rectum, with a slight slushy pop sound.

Timothy feels the unsettling snagging release of Jason's finger probe, and trembles to break free from Jason's arms, running hazardously to the bathroom completely naked, falling several times along the way. Jason calls out to him, but he doesn't respond.

Sexually aroused, and seated on the floor, Jason is left in a daze of confusion. *How did he get to the floor naked with Timothy on top of him? And what possessed him to explore Timothy's body the way he did? Did I just assault him?* A horrifying question, Jason is afraid of answering.

In the bathroom, curled up on the floor against the closed clear

shower doors, Timothy is naked and afraid. 'Why was he being violated yet again? First Craig and now a boy he felt safe with. There's a
knock on the door. "Timothy, please. I am sorry. I don't know what
just happened and why." Timothy remains silent as Jason persisted
in pleading with him. Finally, Jason tries the doorknob. He finds
that the door is unlocked, and so he cautiously enters the room. He
sees Timothy sitting on the floor, his head on his knees, completely
exposed. Jason snatches a towel from the shelf and walks slowly
over to him. He gracefully places the towel around him to cover
his body. "I am so sorry, Lad. I never meant to harm you, especially
in that way."

"So why then? I thought you weren't that way."

"I don't think I am … or at least I never thought I was."

"You just —! I thought I could trust you."

"Believe me, please. I didn't mean to. I don't know what came
over me. I had this need to feel your warmth for some reason, and
I couldn't stop."

With hurt in his eyes, Timothy says, "How could you, Jason. I
don't mind you being in me. But, you know I am not clean." His
voice cracks hard, thinking back to what Craig did, after playing
with Jason's butt,

Jason didn't realize just how unsanitary that really was … or
how humiliating it must have been for Timothy, especially if he had
pulled more than a finger out of him. But he didn't feel grossed out
by it all. He seeps into Timothy's scared eyes. "There is nothing
dirty about you, Timmy. You're not unclean. I don't know why I
did it. You trigger something unique within me that I can't control.
It's crazy. I want to feel you, hold you, and be inside you, Timothy.
I need you like a fish needs water, Timmy."

Timothy scoots slightly away. "You what? That's fucked up! You
know, that, right? I was not clean down there for you to be probing.
I could have given you an STD or—"

"A blimey boner, maybe? That ye did. You're pure Timmy, this I know. Waking up and seeing you on top of me, I couldn't help but feel something for you. I just need to know now. Do you have any feelings for me, beyond friends?"

Timothy looks at him like he's been granted a miracle and smiles. "But what you are asking can never be, Jason. I feel I may be gay, and the last thing I would ever want is for you to be something you're not. I wanted your friendship since the moment I saw you on the field. Boys don't excite me, never have. But I can't stop thinking about you. God knows the last thing I want to be is gay and a geek, Jason."

Timothy removes the towel, fully exposing his aroused penis for Jason to see.

"I wasn't mad when I ran out. I just didn't want to be unclean for you. As you can see, I got a boner too."

"Straight boys don't get boners from other boys. This much is known. But you and I are something different, and if this is a thing, we are going to have to accept whatever this is."

Jason reaches for Timothy's face. "Let's not label this shit, okay? I know I love girls. I've had quite a few and enjoyed every moment with each of them. But this is something different. I feel connected to you, Timmy. I don't know why. I am just connected to you. If you are willing to share this with me, I am all yours too. Believe me. There is nothing wrong with your beautiful body." Jason kisses the tip of Timmy's erect boyhood. The sticky sensation of his kiss sends tingles throughout Timothy's body.

Jason reaches for Timmy's face, but Timothy quickly slaps his hand away, surprising Jason. "Um, not with that hand you ain't. I know where it's been. Remember?"

Jason starts chuckling but then places the dirty finger into his mouth and sucks it. The sight almost makes Timothy cringe, but it excites his sexual desire for Jason too.

Timothy takes charge, reaching over and taking hold to Jason's face, and then he presses his plump and warm lips against Jason's. Their tongues engaged in a playful dance, consuming completely. This kiss starts a new chapter of love and wonderment for Timothy and Jason, not to mention a morning of sexual explorations.

CHAPTER 26

After a couple of hours, Jason is scrambling on the floor beside Timothy, slipping on his trousers. Timothy laid there silent, naked and spent on the bathroom floor. "I hope I didn't hurt you too much, Timmy."

Timothy says, "Not really. You were so gentle inside me. I feel empty without you now. I ... just hope it was okay for you."

"I'm no brute, Timmy. I knew it was your first experience. The last thing I want to do is hurt the one I love. I care deeply about you. And you felt so perfect. You are definitely the best, I have ever had."

"You're my first, Jason! You did this before? You know, in the—?"

"Oy' Lad, I am NO—virgin! I lost my innocence some time ago. You are my first bloke, however. I had several girls, who were virgins, and wanted it in the caboose. I didn't want your first time to be as painful as there's seemed to be. That's the reason I kept telling you to relax it and why I took it nice and slow."

Timothy says, "Oh, my God! You were holding back? I thought my insides were going to pop my stomach for a minute there!"

"So, so sorry, sweet lad. You should have told me I was making you uncomfortable. I want you safe."

"I thought that's what normally happens—that's all."

"Look, Timmy, if this is going to work, we have to be totally open and honest. This is just as much for you as it is for me. With more practice, we will feel each other's rhythm completely."

"Practice? Are you crazy? That thing between your legs is a freaking one-eyed demon."

Jason stares at his visible bulge and then looks back into Timothy's eyes. "I promise that if you allow me to ever penetrate you again, I will be gentler. I promise." Timothy stands slowly, exposing his anus to Jason's face, his junk dangling and spent between his opened legs. Timothy hears a lustful grunt from Jason behind him. Before Timmy can say anything, he feels Jason's tongue tasting the labors of his love from Timothy's spread cheeks. Timothy instantly blushes, and then he moans so delicately.

"Jason, I don't know what this is, but I am yours completely. However long you want me, I am yours." Jason's expression draws deep with each lap of his tongue.

"Timothy, I've never tasted anything so delicious as you. You make me feel amazing. What I feel for you is special. I am looking at the most beautiful person in my whole world, and nothing can ever compete with what we just shared. You opened yourself to me completely and literally. That is magical in any realm, my sweet lad. You are just so beautiful to me right now that it hurts my heart. I can devour you whole … and that hole too. I am smitten with you, Mr. Daniels, my lover, and my friend."

"Hey, you can't say that, can you? I mean … is this really happening between us?"

Jason can't quite focus as he sees Timothy's Johnson bouncing freely about as he is talking. Bashful, Jason smiles and says,

"Honestly, Timmy, me boy, it is hard for me to concentrate seeing your monstrous thick banger dancing all about."

Now dressed in his tight black T-shirt and beige slim-fit trousers, Jason showcases his semi-aroused bulge. Timothy feels embarrassed. "Oh, crap. Guess I should cover up or something. How rude of me. I just feel so comfortable with you. I know you don't want to see my stuff."

"Timothy, are ye listening to anything I'm saying to you, my dearest heart? I just made love to the most amazing lad in all the world, and your floppy parts are fucking beautiful to me. I am crazy about you, lad. I can honestly say that I will play with ye banger all freaking day with a big poofter smile."

Unable to respond, Timothy drops his clothes and leaps lovingly into Jason's arms. They embrace each other, and they are now a true couple.

"Jason, you are amazing." Jason smiles, seeing Timothy so emotional.

"Shut up, and fucking kiss-me already, Timmy-lad."

While Timmy is off showering in delight, Jason feels some deep apprehension. His devotion to Timothy isn't like anything he has ever experienced with the girls he had been with before. His other anxiety comes from not knowing what exactly happened to him while running on the treadmill at full throttle.

Something is off. Jason thinks about how weak he felt the day he and Timothy had their confrontation with Craig. Jason realizes the jaunt on the treadmill was the fastest he has ever run before. Blacking out though is something new to him. Well, along with his new insatiable craving for food and Timothy all the time. Now he feels like he wants something, anything to eat. With lightning speed, Jason raids everything in the pantry and the walk-in refrigerator, which actually stored enough food for two to three weeks.

The bizarre thing is he finishes all the food before Timothy gets dressed and returns to the lab area.

"What the hell?" Timothy yells in amazement. "Jason, where are you?"

In the next room, Jason hears Timothy's outrage and quickly makes his presence known. To his surprise, the lab looks like a tornado has come through, swallowed the room, and spit it back out. Jason looks at Timothy like a child with cookies all over his face.

"Jason, what did you do? How much food did you consume?" Bewildered, Jason looks at him with a confused expression. Even he can't recollect how much he has consumed, but he still feels like he's starving for some reason. He explains his hunger and fear to Timothy.

After some serious thinking, Timothy stumbles on a possible theory. "Look, I remember the first night you stayed here, and Mrs. Eileen fixed you a big breakfast the next morning. She said, she also never saw someone look so hungry before. You suddenly started to heal faster and thinking about it, you were in a feeding frenzy for the next couple days actually."

"So, what are you saying?" Jason showing real curiosity and a quirky smile.

"When we fought Craig and the others, you told me you felt really drained for whatever reason. You told me, it all seemed to start when you met my friend Kyra. I don't have a reason for you just yet, but it appears you, were burning out that day, and all your excess energy dealing with your speed, was making you physically weak.

Eating somehow refuels that energy force and starts your healing factor. And today you reached Mock 2, and your body started glowing. And it was glowing, mind you. I believe that may have been your actual life force resonating around you, and when you overexerted yourself, all your thermal energy reseeded and basically was snuffing you out through super hypothermia. In using my own body to cover yours, you somehow absorbed my internal life energy and drained me, knocking me unconscious. When you probed me, you were energized by the rush of the thermal flux. However, when you made love to me, your body was weak still, and the cravings must have been unbearable."

Jason is overwhelmed by Timothy's brain. Timothy takes him to another lab and injects Jason with a serum. Jason doesn't question Timmy, but he's still very curious. Timothy explains the serum is a nutrition supplement for astronauts who are undergoing long-term orbits in space. It gives the men the nutrition they require.

A few minutes later, Jason's intolerable cravings for food diminishes to a mere little grumble. Jason smiles with tender relief, and his green eyes sparkle most affectionately for Timmy, his salvation. Timothy has the evidence he needs about Jason's remarkable abilities and his dire weakness. He feels it's time to introduce Jason to the thermos-flex genesis suit he has been revamping since learning of Jason's speed potential.

With anticipation, Jason follows Timothy to a new section of the lab to see his working product. With the most inexplicable timing, he receives a text from one of the boys back at the center. The text asks if Jason will meet with him later that evening at the Harvest Fair. The boy says it's urgent and even uses the flame emoji.

Jason feels something serious may be going on, but he knows he won't feel right not inviting his greatest friend and now lover. He asks Timothy if he wants to go to the Harvest Fair to meet up with a kid and maybe check out the fair too.

Although Timothy never once had any reason to go to any social outings, now he has something amazing and sees a life of possible adventures. Jason has walked into his life, and together, they're breaking down walls. He dares not let any opportunities such as this, escape his grasp ever again. Like a madman, he rushes up to Jason and gives him a huge hug. "Of course!" he says.

At a loss for words, Jason laughs warmly. "Okay-okay, me Timmy. I get the point. You want the go. Fine. But we need to chill with all the hugs when we get out there, aye?"

"I understand. What we have is only for us to know." Timothy keeps his head pressed up against Jason's pulsing chest, and they remained locked in each other's arms for some time.

CHAPTER 27

"What time is it, Mr. James?" asks Dr. Kline, his head tucked in a huge pile of files on his desk, about the ongoing DH trials.

Although working diligently, Eric turns away from his computer and replies, "It is 5:15 this Sunday morn, sir."

Dr. Kline sharply lifts his head from his mountain of papers with a stern expression. He has crow's-feet around his squinty brown eyes. Dr. Kline starts, "Damn it, Eric! It's Sunday morning already! I've been working on the numbers for fourteen hours straight." He scrambles through the scattered paperwork on his desk. "I don't have any new answers to give to Mr. Black. None whatsoever! He is expecting a report about finding one of the keys of Ancestria … from that Mathews child. Did the three subjects report back in yesterday?"

Mr. James feels a little apprehensive in replying. "Well, Sir! Michael and Shihan came back early. Cheryl, however, came back somewhat disoriented. She acted as if she couldn't recognize me for the few moment or so."

"Disoriented you say? What the hell are you talking about, Eric? Explain yourself better please! Was she physically hurt at the expo?"

"Not quite. Shihan and Michael can't seem to recall exactly what happened to them all when they reported back. Cheryl spotted Kyra, the very girl we have been wondering about. She then separated from the guys to seek her out. Michael said something came over him, and he couldn't keep focused. Mr. Adam Sparrows was there too. All Michael could recall was that while talking with the young man, he was suddenly gone, and he was missing about twenty minutes of time. Cheryl being lost to Michael's tracking, he knew they must retreat. Finding Shihan Chin, he demanded the Ryuu to shimmer them both out of the building undetected

"Can't we track her?" Dr. Kline, pinching his own chin, while in deep thought.

"He's been trying to no avail. Shihan recalls there was an encounter of some sorts like Michael's, he too reports losing time. Obviously, something very powerful erased their memories of the event. Shihan sensed there were more powers present than they originally expected. A camaraderie of chi strengths culminated together, he said. He felt a union of spirit and chi unlike any he has felt before. An alliance of power. Then suddenly, everything was gone … along with the time."

Dr. Kline questions, "If their memory was affected somehow, how would they be aware?" Eric steps away from his computer to give Dr. Kline his full attention.

"Shihan showed me three deep burn scars, two on his back and shoulder and one just below his left rib cage, all of which weren't present before their departure."

Mr. Kline slowly places his pen down on the old metal desk and steps away. "Burn scars? On Shihan? That would presume an altercation for sure. And they would have to be very formidable to take on Ryuu. For he is basically indestructible in his Ryuu-no-Kage form."

"Yes, that is my only estimation as well. Plus, Michael said their watches had stopped, sir."

Dr. Kline stands erect with his arms tightly crossed. "Just maybe our Ryuu found his mysterious Shira-Kami and fought her only to find out she wasn't the only mystery guest present. We can't rule out the Kyra girl. It sounds like the key's true element may have been activated after all."

"How's that, sir? What do you know of the key's effect?"

Thinking long and hard, Dr. Kline places his index finger and thumb on the five-day-old shadow on his chin. "Not too much, really. Only what Mr. Black let slip out when we last talked." Kline anxiously paces the floor. The heels of his steel-toe boots click on the hardwood flooring. "He mentioned that the key in its many forms is a powerful weapon when put together. Only a true chosen one, can activate a keys power. The key is known to protect its host bearer by using local resources within its surrounding environment or by manipulating time. Each key has a different trigger. Per Dr. Becker's research, many believe that the five key fragments were originally a supernaturally forged crystal heart. It was created to be housed in a mythical creature that could serve as the keeper or guardian. Many believed it was made by the very powerful ancient race. Some say sages, and other says mystics. It could possibly be extraterrestrial. The creature was known as the Jade Dragon."

"A dragon? Was he drinking something? There are no such things."

"I will not get into that philosophical mumbo-jumbo just yet. But I will say that from what his research showed, the dragon was a guardian of the inner realms and nether worlds, governing over time and space."

Eric doesn't say a word. When Mr. Kline is sleep-deprived, he behaves rather disconcerting and unruly. "So, if we believe that two keys are within our grasp, what of the others? Do you have a theory to shed some light on that subject?"

Dr. Kline chuckles briefly. "I am glad you asked. That's the interesting part! He believes five pieces were purposely scattered in safe locations with the hopes of never being recovered and placed together again."

"Who would have done that?" Eric asks, acting curious.

"I am not sure, but some Alexander Maximus guy back in the BC era was referenced in some ancient scrolls Dr. Becker found, while on his archaeological excavations in Italy. The scrolls say that he had slain the mystical beast that breathed the eternal green flame. He ritualistically drank its blood after he ripped out its beating heart, which turned into a jade crystal. He made a personal trophy of the heart, and he couldn't seem to lose in any battles henceforth. He quickly rose through the ranks of the guard to sovereign lord commander, ruler over beast and men by the Roman Regimen Army."

"This is really an interesting fairy tale!" Eric says.

Paying Eric, no heed, Dr. Kline continues, "It was rumored his heroic feats of victory were looked upon by laypeople as inhuman and ungodly. But strangely, many years later Alexander never seemed to age a day and remained a strong young man. He soon hid his face from the world so that no one would notice his eternal youth. He was known by all to be the strongest and most feared knight in the order of the Crescent Knights, and the last dragon slayer of the Draconian Knight Order. So, it was written."

"Wow, remarkable tale. Mr. Kline. Do you presumably believe, any of that be true?" Eric asks with concern. "What became of the heart trophy or the man?"

"The scrolls said that centuries went by. Alexander had to change his name through the generations as not to bring unwanted attention upon himself. But as for the stone, that is the key point here. A woman came into his life. She seduced him, stole the heart, and broke it into five pieces, known as the keys of Ancestria. The keys took on many forms and were scattered from his sights, except the one piece the seductress left in his care."

"So, Mr. Black is looking to combine the keys to open a gateway to something unimaginable?"

"I believe so. But Mr. Black doesn't suspect that I know this much. So, whatever you do, this is going no further than this room!"

"I guarantee, Dr. Kline, that nothing you said here will go any further than this moment."

"Good. I expect nothing less."

"Where is the female subject?"

Eric doesn't like the way Dr. Kline still refers to Cheryl as a subject. "Cheryl is in Isolation Bay 2619 Alpha. She has been drifting in and out of consciousness all through the night and this morning. I last checked on her about an hour ago. I gave her a stabilizing serum, so she will be well rested and hopefully more cohesive when she awakens."

"About how long, will this take to happen?"

"I would give her about five to six hours of sleep. Then we can see."

Dr. Kline looks at the clock on the wall. "I'd better give Mr. Black a call and see if he can move his time frame to later in the evening."

In the meantime, deep in the underbelly of the facility, Cheryl is lying on her back, resting on a cold metal table with sensors attached to both of her temples. The room is devoid of staff and medical personnel, and all appears quiet and restful everywhere—that is, except for Cheryl's unconscious mind.

Deep in her mind, there is a little war happening. She is reliving events that she is unfamiliar with … or that she has forgotten somehow. She sees herself much younger, wearing old clothes. She has dirty hands and worn shoes too. She sees herself in an abandoned building with trash, rats, and homeless people scattered all about. Everything seems all too real to her. *Where am I? What is this place?* She yells, hoping someone will respond to her. But the people she sees look at her and say nothing.

Suddenly, little hand grabs hold of hers. "I am here, big sis. I am sorry I got lost again." *Is that the sound of a tiny male child?* Before Cheryl sees who's holding her hand, she finds herself standing amidst an incredibly active marketplace with lots of busy people swarming about with urgency.

She doesn't recognize anyone around her, but she notices the huge fruit stands across from her and instantly feels uncontrollable grumblings from her stomach. She knows she must eat something quick. She checks her pockets for some money with no luck. She tries asking the people walking past her. They won't even slow down long enough to acknowledge her. "Hurry, big sis. I am hungry." She looks around and sees a little boy, maybe no older than five, with torn clothes and a hole in his shoes. He has scruffy sandy brown hair, and a partially burnt teddy bear clutched tightly in his arm.

The boy points to the cart that is loaded down with apples. "Look, Sis. Apples! Let's get some of those. They won't miss apples, will they?" the boy says. But he doesn't turn his head around so that Cheryl can see who he is. Something is oddly familiar about the whole thing, which makes her uncomfortable. It's like she forgot something that she should never have forgotten.

This dream has manifested more than once in the last year, but like a dream, she forgets it the next morning until she dreams it again. "I want an apple, Sis. Get me one, please. I am so hungry, and Maxi is too!" exclaims the unrecognizable boy as he looks at his teddy.

"We can't! We have no money! Those apples are two dollars. I don't have it. I would like one too."

"Well, use your superpower then, sister, and get us some."

"Superpower?" she says to herself. What was this boy to her, and what did he know of her abilities?

CHAPTER 28

Miraculously, Cheryl finds herself standing in an oddly familiar house. She hears running water and the voices of two grown-ups, which draws her attention. Lenny Crain says, "Damn it, Frannie! I had enough of this crazy shit! Things move about at all hours of the night. Wild, weird noises come from that little bastard boy's room. Why on God's green earth did you agree to bring these two ungodly creatures into our home?"

Seeing a younger version of Cheryl standing there with tear-filled eyes, Frannie calmly tells her to go back up to her room. Frannie turns and sees Lenny a breath's length away, staring at her impatiently. "Look, Lenny. You wanted the damn family. At least you said you did, and I couldn't have children. Cheryl and Liam are ours for maybe a short time. It's only been 3 months. They have no one and nowhere to go. Yes, there is something strange about them, I admit. But that doesn't make them evil."

Cheryl slowly reaches the top of the clearing, overhearing the whole dispute. "If those … kids—if you can call them that—are still here when I get back, so help me, Frannie!" he bellows, putting his old John Deere baseball cap on his partially balding head. He slams the door, almost shattering the glass panels.

Cheryl walks toward a bedroom that appears to be hers. She hears a subtle whimpering sound coming from the room adjacent to hers. With a stealthy approach, Cheryl peeps in to see who is crying. To her startled amazement, it's a four-year-boy with course, dark chestnut, shoulder-length hair dressed in his SpongeBob pajamas. His body is facing the wall, and he's curled into a ball on his bed and hugging a worn-out teddy. Slowly opening the door, she softly steps inside. In a soft voice, she says, "Little boy, are you crying?"

The boy doesn't move, but sniffles. "No!" he replies, which was an obvious lie. Cheryl feels overwhelming sympathy for this boy, although she's unaware of who he is. She fears he has heard the arguing from downstairs.

"Don't worry about them, kid." She tries to comfort the little boy.

"They don't like us, do they?" Cheryl feels so confused by all the events happening around her. *How is all of this related to her?*

"I can't say for sure. Our foster's kinda taken us in when no one else would, I guess. Maybe Lenny is just angry about work, or probably just drunk." Cheryl finally moves to his bedside and uses the name she heard. "Liam?" she pauses for a response.

Liam slowly rolls over to face her. His little face is pale, and his wide eyes are hazel blue in color and filled with tears. His lips are soft and peachy, and they are trembling a little with fear. "Sis, I don't want to be here anymore." Hearing him call her sis startles her. In her mind, she doesn't have a little brother. But why is this dream so vivid? It's more like a memory than a dream. She feels that something is dreadfully wrong. What is this? Her thoughts become entangled as her memory rushes back to her mind in harsh waves, *Is this Liam? My Liam? How could I ever forget Liam?*

"Oh, my God. Liam, it's you. How could I have forgotten you?"

"Forgotten me? You promised you would never leave me or forget about me. You promised, Tessa. Did you lie like you did when you said that Mommy and Daddy would come back to get us?"

With tears, Cheryl says, "I didn't lie. You've got to believe me. I didn't know. I won't forget you again. I promise!" Then she gives him a huge hug.

Unexpectedly, the red bedroom door slams open, vibrating the walls. Lenny storms into the room, a foul stench of booze and old stale cigarettes oozing from his pores. He takes a firm hold of Cheryl's frail arm and marches her out of the room and over to her alleged room. He brutally throws her to the floor, slams the door, and locks it behind him.

Lenny starts, "No funny voodoo bullshit from you, you little witch!" She bangs on the door to get him to let her out of the room.

A garbled voice with hiccups exclaims, "Shut up, you little witch! I will deal with you … soon!"

Cheryl hears a struggle between the married couple. Frannie is pleading with him to leave the kids alone. Cheryl hears a loud slap and a loud crashing sound like a body falling onto the glass table in the hallway. She can't hear Frannie any longer.

Desperate, Liam starts calling out for Cheryl. Lenny slams the door to his room, and he and Liam are alone inside. Cheryl can hear his loud and abusive profanity through the thinned walls. He audibly removes his belt, hearing the buckle clinking.

"I should whip the devil out of you, boy! I know you burnt my lucky sports blanket!" Pleading for him not to hurt her brother, Cheryl hears several swing attempts. But Liam wasn't staying still. She can hear things falling off the walls and breaking.

Cheryl's worst fear is realized, when she hears Lenny belch out with a massive grunt, "I got your little ass now, boy! Little demon, your running days are over!" Lenny's voice sounding ominously victorious. A horrific sound fills Cheryl's ears, as Liam screeches a horrific cry, a thunderous thump of something with weight slammed violently against the wall divide of Cheryl and Liam's rooms.

The scream is instantly silenced by a thump against the backside of her bedroom wall. Was it Liam being thrown against the wall and crashing solidly to the hard floor. Everything goes eerily silent, no whimper, screech nor cry.

Liam is deathly silent now, and so is Lenny.

Frannie regains consciousness in the hallway and now bangs on Liam's door, demanding Lenny stop what he is doing and let her in.

"I am teaching this little shit who the boss is around this house. I have his Max bear! You destroy my shit, and I'll destroy yours!" Liam yells out. Lenny stands above Liam lying vulnerable on the ground, screaming at the top of his lungs.

Lenny's ears ... and then his nose and eyes start bleeding. "What the fuck?" he screams out. "What the fuck? I can't see-I can't see!" Suddenly, the hand holding Liam's teddy bursts into flames as Lenny screams again. Frannie manages to get the door open to Liam's room and screams when she sees Lenny engulfed in flames.

Cheryl hears nothing but terror and fear from the next room. Focusing her mind, she manages to open her door. Before Cheryl can make it to Liam, Frannie is thrown clear from the room into the hallway, busting a hole into the Sheetrock. The mere sight stuns Cheryl. Frannie pleads with her to get her brother and run. "Hurry-Hurry-hu—!" she exclaims before fainting.

Cheryl finds Liam holding tight to his teddy with giant tears in his eyes, his room filled with raging flames. Lenny was no longer recognizable in the burning ashes. Cheryl grabs hold of Liam, and she is instantly transported to the very marketplace where the government abducted her a year later. Liam is now five, and he points to the apples on the stand, practically demanding one. Suddenly, a spark of flame catches onto one of the awnings.

"No, Liam. Not good!" Cheryl realizes that a five-year-old boy with power is still a five-year-old boy. She charges over to the stand to snuff out the flame with her jacket. Suddenly, a merchant yells at her, saying that she started it. Cheryl is scared and confused. She's only ten years old herself. She tries to explain, but another merchant takes hold of her. Liam cries out and tells them to let his sister go. One of the men's eyes begins to bleed. He shrieks as Cheryl tries to break free from his grip. Then she unknowingly releases her gifts, and nearby objects begin smashing wildly. Cheryl tries to make her way back to Liam when everyone starts running away out of fear.

Lost in a frantic crowd of people, Cheryl calls relentlessly out for her little brother, but she can't find him in the crowds. With great fear in her heart, she desperately fixates on the smoke-filled skies and screams a horrific, inhuman sound.

Miraculously, manifesting from out of nowhere, a mighty arctic blast of torrid winds descends upon the open market, thrashing everything in its path and tossing people from their motorbikes. Car alarms sound off as debris flew about chaotically. A man wearing a black suit and dark shades stands before her, holding something in his hand.

Finally, she sees that it's a tranquilizer stick, and then she feels a jolting charge course through her young body, rendering her unconscious. As she is falling to the ground, all she can do is try to yell out for Liam over and over till she hits the ground hard.

Cheryl wakes instantly. Disoriented and confused, she scans the unfamiliar room. She's not sure if she's still dreaming or not. She yanks away the probes from her forehead. She forces herself to stand from the table in a hazy daze.

For a medical room, it feels very military. Suddenly, Cheryl remembers. *Dr. Kline. My mission.* Everything feels strange and disorientating. She feels her way around, instinctively knowing she must flee before she is seen. If nothing else, it's clear that she has a brother out there. Five years is a long time to be on your own in a messed-up world.

While sneaking out of the isolation room, she starts to remember the layout of the dim corridors and tunnels. Maneuvering with great skill, she halts, spying on Michael and Shihan engaged in a hostile conversation, both still baffled by their lack of memories.

"Shihan, I don't know how we lost our memories yesterday. Obviously, something went down because my jaw is bruised and aching. I don't remember anyone sucker punching me. Do you?"

"It was a strong cast laid upon us by a formidable crafter. We may have the answers we need when the girl awakens."

"Hmmm, if you are hoping for that bratty-ass piece of garbage to solve this, you are deeply mistaken, buddy."

"I am not your buddy!" Shihan says with a wicked grin.

"With all the extra crap they have been giving her, she still isn't totally dedicated like the rest. I say we should just put her out of her misery and call it a day. But the boss thinks she is important for something."

"I agree, Dark Hunter. In time all will be revealed. Once she outlives her usefulness, you may have that chance. They are still trying to crack her genetic code."

She's heard quite enough. Cheryl makes a stealthy exit from the facility, and then she makes her way off the premises, clear of detection.

A few hours pass and Cheryl finds her way into the town. Speaking to some people, she learns of a nearby shelter. Locating the shelter wasn't that difficult. However, the staff informs her that the place is completely booked. One of the administrators asks how old she is. Cheryl tells him her age and the admin smiles. He grabs a clipboard off the wall behind her. "You are still a minor. There is a place you can go that will be more accommodating for your age group and give you better security than this place." He tells her to visit Mrs. Prescott and gives her a number and address.

Cheryl graciously thanks the admin and searches for the place. Her head swirls with vertigo. At around 10:00 a.m., she finds the place and speaks with Mrs. Prescott, who seems pleased to help Cheryl with her dire situation. She explains how a room will be made for her within a couple days. For the time being, she can borrow a room that belongs to another teen who is out temporally. "Just don't bother his belongings. It may not be much, but they're his. He is a bit of a loner!" Mrs. Prescott says while opening the door to the room. Some of the teens, mostly the older boys, watch with amazement as Cheryl is escorted to Jason's room. Once inside, she pays the unwanted attention no mind. She gives everything a quick glance and crashes on the bed, her face to the opposite wall.

Back at the facility at around 11:00 a.m., Eric makes his way to check on Cheryl. That's when he discovers that the girl is missing. He scrambles to each room, searching for her. Michael sees the scientist running around a worried frenzy. "Mr. James? What seems to be the problem?"

Eric says, "Have you seen Cheryl this morning?"

Michael shakes his head. "No. Was I supposed to?"

"Oh, dear. This isn't going to go over too well. Cheryl is missing, and Dr. Kline needs to talk to her about yesterday before Mr. Black arrives in another hour."

"Missing? I thought she was sleeping?"

"She was. But somehow she woke up and left the area."

Michael looks to Eric. "Don't worry. She won't get far. We will go find her and place this base on lockdown." Michael grabbed Shihan from one of the strategy rooms. Eric quickly explains to Dr. Kline what has transpired. He tells them to do whatever it takes to get that girl back. He will have to handle Mr. Black when he arrives.

CHAPTER 29

In the festive historic township of, Upper Marlboro. The streets date over a hundred years of long-standing lineage and architecture. The autumn seasonal decor all abounds. From the courthouse to the centuries-old Bank at the end of Jefferson St. The town is dressed tight with pumpkins, autumn leaves and orange and black poster's hang on every pole and storefront window.

One of the posters questions boldly, "What do you ask of the Harvest Lord? Come, one and all, to the spookiest time of your lives at the Franklin High's Halloween Spooktacular!"

It's a warm Sunday afternoon just after the noon service at St. Agnes's Church, near the county's courthouse. Kyra and Julie decide to share a picnic bench together on the church grounds while their parents partake in the potluck brunch filled with egg salads, pasta, many types of casseroles, and exotic dips creatively crafted from famous food network stars.

"So, let me get this straight! Miss Kyra Cassandra Mathews? You and Mister, Star Athlete extraordinaire, Scott W. Tanner, are seriously a thing now?"

Kyra turns bright red and smiles from ear to ear. "Of course, you know this already. Remember the day of the break-in?"

Julie nods. "I know. Believe me, I know. It's just spreading like wildfire all around the school these days."

Kyra tosses her hands in the air. "Why can't people mind their own business?"

Julie gives Kyra, the wise woman stare. "Hun, when you are officially dating the most popular, all-star athlete—oh, not to mention a mega hottie—in Franklin High, this is bound to be on everyone's news feed."

Placing her hand on her forehead, Kyra begins. "I guess you're right. It's so ridiculous, this high school melodrama."

Then Julie questions in her best Barbara Walters impersonation, "So how does it feel to have gained the respect of your parents and become an active member of the modern social world? Like having your wheels back? And what are your plans for the very near future? Primarily speaking, after school tomorrow maybe?"

Kyra responds, "Honestly, it's a major relief, and I have made plans to meet up with Timothy after school tomorrow. We needed to go over some plans for the SciTech Challenge coming up in February."

"Eww! Geek patrol! Geek patrol … on the road!"

Kyra gently slaps Julie on the shoulder with the back of her hand. "Hey, don't do that!" she exclaimed with a subtle laugh.

Julie apologizes, "My bad, Miss Mathews. Quite unprofessional of me, I must admit. I can't help but notice, Tim-o-Tron-3000 has really opened up, lately. Do you have any insights on this new development?"

"Excuse me?"

"You know, can you elaborate? Why he doesn't act like a robot these days? He appears to be infiltrating and blending in with the normal populous."

"I think he is coming into his own. That's all, really." Kyra tries to avoid, releasing anything about Timothy's private life, she bounces back with. "Why the concern over Timothy, Miss Walters?"

Julie smiles somewhat awkwardly. "Well, if you must know, since breaking out of that proverbial shell, he is showing major signs of being a relatively hot sophomore."

Kyra shakes her head. "Please leave that boy be, you cradle-robber. Have you no shame, Miss Thang?"

Julie stares with wide eyes. She can't believe how defensive Kyra is about the young students. "It is great that he is finally opening up. He is a very sweet kid. He kind of reminds me of Kyle—when Kyle was a lot younger and before he became an arse."

"Oh, double G's. You think he may develop a body like good ol' Kyle when he grows up?" Julie flutters her eyelashes.

"Um, Eww! Seriously, Julie? My brother? What the hell is going on up there in that sexually charged brain of yours?"

"Hey, your brother may be a douche! He is hell-a-fine though. He has a great ass build, not to mention the obvious fact, he's very blessed down—!"

Kyra thrusts her hand, forcibly over Julie's mouth. "For heaven's sake, you'd best not go where I think you are! I will disown your ass, Julie! Don't even play like that. What are you thinking? Seriously, Kyle?" Kyra exclaims, not wanting to see her brother being reduced to a sexual object, because of his endowment.

"Ouch, tender subject got it. Besides, we were talking about Timothy anyway."

"Yeah, we were. I was just going to say, there is so much more to Timothy, people just don't get."

"I'm sure!" Julie says. "I saw him sporting those cotton hip-hugging shorts."

"Oh, my God! Robbing cradles again, eh? You need some penance for the way your brain is wired."

"All I'm getting at is that since he buddied up with Jason, he's truly a changed man. So chilled, confident and way more sociable." Julie compliments Timothy, and Kyra approves.

"Now that I mention his name, Jason is some young hotness in the making too with the red hair and bouncing booty. Those thick thighs can melt butter. Seriously. Hmmm, and he's a Scottish boy too, which is super hot! Yum."

"Now-now-now! Hold your horses, tigress. That's jailbait yet again."

"Damn, that blows. Jason is a sophomore too, but for the bright creamy ass, I would do a little time. I could really work—"

Kyra points a warning finger at Julie's face. "Don't even think about it!" Julie laughs as Kyra continues, "I think it is awesome that the fellas are so chill with each other, you know?"

"Yeah, apparently so. Don't get me wrong. I have nothing against Timothy, but isn't he a social dampener for Jason's elite babe appeal? From what I've heard, everyone is saying he's destined to be the next Scott Tanner. That's if he chooses to join any of the athletic programs next year. I still wouldn't mind meeting the young guy everyone is so talking about these days. I know he didn't take a picture for the yearbook this year."

"Didn't know that. But seriously, Julie, you of all people think a person is only as good as the companions they keep." Julie looks cornered and gives a funny facial expression. Kyra breaks it down for her, "I don't see that in him. Jason is a genuine kind of guy, a boy of his word and true to himself. I don't believe he looks for the approvals of others to make his life choices. He does what he feels is fair and just to him. He has a big heart, and he's genuinely pleasant to everyone. I can see him being something special to many people as he gets older. Like right now, he seems to really adore Timmy and isn't afraid to let other people know about it. He doesn't play games like a lot of the jerks in our school. I think many people seem to really dig that about him."

"Honestly, Kyra, that's actually major. More of these clowns should be following his lead. I say good things for good people!" Julie raises a fist in the air along with Kyra. "Go, Timothy and Jason, bros for life."

Julie then says, "By the way, you remember Adam, don't you?"

"Umm, yes. Who couldn't? The tall, toned, and native hottie."

"I have been chatting it up with him before the meet, and now we are a bit on the DL because he is two years older." Kyra's eyes light up like Christmas ornaments. "He's really amazing to talk to, and he's helping Coach Johnson in the gymnasium in a few weeks next semester with the beginner's self-defense training workshops. I thought it would be cool to see him again, you know, in the flesh."

"Can't possibly disagree with you there. Just remember to sign up for the workshops. And not too much flesh!"

"You know, things could get messy … if he wasn't such a Boy Scout!" Julie retorts, under her breath.

Kyra bursts out into laughter, spilling some of her drink on the ground. "Girl, you are sick!"

Julie laughs too. "Oops, girl, we are making a scene." Julie notices the eyes staring at them.

"Yep, thanks to you." Kyra jokingly points at her, giggling.

Julie gets a little serious as she peers into Kyra's eyes. "Are you going to the fair tonight with Mr. Wonderful?"

Kyra blushes. "Well, he is picking me up after dinner. He's gonna meet my folks, and then we are going to head on over."

"Oh, shit!"

"Shhhh!" Kyra covers Julie's mouth with her hand.

"My bad. I am so sorry, big guy." Julie remarks while looking up to the heavens. "But that is awesome. I asked Adam yesterday. But I wasn't sure if it was possible. He has labs that need to be done this week. And prep for the tournament took a good portion of his work time away."

Kyra shakes her head. "This is what happens when you are talking to a college man."

The girls burst into laughter once more.

CHAPTER 30

Much later that evening, Scott picks Kyra up from her house and meets the family for the first time. Kyle scopes him out as Rissa is amazed at Scott's shade of blue eyes. She even calls him a prince. Kyle shrugs off the remarks with a cheeky grin. Uneasy with the looks and stares, Scott stays silent. Kyra's mother seems overly hospitable to him. Scott gets some one-on-one time with Mr. Mathews and Kyle.

With Mr. Mathews, it's more about this boy respecting his daughter and taking care of her. He also wants to know what colleges Scott is thinking about and which ones have sent him letters of acceptance. Meanwhile, Scott meets Kyra's twin brother for the first time. It's funny how much Kyra and Kyle look alike. Kyle was obviously a very handsome stud with a bright smile and well-groomed faded haircut. The straightness in Kyle's hair tells Scott that this boy has some Indian or Hawaiian in him. He's very attractive boy either way.

Kyle wastes no time just like a protective brother would. "Look, Scott, I know who you are, and I know your rep around the school. I don't get into my sister's affairs because I don't want her in mine."

Scott has a hard time imagining this guy in front of him is actually a virgin. He clearly shouldn't have any problems with the ladies. "I don't want you hurting my sis in any way. Got it!"

Scott responds with a nod.

"I will be on you like stink on a skunk, Mr. All-Star Tanner. I know my sis is going places, and she is going to do great things. I aim to make sure she does."

Scott is impressed with Kyle's directness and obvious love for his sister. "I will be a true gentleman with her. I will never make her do anything not becoming of her. I want her happy. If I hurt her, I will personally let you kick my ass."

Kyle gives a smile. "You are okay, dude."

"So are you, Kyle. I don't think your sister really knows how much you care about her, man. You know she loves you dearly and wishes great things for you too."

Kyle starts getting a little bashful as his boyish charm starts creeping in. "I know. But don't tell her. I like to keep her on her toes."

Scott shakes Kyle's hand and then gives him a manly hug. "Your secret's safe, bro!" Scott whispers in his ear as Kyra reenters the family room. Mr. Mathews assures Scott that he will be taking Rissa and the Mrs. Mathews on Monday afternoon to see the work they did on Mr. Bowman's fairgrounds this year.

As a gentleman, Scott opens Kyra's door before getting in the car. Scott and Kyra can feel the eyes staring at them from the house as they pull out of the driveway. Mr. Mathews looks to Kyle. "So … when are we going to see your plus-one, Son?"

With a miscreant grin, Kyle says, "My bad, Dad. But sweaty, hairy jocks aren't really my thing." He taps his father on the shoulder while grabbing his thin jacket. "Gotta zip, Pops! Benny and I are going to shoot some hoops at his place."

Shaking his head, Kyle's dad simply smiles. "One day you'll be normal, kid. One day."

"Don't hold your breath, Pops. Too boring." Kyle darts through the front door hops on his crotch rocket, and skids off.

Scott starts. "Kyra, your brother, is a piece of work, isn't he?"

Kyra glares. "You think? I am forced to live with that total pain."

Scott chuckles. "Maybe you shouldn't be so tough on him. Under all that sarcastic armor—"

Kyra interrupts, "A stinky, butt-wipe jerk for a brother! That's what you mean, right? He's an enormous prick."

Unfortunately, Scott recalls Kyle's natural endowment below the belt, "Ah, Eww! So not what I want to have in my head right, now. And yes, the rumors where true, I saw." Kyra's eyes pop wide, Scott would even admit it, Scott continues, "Anywho, what I was saying, Kyle is a good guy, with complex outlooks on things, yet he tends to deliberately lead you to think otherwise. It's strange!"

Kyra sees how serious Scott is about her brother. "Seriously, come on. Don't tell me you fell for his macho bull crap too?"

"I wouldn't say that. I am just saying your brother may actually surprise you, Kyra. That's all."

"Oh, wow! You've got to be kidding me. He's got you with his secret mojo thingy, Next thing you know you two will be wearing matching friendship bracelets, and boxers, OMG!"

Scott almost chokes. "Excuse me? OMG! How did we get there? Boxers?"

Kyra laughs. "My brother is a grade-A jerk. Enough said!"

"Okay-okay! Yes, he comes off rather crass and strong! But I was right about one thing. Be honest. Your bro is one hell of a good looking guy. Not that I judge remember? Some girls from the squads know him and consider him something of a hot unattainable item. They dig his cocky confidence. I don't see him as girl shy at all like you suggested earlier. I think he wants something more, someone, who will meet up with your approval. I bet."

Absolutely dumbfounded, Kyra sees just how serious Scott is. "Really, Scott? You got all that just by meeting him today? What on earth did my brother say to you?" Kyra eyes and ears perked high.

Scott grins. "Sorry, sweets. That's only for us fellas. It's the bro-code thingy."

Pfsst Kyra gasps out air. "The bro—what? Seriously?" She shakes her head, blows it off, "Okay, whatever!"

"Give'em time. The guy is heading somewhere! He hasn't found it yet, but I see real potential in your brother to be a leader much like you."

Kyra laughs into the palm of her hand. "Ah! Too funny! Those are my father's exact words about him. I really must have missed that briefing somewhere."

"Well, think of it this way. Your father is a very strong, independent guy with a real head on his shoulders. He might just know a little something."

Kyra smiles. "You are right. My father isn't often wrong about people. Even when he gave me the wink earlier, saying I did well with you."

Scott's cheeks turn rosy with such approval from her father. "Anyway, enough about those guys in your life. How are you doing this evening?" Scott changes the subject. He takes a nice firm hold on her hand and gently starts massaging it. Their conversation blossoms as they continue their journey toward the fair.

Once at the fairgrounds, people start pouring in from every direction. With delight, Kyra admires the larger-than-life Ferris wheel in the evening's moonlight. The aroma of salty, buttered popcorn, steamed bags of freshly roasted nuts, sugary treats, and bright red candy apples fills the air. The joyful laughter and the polka music fills the entire fairgrounds. By the looks of the fair, she would never have suspected the place had been a barren, unplowed piece of land only days before.

Like a child on Christmas morning, Kyra takes in all the sights and sounds. Scott feels such a satisfaction just watching her delight in everything.

"Oh, Scott? Where is your friend?"

"You're talking about, Mrs. Levette?"

Kyra nods assuredly.

"She's not far. Just on the other side of the carousel. We will go there shortly after I get a picture with you at the photo booth over there."

Kyra agrees with a smile.

Making their way to the booth, Kyra notices that someone is inside, and she brings the presence to Scott's attention. "Don't worry, hun. Whoever it is, won't be long. We have next go."

Not more than a minute passes, and then the people within the booth slowly emerge from behind the purple curtain. Kyra's face becomes as pale as a ghost, which takes Scott by surprise. He shoots his eyes around and sees it is Kyra's best friend, Julie, is in the arms of a tall, good-looking Native American. Each of the girls appears surprised.

"Hey, K-girl." She stops to give Scott a once-over. "Hi, Scott. How are you guys?" Julie's voice is obviously shaken, which bewilders Scott and Kyra.

"Julie, what's up?" Adam closes the top button of his shirt.

"Adam?" Kyra asks with a hint of alarm. Julie never mentioned she was coming to the fair ... with Adam. As a gentleman, Adam reaches out a warm, inviting hand to greet Scott and Kyra. Taken in by the muscular physique and height, Scott smiles and returns the gesture. "Hi, I am—"

"Scott Tanner, MVP for the Franklin High football team. A pro-style quarterback. Am I right?"

Scott is completely blown away and boastfully proud with Kyra in his arms. "Wow! That I am."

Adam laughs. "I follow local sports, especially when there are great players." Scott thanks him for the compliment, and Adam explains who he is and what he is doing at their school after winter break to help Coach Johnson. Scott thinks it is great to have a self-defense program, especially after the recent events. The four become better acquainted with each other as time passes. They all seem to really click as a group.

Standing in line for the Ferris wheel, Scott sees a fairly familiar ginger-headed boy off in the distance with a shorter kid about to enter the house of mirrors. Scott excuses himself for a quick moment, assuring Kyra he will be quick. Kyra gives a stern expression. "You'd better hurry, or I'm getting on by myself!" That actually sends a chill down Scott's spine.

Scott jumps clear from the line and jogs off. Finally, Scott sees Jason firmly squeezing Timothy's bottom and quickly releasing it. Timothy is giddy with laughter. He turns to him and playfully punches Jason's arm. Jason laughs and tussles Timothy's curly locks, and he then proceeds to kiss his forehead, not concerned about who can see them.

Scott is deeply shaken by the interaction, considering what they went through not that long ago. With an uneasy feeling in his gut, he quickly returns to Kyra, never saying a word. When she asks who he saw, Scott thinks for a second and then says, "Oh, nobody. I thought I saw someone from school, but I was wrong."

"Next!" announces the attendant for the ride. "How many in your party?"

Julie climbs on board without haste, yelling out, "Four, good man. There'll be four!"

Adam climbs swiftly behind her, minding his head as he adjusts himself inside the ride. Scott lends a helpful hand to Kyra and helps her into the big carriage with plush leather seating.

The vessels can easily seat eight normal-sized people, but with Adam's longer legs, he requires a bit more stretching room. The cabin feels just right. Scott finally brings up the rear and climbs on board, nestling tightly with his arms around Kyra's shoulders, allowing her head to rest of his broad, warm chest. He reaches over gently and pecks her forehead with a kiss.

CHAPTER 31

Not far from the ride, observing from the shadows, Madam Levette, unbeknownst to them all, has her keen eyes securely locked on each of them. With a spark of interest, she swings her attention over to Jason and Timothy, observing their subtle cheery closeness as they depart the house of mirrors together. Jason is sneakily squeezing Timothy's butt, while no one is aware of his loving affections—except for Madam Levette.

Madame Levette knows a test is coming for the young people in her charge, and she is also exceedingly aware that this test might be enough to destroy the very fragile fabric of Kyra's unsuspecting circle. The strength of their unity will be the defining factor.

"Hmm, so it begins. So, it begins!" Levette whispers just loud enough for the mysterious figure amid the shadows to hear.

A smooth but cryptic voice responds, "As you knew it would be, my faithful companion. The time is at hand, and you know there will be great suffering to come for these young ones. The Linking Circle must undergo the final tests, like those before them. Don't lose your resolve young heart, for the seventh must be assimilated by the chosen. First, you must establish loyalty among the six. Has the Kyra girl, channeled each of the six's gifts?"

"Yes she has, and I am quite aware of the importance of the seventh, my dearest lady. I feel the tides are moving in the right direction for this chosen collector, Kyra Mathews. The one she needs to seek is fairly close and still hasn't unlocked her true potential at this point. May these poor, innocent children quickly grow into their chosen paths with grace and mercy." Levette heart feels for the kids.

"I agree, Isadora. Tonight is the first test of many to come for these … young ones. You must see it through with no interference. Understood?"

"Yes, I do. I just pray it won't end as tragically as the ones before them, my dearest mentor, Lady in White."

"How are the two pupils of your's fairing, Iziariaha, and Ambrose?"

"Balance is tilted toward the dark, I fear. Iziariaha and her brother Zaineb, the Kitsune siblings, are safely hidden away. Yet, I fear my longtime acquaintance Ambrose, the alpha prime wolf has turned dark. He has become the black cursed wolf. Now the other side has acquired a young hunter to locate him, which means they have learned of the alternative means of opening what should never be opened, outside of the crystals of Ancestria. So, we mustn't fail this time around."

"Things are moving much faster than the last time."

"Yes, I think we must prepare like never before, Isadora."

"I will do my part, my lady." Levette crosses her arms tightly against her own breasts.

Just as she finishes her words, her shadowy friend vanishes into white vapors. "Let come … what may. We shall stand … till the end." says the disembodied Lady in White.

Meanwhile, Julie and Adam are enjoying their splendid time in each other's company, sharing cotton candy and grand humorous moments of laughter. Both are competitively calculating who will bring home the most stuffed prizes by the end of the night; however, all sides agree that they will not use their unique skill sets during the challenge. Since neither of them is big on collecting giant stuffed animals, they both promise to give all their winnings to the local children's cancer ward. Bringing happiness to the little ones is important to them both.

There's a gentle breeze tonight. Adam and Julie are both fixated on the beauty of the night and each other. Everything feels right with the world now that they have each other.

Scott is enjoying Kyra's soft cuddles while holding hands, and Julie is enjoying Adam's free spirit. So too, Jason is enjoying his secret intimacy with Timothy, not knowing the others are only a heartbeat away. The six individuals are basking in an amazing state of delightful bliss. Julie and Adam decide to take a walk through the haunted hay labyrinth after dropping off several dozens of their prizes at the front ticket booth for safekeeping. Kyra asks Scott about checking out the house of fortunes since he promised earlier that day. Scott looks at her enchanting eyes, and they kiss as sparks fly. This is the first time they're able to fulfill their desire for intimacy.

Meanwhile, Jason and Timothy accidentally stumble upon an unexpected development. They have no desire or plans to share their intimacy with the public because they know the intolerance of most of their peers, especially the straight-laced Scott Tanner. Just then, however, Jason catches Scott in the throes of a passionate embrace with the beautiful Kyra, undeniably glancing right toward Timothy and him.

Jason's anxiety engulfs him like a tsunami. He realizes his hand is still nestled snugly within Timmy's lovingly tight grip. Jason quickly rips his hand clear from Timothy's.

Uncertain, Timothy scowls at Jason with baffled concern,

shifting around to possibly learn what has spooked his brave, loving partner, Jason. Soon he notices Kyra and Scott together a distance away.

The couple is now gazing in their direction. So too, Julie and Adam approach from another direction. Their joyous giggles abruptly stop as they sense an intensity between Scott and the younger boys, mainly Jason. Suddenly, there is an awkward moment of silence between the three couplings.

Praying desperately for any deity that will answer him, Jason hopes like hell Scott didn't witness their intimate embrace. His mentor and close friend, who often joked about guys who lived as weak bastards, will assuredly be devastated by this new development.

Jason steps forward to greet Scott and Kyra. "Scott? Kyra? Hey, funny running into you guys here!" Jason waves his hand and wears a very unconvincing smile.

"Stranger things have happened, I guess." Scott's cracking voice shows great distress on his mind. Kyra smiles at Jason and gives a gentle nod. Then she turns her attention to Timothy, who appears a bit confused by their presence.

"Timothy? Wow, you actually came out to the fair, lab partner!" Kyra's voice greets Timothy's ears with a joyous sense of invitation. Timothy's stress levels decrease immediately, and he becomes a little more relaxed. Jason wants to reach over and kiss the hell out of Timothy's pretty little boyish face, seeing such happiness. But he doesn't know if this group will accept the news about him and Timothy, so he chooses to remain detached, not wanting to raise any red flags yet.

"Hi, Kyra! I thought I'd finally partake in a sociably acceptable construct. If it weren't for this big guy, I am rather certain I wouldn't be here." Jason's palms start to sweat while observing Scott. He has never witnessed a look like this from Scott before, and he doesn't care much for it. He wishes he was a million miles away. If it weren't for the cute boy with the cheeky grin, he would have blazed out some time ago, never to be seen again.

Unbeknownst to Kyra, Scott clearly feels a personal betrayal from a guy he mentored and thought he knew so well. She nudges Scott's ribs, wanting to move closer to the boys. Scott, however, presents a noticeable resistance in moving. So many things inside of him are screaming for him to walk away right now. The last thing he wants is to be confronted once again with one of his deepest fears—another strong male in his life betraying their symbolism of masculinity. But he doesn't want to disappoint Kyra, so he buries his emotional upheaval about the possible union of Jason and Timothy. Ironically, Jason senses something is about to dramatically change, in Scott and his current relationship with him.

Scott gazes upon Kyra, hiding his insecurities with a charming smile, turning his attention to the surprisingly enthusiastic Timothy. Julie and Adam graciously walk up and greet the newcomers with a warm hello and introduction. Jason can see that Scott doesn't want to make any direct eye contact with him, which leaves him with a terrible twisting feeling in the bottom of his stomach. *Is this my new reality? Did I lose the only friend I ever had because of this thing I have with Timothy?* Jason ponders.

Kyra welcomes Timothy and Jason with a heartfelt hug, but unexpectedly, she senses a little trembling in Jason.

"Wow, it's so great to see you guys. Isn't it, Scott?" Kyra doesn't understand Scott's sudden withdraw in personality. Everything was so warm and fuzzy at first.

Without any cheer, he says, "Ah, yeah … sure."

Julie easily picks up on the tension without needing to use her extrasensory perception, but she decides to keep her peace and simply observe.

"You know, just seeing you guys here and together is a real treat, especially you Mr. Daniels. Jason must have really performed some magical feats to get you out of your fortress of solitude. Here you are, looking so relaxed and unwound. How's the arm?"

Timothy nods with giddiness. "Arm is much better, and Jason is an amazing buddy. He has been something of a muse to me, to be honest." Timothy still looks for some sign or reaction from Jason, and still, there is none but a mute expression.

"It is such a great night to be out under these amazing stars. Probably the biggest display in forever." She wraps her arms snugly around Scott then. Timothy almost says something about the night sky, but he manages to hold back, not wanting to be too geeky and embarrass Jason.

"And this weather is simply divine. It just seems like magic is in the air." Timothy smiles with such joy. Kyra sees a glow about him. Timothy acknowledges Jason with warm infatuation, but the look isn't returned. He tries to reach his hand over toward him, and Jason sharply flinches away.

"What did I tell you, Julie? The red hair, right?"

Julie's eyes practically come out of her eye sockets, "Oh, my god! You weren't kidding. It is mega cute on him. Loving the red! He is the real deal for sure, unlike yours truly."

Jason isn't feeling amiable enough to smile, so he simply nods with a slight grin, thanking her for the compliment, which makes Timothy even more concerned about Jason's sudden change in personality.

"Hey, is something wrong? This isn't like you!" Timothy whispers into Jason's ear.

Scott chimes in with sarcasm, "Yeah, Jason! Something is different about you tonight. I can't quite squeeze my—hand on it! (he cuts an eye at Timothy) You know what I mean?" He emphasizes the word *hand*. Now Jason knows his greatest fear is an undeniable reality. Scott did see him and Timmy together romantically, and most of all don't approve.

Jason feels instant rejection from a guy he deeply admires and looks up to as his role model and brethren. Jason stares at Scott with such unspoken hurt in his heart, affecting him in the way he doesn't expect. Timothy peers up to Jason and can't believe his eyes. A single tear escapes Jason's eye and pale cheek. Kyra, Julie, and Adam see the tear fall too, while Jason stares motionless at Scott.

Julie sees Jason struggling with something emotionally and calls out to him, playfully. "Jason? Ginger-king? You okay there, big guy?"

Timothy sensing the tenseness in the air and reaches out to his beloved friend. Jason snaps out of his stolid stare and clumsily stumbles a few steps back while staring at Timothy as if the boy was a complete stranger to him. Timothy reaches out for him with heartfelt concern, sensing a fight or flight within Jason. Peering into his true loves worried eyes, with the greatest of regrets, Jason's voice shakes. "I am so sorry Lad. This simply can't be!"

Timothy snags tightly to Jason's quivering arm, knowing deep down in his spirit, if he lets him go, Jason maybe lost to him, forever.

"No! Please, Jason! Don't say this, don't do this, please, Jason! I need you—" Pleading Timothy, as Jason abruptly cuts in, "No! You don't need shit, my Lad!" Jason sharply looks to Scott, seeing a look he doesn't like.

"You are a wee bloke like me, Timothy. You don't need shit, from another bloke, and that's it. Now let me go, Timmy!"

"What the hell are you talking about, Jason? You know—!" Timothy struggles to hold onto him.

"I don't know shit, Timmy! I don't know what the hell I was thinking! Everything is so fucked, and you know it." Jason can't take his eyes off Scott's disapproval of him.

Adam, Julie, and Kyra are witnessing a breakdown in Jason, which seems to have come out of nowhere. Great confusion is going around about the dialog between the boys.

"It is all wrong, Timothy! I am not what you need. I am not!" He looks to Scott again, tears freely falling. "I am not what anyone needs." The words hit Timothy like sharp daggers.

Kyra is struck with confusion, while Adam clutches tight to a confused Julie, sensing the unspoken nature of Jason's internal conflict.

"I am really sorry, Timmy, my lovely boy. I don't need to be a part of this world—if I am only destined to be a miserable disappointment to everyone I care about."

Scott watches intently like a child who can't play the lead role in the play but then learns the role is far more intricate than he originally thought.

Jason rips away from Timothy's grip and jogs toward the darkened path leading to the giant hay labyrinth. Timothy yells for him to stop. "You know I can't catch you, Jason. Please stop. Don't go!" At this moment Timothy doesn't care who knows how he feels for that sweet redheaded Scottish boy.

Kyra shakes her head and looks at Scott with such disdain. "What did you do?"

"Me?" Scott becomes defensive. "Why is this my fault? The boy is obviously not right. It's not like I told the queer-wanna-be, to run off crying like a goddamn, Drama-Queen!"

With a tone very familiar to Eric, Carlos and Craig's, Timothy glares at Scott viciously. "No?! Seeing it is your self-righteousness! You didn't have to, Jerk?" Timothy protests boisterously.

Kyra, gives Scott a stern look of confusion, "You weren't aiming to stop him, were you? The way he was looking at you with such want and fear, and you were avoiding him in every way you could. You might as well have been the one chasing him with a stick, Scott. This isn't like you. You have so much heart, and I thought you cared so much for that kid.

You talked my head off about him, and then you instantly go

cold on him tonight, for what reason? What has Jason done to deserve such desertion from the guy he looks up to the most, Scott? What did he do to deserve your rejection of him, now?"

Julie and Adam stand back silently, not sure what to do in this situation.

Scott looks at everyone around him, with a disdained look of bitter betrayal.

Finally, he looks at the confused, tearful Timothy, and back at Kyra. "It's something I can't quite explain. I saw something I didn't want to see. It's like my father all over again. I believe I knew someone, and then I learn a startling secret, which only breaks my heart later."

Timothy feeling distraught, hearing such words from Scott after Jason has told him about Scott's great compassionate heart for others, especially when battling to gain his friendship and later, brotherhood. A trembling fear befalls Timothy, watching his whole world run off into the dark night with no sense of coming back. The uncertainty of what Jason is thinking and doing; All the while, knowing he isn't protected, should he decide to use his power.

"Come on Scott! Get a clue, asshole!" Timothy raises his voice with pent-up anger. "You really think I don't know why ... Jason is out there, not wearing the suit I made for his own protection tonight? (looks flutter between everyone surrounding him, for none of them know of the suit or why one is needed.) He is out there doing god knows what! All because of you! (pointing to Scott) You the fucking homophobic role model and mentor, who just looked at him, as if he was the garbage of the freaking earth! Are you so damn insecure over your father's bullshit, you'd prove to be no better than the three assholes from school, like Craig and his backup butt-buddies?"

Scott scrambles to get a hold of Timothy. However, Adam is right there to take hold of him, stopping him short of engaging

Timothy, physically. Clamping firm to Scott's arms like mighty vice grips, Scott is instantly alerted to the sheer physical strength of Adam.

"Hey, if you know what's good for you? You may want to let me go, Buddy!" Scott threatens, while seeing a look in Kyra's eye, he never wanted to see. A look of fear and uncertainty. Kyra sees darkness within Scott, which wasn't there before, or was it always there, just below the surface. She pleads with her heart for him to back down. Surprisingly, for Adam, Scott does just that.

"Oh Yes, Scotty Dearest! It is common knowledge! Your father left your mom for a male whore. He was a prick, for doing that, yes! Not Jason. He is scared and now out there, on his own!

You're so hellbent, feeling like you've been betrayed! Jason is fucking straight! You homophobic prick! He and I, share a bond that's above the physical and we truly love each other unconditionally!" Timothy exclaim as the spittle flows from his lips.

"You don't get it! Jason, your so-called buddy? Went through hell! Craig did some messed up shit to him, and you will never understand. I hated being the ringside participant of his torture, watching him defile Jason's beautiful body in such a way, Scott! I know your thinking, Jason betrayed you or your trust, like your father did!"

Unaware of Timothy, his very words are like devastating daggers to Scott's very soul. Burning with rage and internal hurt, while all within one cyclonic whirlwind of emotion, Scott desperately wants to stop Timothy, yet understands how right Timothy truly is.

"You don't care! …or should I say, want to care! You think every boy who feels the way Jason and I feel for each other, is like reliving your father's betrayal of you and your mother? Ultimately, hitting everything against your cherished ideals and embedded beliefs of what a man should be, don't you?"

Scott, stares Timothy in the eyes, in the middle of his speech, in a voice which seems to be implanted in Timothy's head somehow, "Back down... Go sit!"

Meanwhile, Timothy states, "You are a hypocrite S-Sco—." Timothy pauses instantly with his mouth open wide, a sight concerningly surprising both, Julie and Adam. Timothy gives Scott the blankest stares as if Scott's command was the only thing surging in his brain.

Without another word spoken, Timothy moves away, sniffling to himself. He wanders a few feet and uncharacteristically plops himself lowly on the dusty road, just as directed by Scott.

With eyes filled with bent fury, transforming into utter shame as he watches Timothy sitting on the harsh ground in tears, yet again. Scott recalls how happy Timothy was, not so long ago. The image of the boy's, coming out of the house of mirrors, repeatedly plays in his mind. There was true love there, he can't deny.

Scott, standing solitude, void of emotion or words. He hates the low-ball move he performed on Timothy without his knowledge, forcing his will away from him, with a mere thought.

Adam, with questionable uncertainty to what has just occurred, steps up and tap Scott's shoulder.

"I can't begin to know your spirit, Scott. It appears you are caught in an internal conflict within yourself. I also don't know what it is you did, to make the boy so submissive. But, you need to come off the mighty horse thing you have and correct this. Jason and Timothy, are two broken spirits who managed to connect while surviving a life-altering event.

They traveled a rocky road, no one should ever have to. The boys found unity and spiritually bonded in a way only their two souls could understand. They are internal brothers now, inseparable hearts. Convened by a love, far beyond the mere understanding of social labels— gay, straight, Bi-sexual, or anything of the sort. Don't place your misguided prejudices against them, without first understanding, the desert they crossed, all alone. Not cool, for a leader among men to do."

Julie kneels by Timothy's side comforting him, with Adam standing at her right side.

"Understand this, we aren't going to let anything happen to your sweet friend, Timmy. This is a promise!" Julie and Adam simultaneously agree, collect the shaken Timothy, and make their way towards the entrance of the fair, to ensure Jason didn't leave the fairgrounds, yet.

Kyra, not in the greatest of moods, gives a bewildering stare, filled with hurt, toward Scott. Before taking off in the direction Jason had originally run, Kyra shakes her head with silent disbelief. All the while, leaving Scott, standing alone on the deserted, dank, dark road.

CHAPTER 32

Searching the dusty road leading to the man-made labyrinth of hay, Kyra spots Jason farther ahead on the trail. He's on his knees, sobbing. She calls out to him to get his attention, but he doesn't respond to her. She jogs down the trail toward him to get closer, and she attempts to call out to him once again. This time she manages to spark his hearing. He glances back down the trail and sees a girl advancing toward him. He wipes his tears away like a little boy who doesn't want the bigger kids to see him crying.

"It's okay, Jason. Come on back to the fair!" Kyra pleads as he staggers to his feet.

"Leave me, lass. I should not have been here or anywhere for that fact!" Jason yells back, which makes Kyra very nervous. She wonders what he might do to himself.

"Jason, stop."

"You can't stop me, lass. No one can. I know what I must do to make everything okay for everyone."

Know what to do? She questions to herself again. Using her cell phone, she texts Julie that he is headed out toward the maze and that he is in a self-destructive mode.

Julie alerts Adam as they run back to a distraught Timothy and a disenchanted Scott, explaining the text. Julie, Adam, and Timothy run to get Julie's car, trying to get to the other side of the fairgrounds to block him off from the other side of the maze.

Scott stands by himself, pondering heavily. He paces back and forth, pulling at his hair, slamming a fist into his palm. *What the hell am I doing? I shouldn't feel like this. I have this aching pain in my heart, and my stomach feels like crap! Jason is a great kid with a big heart, a true blessing to get to know, and for God's sake, Timothy is no different really in his compassion and friendship with Jason. It's not like I haven't already suspected a spark of something lingering between them. I should have been supportive of Jason for finding someone who makes him so happy. I know his sad and troubled life. If he hurts himself tonight, it will be my dumb-ass fault.*

Suddenly, a voice whispers from behind him, "Things happen for a reason, young Scott. They always do." Scott turns to see Madame Levette standing there, reaching out to take his nervous hand.

Julie, Timothy, and Adam take a quick ride to the end of the fairgrounds to a neighboring hilltop that overlooks the entire maze. There are just enough lights outside to see the people moving inside.

"Please stop, Kyra. Once I start running, you will never see me again. I promise."

"I can't let you just run away, hun. Timothy, I can safely say, loves and needs you in his life. We all do."

"Not fucking Scott! Tell him I won't be a disappointment to him any longer. Oh, and tell him, he can be the fastest guy in school again. I won't be there anymore."

With his last words, Jason charges off at a blistering speed, leaving a mighty dust trail behind him. Kyra doesn't believe her eyes. She never suspected that was even possible. Even though she knows she can never run like that, she runs after him with great desperation. From the hilltop, Adam sees the dust flowing toward the maze, "What the hell is that?" he points to the dust trail.

Timothy peers out. "That's him. That's my Jason. I told him he can't do this right now. He is going to burn out his life force."

Julie looks. "What is he? He must be breaking sixty miles per hour down that road."

Instantly, the dust storm stops. Jason falls to the ground yet again, obviously hurt, gasping for air. He hasn't fully recovered from his last burnout. Kyra sees him about three football fields away. Without a word, she goes into a full sprint, and like the time with Scott, she feels the energy build in her. Her speed quadruples, and she feels the rush of wind compounding her body. She makes her own dust trail as she quickly approaches Jason. Timothy sees Kyra as if for the first time. Her unbelievable speed is much like Jason's.

Is it possible to have two speedsters attending the same school and not know? Kyra, is that really you? What the hell? Timothy thinks.

Julie flashes back to the cafeteria incident and remembers Kyra's lightning-fast reflexes, grabbing the falling cup out of mid-air. Adam looks to Julie and Timothy. "Today is the day the Great Spirit is calling its children. Kyra, too, is a chosen spirit on the pathway of a destined rite of passage." Timothy doesn't try to understand Adam's words now. He only wants to be down on the ground with Jason, and that's all he can concentrate on.

Kyra stops a few feet from Jason, who is climbing to his feet. He doesn't expect Kyra to advance so quickly. He is sweating profusely. His shirt and shorts are completely saturated.

"Jason, please come with me. You aren't looking so great."

Jason can't believe how fast Kyra caught up with him with no vehicle. "I don't know how you manage to get here, but—" He struggles to speak because of the lack of oxygen in his lungs. "This is it, Kyra. I am tired of fucking things up with the people I care about. My folks, friends, and the foster family who actually cared about me. Now it's fucking Scotty, your boyfriend and the only guy I could ever really look up to. He can't even look at me now. I am so done with this crazy, fucked-up existence, Kyra. I am getting off the train ride. Tell Timmy I am sorry, but he deserves much better."

Kyra pleads with him. "What about Timothy, Jason? What do you think about him losing you? You are willing to desert him when you are the first person he has ever opened up to?"

With tears in his eyes, he says, "That's why I can't, Kyra. He is all I think about, morning, noon, and night. I hate that that's the case. It's not normal to feel the way I do for another boy. He has a great chance at a great life with real friends and people who can love him unconditionally."

"Jason, that's your sweetie, and you know it. Am I wrong in saying this? You are the one guy who unlocked his heart and loves him unconditionally."

"Yes. Maybe so, but I am a fucking boy like him. He doesn't need a nasty, disgusting bloke. He needs a soft, pretty lass like you to be his heart. Not a hairy, smelly dude like me. I always liked the girls, never any fucking blokes."

Jason drops to his knee, bawling. "I don't know why Timmy is so strong in my head, my heart, and my soul. I cry inside when I gaze upon his soft brown eyes. I forget he's a lad like me. We did the happy-happy for the first time, and instead of being disgusted by it all, I found myself ultimately enjoying every fucking moment of being with and in him. I stole his sweetest innocence before it's time. He gave up his virginity to me like a freaking birthday gift, Kyra. A nasty ass bloke like me, and not a sweet pretty thing like you. What kind of ass-backward, sick friend am I … I rammed my junk up his perfectly innocent plump sweetness? All because I was freakishly horny or some shit! I knew it was uncomfortable for him doing it, but he didn't protest once but loved me the more for it. I don't know how to feel about any of this shit anymore. I see the look in his eyes like this is eternal love or something. I may have fucked up his life forever, Kyra!"

Kyra tries to wrap her head around the imagery and the fact Jason is so open in his tearful confession about their very privately intimate, sexual relation, which is a lot for Kyra to process in her mind. As Jason paces frantically pounding his legs with his fists, he watches with a hawk-like vision for Kyra's reaction or response to everything he said. It is boggling to him, her subtle silence, and what it actually means.

"You must be totally disgusted with me for fucking your friend Timmy when we all thought he was a straight boy. I can see you judging me, as we speak."

"No! …never, Jason! I wouldn't do that. Timothy has a mind of his own! I just think you guys may be a little too young—"

Before she can complete her thought, Jason says with fire in his eyes, "Don't even say it. Please don't. I was too fucking young for half the shit that went down in my miserable life. Honestly, Timothy is the only true happiness I have ever accepted or will ever experience again. Goodbye, Kyra! This will be my last time I gaze upon such a delicate flower. I am happy to have known you. I shall leave this world tonight."

With his quantum force at full throttle, Jason blasts away at a blazing speed, far faster than anything she can see with her eyes. Jason blazes in the distance and sees the labyrinth rapidly approaching. He changes in his direction, and pops out of the quantum speed, continuously loops around the outer walls of the maze, in speedster flair, to drain off his own life force. He loops the maze within mere seconds at a time.

His speed was so fast the gang on the hill couldn't even see his movements, until he dropped out of the quantum and his body starts to burn up, his life energy becoming visible. He starts to glow a bright golden, leaving a trail of light in his wake.

Timothy screams at the top of his lungs while releasing tears, pleading for Jason to stop running! It's a sight that's breaking Julie's heart. She retrieves a hand towel from her handbag to comfort him.

Please stop him, Kyra! I beg of you! Julie prays. She walks over to console the distraught Timothy by wiping his face clean and wrapping her arms around him, assuring him that Kyra will do something to make him stop.

Kyra isn't really sure how to accomplish such a feat, but she can't pull her eyes away from the blistering display of glowing energy being emitted from Jason. She can't see him any longer. She can only watch the streams of light exuding from his energy trail. People within the maze are completely clueless about what is transpiring outside, behind the barrier walls, enclosing the perimeter.

Kyra understands she needs to reach him in some way. *C'mon, Kyra. You are the only one who can do this now. So, get off your ass, ol' girl. Get in there and help that poor, broken spirit. If only I could keep up with him, that would be a blessing.*

With bewildering wonder, her medallion opens, revealing the jade stone. The stones pulsate with a glow as an overwhelming charge of energy touches every cell in her body like blazing fire. Although she is getting accustomed to these experiences, this one seems to be more intense and stimulating. It feels like she just finished drinking a gallon of caffeinated energy drinks.

She figures this new sensation must be related to her request for more speed. Then she dashes off with everything her legs can muster.

Kyra feels herself zooming along with more speed than before. Ironically, she is feeling no discomfort or any exertion. She gains an acceleration of speed with every step. Suddenly, everything is no longer whisking past her in a blurred haze, but the world appears to have come to a complete standstill all around them. However, everything is moving at a microscopic speed while she and Jason continued running. Seeing his actual life force oozing from his body, Kyra quickly understands why there is a trail of streaming light behind him.

Jason looks back to see Kyra at arm's length away from him. From the hill, all they can see is a yellow streak followed tightly by a green streak whirling around and around.

Adam looks out over the fields to see if there are any stragglers out there. To his satisfaction, there are none he can see, and so he turns to Julie, who has a look of concern. Timothy just stands there, looking at the two pulses of lights.

"I think we need to cover this event so that others can't witness it."

"I agree, hun. But you know what that means, Adam?"

"I know. We must reveal ourselves to a normal. Do you see any other choice? Kyra has shown her hand. So, has Jason." Adam points out.

Julie shaking her head. She can't deny Adam's logic, "Fine. We shall do this."

Timothy overhears Julie and Adam's conversation, a bit puzzled.

"How you wanna play this, Adam?"

"Can you summon your Shira-kami cloud cover?"

"Sure, but I can't send it all the way over there. It usually shrouds me."

"Hmm, let me handle that part."

"Okay. As you wish, babe. One Shira cloud coming right up." Julie steps back, closes her eyes, and reflects on words of inner chi strength. "I am the sun, sky, moon, and air. Shira-Kami, I am one with thee and thou with me."

Gradually opening her eyes, Julie's irises emanates a radiant white light. Julie puts her hands together in a prayer-like symbol by joining the tips of three fingers; the thumb, index finger, and pinky. A fog-like substance starts billowing around her body and pouring itself outward from her center. Timothy watches with awe. Adam holds his arms up to the night sky and says, "Great Spirit of my ancestors, I call on my birthright of the air. Grant me your blessing." Then the air around him starts to turn and sway, lifting Julie's cloud. He guides it to the labyrinth down below. With subtle grace, the massive cloud fills the inner workings of the maze and blocks Kyra and Jason's energy trails.

CHAPTER 33

W hat the hell is that?" a familiar voice says from behind the gang. Timothy looks back to see Scott standing there, stunned. "Those blazes of light are our beloved mates. The yellow stream is my Jason. Because of your disapproval, he is running to end his lifes existence. The green light you see is—"

"That's Kyra?" Scott erupts, sounding totally shocked by the revelation. "Dude, I knew she was fast, but ... what the—"

Julie interrupts him, "You already dropped that F-bomb today, Bigot-boy."

Scott says nothing in defense, for in his mind, he knows he deserves everything he gets.

"Why is there a cloud only covering the maze? I can't see any-one." Scott examining with quiry.

Julie points to Adam and her, to give clarity, it isn't a natural act.

"I see. So, this is really happening." Scott finally coming to grips at all he is witnessing.

n's yellow streak is becoming darker by the second.

no, Jason, please stop this!" Timothy's reaction alarms the

"What happens when his color changes?" Adam inquires.

"If his glow turns blue, his life force will have been spent, and he will die."

"And he knows this?" Julie questions with alarm.

Timothy gradually nods his head confirming the answer as true. Adam, Julie, and Scott stare at each other as with concern for Jason's well-being. Jason's glow darkens from medium crimson to a deep purple, which means that blue is the next step in the color wheel.

"Kyra isn't quite fast enough to stop him. No one is at this moment." Timothy states, seeing the green light lagging behind.

"I am really sorry, Timothy. This should have never happened!" Scott says, trying to apologize.

"No shit, Sherlock! Bigot much super jock?" Julie retorts.

"You're right. I wasn't at my best maturity level this evening. I know what I must do now. I can't allow the boy I fought so long and hard to feel like he can fit in with the real world, just to lose him like this? Ain't f'ing happening! Not today! Seeing this is Show-and-Tell day … It's time for Scott to start sharing with the class."

"Show-and-what?" Julie questions him.

"What is he rambling on about? What can you possibly do?" Adam joins in the conversation, "Especially from way up here?"

Timothy using his logic, "He will surely go blue-phased before any of us could make it halfway down this hillside. Meanwhile, Kyra with her extraordinary speed is reduced to an arm's length away, unable to advance further. All she can do is witness Jason's undoing, up close and personal, which is only possible because Jason didn't go Quantum."

Scott places his index fingers to his right and left temples. He closes his eyes in deep concentration, focusing purely on Jason.

Jason, Jason, listen to me.

Jason hears a voice loud and clear in his head, that isn't his own.

"Get out!" Jason screams. While in his mind, Jason thinks about the past few days.

Scott struggles because of the emotions coursing through Jason's mind, but he must overlook the emotion and breakthrough.

Listen to me, Jason. Enough already. It is time to stop.

"Why? I mean nothing to you like this, right? I saw the look in your eyes." Jason screams to the voice in his head, knowing it is Scott.

As Scott touches his mind, Jason's life force turns blue.

"Oh, God! He is dying Scott. He is going to die!" Timothy shrieks out.

Julie looks at the blue and green streaks zooming around and around. When she turns to examine Scott, she witnesses a stream of dark blood oozing from his nostril. Jason is fighting him out, and Scott can feel death coming.

"I can't take this safely anymore!" With both fingers on his forehead, Scott yells out, "Stop now, God-damnit! I command you, Jason!"

Timothy and the others don't know what to do. They can't figure out what is going on.

Julie looks back and sees the lights have stopped. Julie can no longer hold the fog in place, "Oh no! The people are going to catch Jason and Kyra down there!" Julie exclaimed, apprehensively.

Shaking his head, Scott asks for the number of people in the maze. Adam counts them, "There are thirteen of them." Scott nods, sending out a subliminal suggestion to the thirteen people inside the labyrinth to fall sleep. Within seconds, all thirteen people fall instantly asleep, right where they stood.

Julie, Adam, and Timothy have completely blown their minds. Scott drops to his knees, completely spent, tearful and bleeding from both nostrils.

Timothy runs to his aid, "What did you do? Are you okay?"

Scott for the first time understands Jason appeal for the curly-haired boy before him, with the waterworks flowing.

"Don't worry about me, Kid. Go get Jason, Timmy. He needs you right now. I will get plenty of food for his energy."

Timothy stares at him. "How did you know about the Food?"

Scott looks down at the ground, "I Just know. I know a lot more than I did before, kid. Please go get him. He is deeply in love with you and really needs you more than ever right now."

Julie grabs Timothy to take him down to the labyrinth, while Adam tends to Scott's immediate needs. "Adam, please don't tell Kyra about this. I wanted to tell her in my own time."

"I won't, but you know your gift can kill you too. You are a mind walker, and mind walkers eventually lose their own minds with too much exposure and reach."

Kyra holds Jason in her arms as he looks up at her.

"You are amazing, Lassie. Never, have me seen anyone keep up with me like you did. Your Scotty-boy is much more than I ever thought he was too. Tell Timmy I'll love him always." Jason coughs, "I think he is my first true love, too."

Jason's head slumps to the side as Kyra sheds a tear, not wanting to believe everything was for not.

"No, you can tell him your damn self, Jason! You must hang in there, sweetie!" Kyra hears a car rapidly approaching. "See, Jason. Help is coming. Hang in there, Please!" She pleads with all her heart.

Jason's face turns a shade paler, as Timothy rushes out of the car. Sliding to his side, Timmy takes hold of Jason cooled hand. No words are said, but it was clear to them, Jason has passed on.

"No Jason, wake up!" Kyra doesn't realize he passed in her arms. With tears, Timothy reaches down and kisses him on the forehead and his blue toned lips.

"I am so sorry, my love. I am selfish. I want you here with me,

Dang it! You are my beautiful angel, Jason, and my hero! You made me want to live. You gave me new life."

Kyra places a gentle hand on Timothy's shoulder as he leans over Jason lifeless body. She looks to Julie, who stands there in shock, her hand over her mouth. Kyra looks at Jason's lifeless body, void of breath and getting colder to the touch.

A moment of silence passes, and there's no sign of life to be had in Jason's emptied vessel. Timothy knowing the one true love of his life is now gone as soon as it came, and Julie stands solitude and quiet.

"No!" Kyra blast out with fever in her tone, " I can't accept this! None of this! Jason, you need to wake the hell up, right now! You hear me, Highlander boy. Your man is right here pouring his heart out for you, and you just want to lay there and ignore his ass? Not happening, are you hearing me, Laddie?"

Timothy looks up at Kyra like she is a mad woman who has lost her mind.

She looks up to the sky. "The power which has been by my side thus far, I need you now more than ever. This boy deserves to live. He is needed, by Timmy and surely by us all. Help me bring him home, please!"

Julie and Timothy look confusedly as to whom Kyra is reaching out to, in her plea.

As if on cue, the medallion glows bright and strong, fully emanating with ambient life. Energy surges through her body, and she instinctively places her hands-on Jason's limp body. The energy passes through Kyra into Jason. Within seconds of her touch, the color quickly rushes through his cheeks and lips. Kyra can feel the healing energy entering his body, mending each cell, rehydrating his muscle, and warming his body temperature back to normal. This healing process is taking a lot out of Kyra. Jason is so close to death's door.

Another vehicle races to the scene. Scott jumps out of the car with bags of food. Adam has an armful of drinks. Scott sees what Kyra is doing and can't believe his eyes. *First supper speed and now this?*

CHAPTER 34

Timothy hears two faint coughs from Jason. "Oh-God, thank you, thank you. Come on, Jason. You can do it." Weakened, Kyra looks to Scott and Julie. Jason slowly opens his eyes and sees Timothy. He looks him directly in the eyes. Jason just bursts into tears as he reaches for Timothy and pulls him close. Scott feels major relief.

Suddenly, Kyra faints beside the boys. Scott drops the food and rushes to her aid. The glow fades, and the medallion closes. "Kyra! Kyra? Are you okay?" Julie grabs water from Adam's arms and sprinkles it over Kyra, which brings her back to consciousness.

Timothy and Jason are crying in each other's arms. Scott looks deeply into Kyra's eyes, while Julie rests her head on Adam's chest. Like a breeze in the night air, Madame Levette stands before them all. "Yes, it has begun. Your destinies are forever entwined." Julie and the rest question where the woman came from. She instructs Scott to bring Kyra and Jason to the fortune booth so that she can tend to them. Without question, they do as she requests. Something about her feels familiar to them all. It's like they know her intimately.

Jason has plenty of time to heal and recoup his energy. Thanks to Kyra's very effective healing, Jason is recovering much smoother than he did the first time he collapsed. Timothy does not leave his side, tending to him personally. Kyra rests in the back room, and Scott is vigilantly watching over her.

Outside the fortune-teller's booth, Julie waits with Adam. "Wow, this is so crazy with the weird happenings at the complex center yesterday. You and I both know that we were definitely attacked by a dark force before everyone lost their memory."

"We fought on a spiritual front when everyone seemed to lose time. I think we retained our base knowledge because of our unique spiritual powers."

Julie nods her head in agreement. "You are very right. I miss my sensei so much now. I didn't give my studies my fullest attention, but now I understand that I have much to do to become the warrior my sensei believed I would become."

While standing restlessly outside the tent, Tiffany says, "Girl, tonight is a total freaking bust, Trish. Scotty is nowhere."

"I could have sworn they were going to be here, Tiff. I heard it myself!" Trish answers without confidence.

"No matter! Tomorrow is another day. Let's get out of this abominable dump!"

"Yeah, why would you want dirt on a floor, anyway? I mean, seriously! How barbaric! Your Prada's don't like peasant dirt. Ugh! Besides, Tiff, hun, if he was here, he might have realized how boring that geeky princess Kyra really is and left already."

Julie overhears their entire conversation, *what a pair of lame-O's!* Julie is chuckling in silence, shaking her head, she pretends to zap Tiffany's butt with her laser finger. Suddenly, a wisp of white flair in Julie's eyes, and amazingly discharges a small spark of white light, striking Tiffany as she is sashaying, forcing her to yelp while clutching her bottom. The sound alarms Trish, as they scramble to know what struck Tiffany. Narrowing it to a bug bite, Tiffany storms off angry and sore. Julie is left baffled by the notion she used a new skill, she hadn't learned yet.

Kyra opens her eyes and sees Scott sitting at her side. A voice comes from somewhere in the room. "I see you have awakened." Madame Levette alerts them all. Jason looks over and sees Kyra looking up at him.

"Hey, Kyra, how are you feeling?" asks Scott, brushing her hair with his fingers.

"I am okay. Where am I?" Kyra replied while gathering her barrings to the unfamiliar room.

"You are where you are meant to be, young one. This isn't my home, but you are safe here, Child!" Madame Levette says with a raspy voice.

Kyra sits up and sees the elderly black woman dressed in vibrant colors sitting in a chair on the opposite side of the small room. Kyra smells smoky ash and finds a twig along with a small pouch resting in her lap.

"What is this?" she says, looking at the twig and cheesecloth.

"That is an old remedy used for many generations to bring strength and stability to the faint or unconscious." Madame Levette answered.

"What about Jason? Is he okay? Where is—?" Kyra inquirers with urgency.

Scott confirms "He is good."

"Yes, thanks to you, young one. Didn't know at first if you would be able to do it. But, you did. You have come a long way in the past few weeks. I am pleased to finally meet you, Mrs. Kyra Mathews."

"Um … excuse me, but who are you?"

With laughter, the woman says, "I am Madame Levette. I am the one who can help you."

"You were the one who helped Scott in the hospital?"

"One and the same, my dear." The woman stands to her feet and walks over to a little round table in the center of the next room. Reaching her hands towards Kyra, she says, "Come now. It is time. Help her sit over here." Scott does as she commands, helping Kyra to the chair opposite of the Madame herself.

Sensing Kyra's apprehension, Madame Levette calms her tensions with a light reading, about her health and family life. As Kyra realizes there isn't anything to fear in the readings, she loosens up quite a bit, allowing the Madame to delve deeper.

Leadership, family, powerful acquaintances and dear friends, are the heart strum Levette's reading to Kyra. She soon speaks of far exotic future travels to the north and far beyond. She also conveys, of things being lost and yet found renewed. Madame Levette slowly unwinds telling the story of Kyra's destiny by examining near and very distant past.

"Nature was once governed by great powers before the dawn of man. The heavenly powers and the earthly domains, they were called to be." As Madame Levette talks about creatures like dragons, Kyra gets very interested. She always thought they were pure fairy tales and folklore.

"Dragons? Are you sure? I never read about dragons in any Bible at Sunday service?" Kyra question as Madame Levette smirks.

"Exactly. It wouldn't be in the modern-day Bible. Before the Bible was pieced together by man, there were many ancient scrolls with greater detail of events from those long-forgotten times. But many of these scrolls—the ones that weren't lost over the millennia—were discarded by the monks. There's much-forbidden knowledge now that hasn't been released to the common man.

"Chaos would surely break out in this modern world if any of the knowledge within those scrolls were ever to be revealed.

Creatures with fantastical powers might still be roaming the earth!" the woman says.

She explains how the world was governed by four ruling kingdoms of dragons before the dawn of man. Each was very specific and true to its element—fire, earth, wind, and water. The house of Aphuryan was fire. The house of Aquilian was water. The house of Carnelians was earth, and the house of Aeolian was air.

"That's a lot going on!" Kyra retorted, almost overwhelmed by the knowledge.

Madame Levette chuckles as she continues to explain how only the ruling members of these houses were truly sentient just as a human being today. The younger dragons were more instinctive and primal. She tells her of an order of celestial dragons who are spiritually ascended sentients who worked with the celestial beings; otherwise known as angels.

"All was grand until one dark millennium when a powerful celestial dragon listened to his mighty archangel partner. The creator desired to create a new species, humans, to rule and guard the world. A brave celestial saw darkness growing in the heavens and acted with haste to plan for a countermeasure in case they should need it.

"The Archangel of light, Zaelzoahn, the most glorious and powerful of the celestial dragons, set out to destroy man. The archangel brought anarchy to the heavens, demanding his place in the hierarchy of angels. Realizing that wasn't going to happen, the archangel of war was called upon to remove the light bearer from his lofty position. In doing so, a great war was forged, rocking the pillars of the heavens. Mighty captains were summoned upon to lead vast celestial army's, both Angelic and mythical creations alike. All in the creator's name."

"What happened?"

"Alliances were made among the fallen celestial dragons and the mundane creatures here on earth, creating dark Nephilim, witches, wraiths, and demonic beings. A few celestials of light placed a seed in the newest creature, called man. From these spread seeds sprang forth balancers against the dark. These were the deserving titles of guardians and protectors. Dragons were some of the oldest and strongest among the mythical powers. Others manifested in other ways to combat the dark, like; Charmers, Wielders, Seers, Prophets, Chosen Messengers and finally the Yielder's of the light themselves."

She explains how the battles raged on for many centuries, leaving desolation and carnage in its wake. She also describes how the purge came after the defeat of Satan, his pet, and all his followers. "The dark angel is bound and imprisoned for all eternity in the underworld because he could not be destroyed. Zaelzoahn along with his loyal dragons were stripped of their glorious celestial armor and power and transformed into nightmarish beasts unlike anything ever witnessed before. Malstarzaine is now the black dragon king." She gives a description that strikes fear in Kyra's heart.

"Like the fallen, the celestials needed an answer. The ancients created a ripple in time and space, a place of utter darkness. Lucifer's pet and partner were banished to this inescapable realm, never to bother man or any other creature again. Since the balance of the world has grown chaotic and vile with war, strife, and horror, the ancients alongside the divine order created a doppelganger world just out of sync with the original earth, transplanting all the known elemental guards so that humans can evolve and prosper. So, all the dragons, mystical beasts, sorcerers, possessed creatures, Nephilim, fairies, gargoyles, conjurors, and so on were exiled to this other alter-world, where they could live in balance with each other. The world was called, Alter Dai.

"The ancients tried something very new. They harnessed a vast source of celestial and terrestrial energy into one concentrated source, which became the Jade Crystal of Ancestria, also known as, the Key. This key can open the gateways to other realms and worlds if used correctly. This stone was molded into the shape of the heart of a magical dragon. It didn't take long for the world of mortal man to notice that the myth was a truth.

"People have hunted for the key for centuries, but it's never been found. A single brave knight in training, a squire, stumbled upon the majestic creature of tantalizing beauty with its smooth, crystalline, iridescent scales and feathered wings and a long, lanky body. It also had a tail like the anchor of a ship. As the beast slept alone in a shallow once forgotten cave, the young knight studied it with complete awe. Before the dragon was slain, it briefly awakened. With a voice of mystical wonder, it spoke through its mind. The young and impressionable knight trembled with immense fear, but he was brave enough to stand his very ground. 'I see you have finally come, young Alexander Tiberius Maximus. You are here to fulfill your part in destiny's hand. I am very aware of what it is you seek. I must acquire certain things from you, before allowing you to take your reward. If you can't honor this, then you leave me no recourse but to undo destiny's plot.'

"Wide-eyed optimistic and shivering, the knight listened to the mystical beast, knowing all too well how slaying the dragon could bring him a great ranking among the nobles, within the order of the Crescent Knights. However, the young squire is baffled about how the creature knew his name or how it could speak without using its mouth.

"The dragon assures his safety and draws him near to whisper in his ear. The squire did as the creature requested. When he had approached, the dragon whispered ancient words into his little ears, and then he asks Alexander to be quick about it and remove its beating heart. He was supposed to consume the vital blood within his heart as nourishment, and doing so would connect him with the key."

Kyra didn't like the sound of drinking blood and wanted to shy away. But, Scott was there to calm her.

"Yes, he was destined to partake of the blood to fulfill the great prophecy that was to come. Hungry for notoriety within the ranks, the young knight was willing to do like the dragon so decreed with one promise. He was to never allow its heart to fall into the hands of darkness! Alexander, honor bound by his knightly code, faithfully promised with his very life to never let the heart fall into the hands of evil, even if that meant keeping the heart from his sovereign king. The dragon was very pleased, for it saw a purity of light within the young man.

"With honor and respect to the beast, he drank the plasma from the heart that he had removed. Surprisingly, the heart fits in the palms of his two hands just like a human heart. He put the heart to his quivering lips and drank all the fluid that would flow, draining it completely. While he admired it, the flesh turned solid and crystallized before his very eyes. The crystal pulsed with glowing energy, and the heart completed its transformation. He knew there was something very special about that heart and that dragon. He stashed it away and kept the heart secret per the dragon's request.

"Many years would pass, and yet that knight soon became the second lieutenant in the sacred order of the Crescent Knights. Alexander didn't seem to age or suffer any illness. He learned to mask his identity from suspicion by the fellow knights. He later fell deeply in love with a beautiful Sicilian maiden. He asked her to marry him. Under her enchanting charms, they shared a night of heated passion, and in his recuperating bliss, she took the heart from his hiding place."

Kyra and Scott are completely tuned in now, holding each

other's hand tightly. "What happens? Go on?" they say in sync with each other.

"Long story short, my dears, the woman, takes the heart and breaks it into five pieces. She didn't want any human or creature to possess such unchecked power. Breaking the heart ensures the rare chance of any one individual ever possessing or wielding the complete heart, ever again. Three pieces were separated into different parts of the world, while two were cast to the alternate Earth, known by a very select few as Alter-Dai, what I'd mentioned earlier, to you."

Kyra and Scott catch each other's eyes when they hear about another world, yet again.

Madame Levette continues, "Before the soldier had realized what she had done to his most precious possession, she was gone, never to be seen again. She left behind one fragment of the mighty crystal heart for his personal keeping. It was known to her; his destiny would be intertwined with the crystal. Alexander now roams the earth as an immortal and the sole protector of its power. Much like you are now, Ms. Kyra Mathews."

Kyra admires her medallion with great reverence as Scott lovingly admires her.

"His piece of the jade crystal was mounted into a special sword forged by a dragon's breath. He found the weapon in his lowly routine duties when he served as a squire. The sword of Ancestria, which he later endowed with his jewel, was a very special sword in its own making indeed. Many believed the sword was outside the reach of mankind forever, given to the lady of the lake. It was the sword of kings, and it once was named Excalibur. For hundreds of years, the immortal has been searching for the hidden pieces of the jade heart."

"The keys?" Kyra replies while examining her medallion.

"Yes, my dear, you possess one such key, the medallion of

Ancestria. It's the soul of a long-forgotten dragon who bridged the heavens."

Over the next hour, Madame Levette explains in detail about the medallion's protective powers, the well-hidden charms of its past, and the need for a united circle. "Seven in total makes your circle complete. The seventh member is yet to come. Don't get me wrong, the six are strong, but the seventh is needed to stand in the end!" Madame Levette said.

Taking a breath, She continues, "Unlike the others in your tight circle, this one isn't going to be easy to acquire. You must reach their heart and be their anchor when the time arrives. That is all I can say on this matter."

Kyra now knows that they are missing a very important member of their inner circle, but she doesn't have a clue about who it may be. *Have I already met our seventh and didn't realize it? Only time will tell.*

Later in the night, Scott makes a soulful apology to Jason and Timothy. The boys graciously accept Scott's heartfelt words of love and compassion with hugs, practically knocking Scott to the ground. With great laughter, Adam watches the bombardment of loving embraces and tender kisses from the young boys. Scott can't help but giggle and blush as he tries desperately to escape their playfulness.

Kyra updates Julie about the mystery of their unspoken bond, connecting the six of them to each other. "It's called the Linking Circle, as Madame Levette described it."

Kyra and Scott catch each other's eyes yet again. They feel an uncontrollable longing for each other that goes far beyond the physical need. Kyra feels she must bring the gang together more now than ever and will start, with updating Julie first and follow up with the rest in time, once she's finished catching up with some special alone time with the love of her life, Scott.

A bold new journey awaits these six young friends. They will learn of the reaching darkness that is coming their way. It's time to truly prepare for what there is to come, and the one they will need to complete the Linking Circle, the guardians of tomorrow, while all is at hand this Eve of the Dark Horizons.

The End of Part One of
THE DRACONIAN SERIES.

EVE OF DARK HORIZONS

Dragons, mages, and shapeshifters … Oh, my! Is this to
be Kyra's new reality? Fantasy and reality merge in the
modern world. A seed of darkness threatens everything
that is good. Strange beings are hidden in the shadows.
Kyra, the wide-eyed optimistic senior, is hopeful about a bright
and shiny life when she graduates. However, she is thrown
into a bitter series of events. She is destined to lead the seven
as the first line of defense where destiny and fate will collide.
The quest has begun. Will Kyra be strong enough? Does
she have the will to endure, what is required of her?
The old medallion, an ancient power which
is calling to her from within.
Why is the government so hell-bent and
lurking so close to her and her friends?
When a deadly enemy may somehow be their hope!
Only then will chaos truly take hold of the very fabric
of time and reality, and attune itself as home.
Kyra Mathews must find the answers she so desperately
needs before time runs out her and all mankind!
In the days to come and the nights that follow,
The very Eve of Dark Horizons is upon us.
Where life, love, and destiny are put to
the ultimate test for survival.
And so, it begins.

A new journey in the journals of the *Draconian Series*.

ABOUT THE AUTHOR

MARVIN PROCTOR JR was born and raised in Maryland. He is a trained scholar-musician who enjoys teaching and who has had a lifelong love of science fiction and fantasy. He is grateful for the friendship of many other authors who have assisted him along the way to the publication of this, his debut novel. He currently lives in Clinton, Maryland.